Praise for
CALL TO ARMS: NATIONS FALL

"*Call to Arms: Nations Fall* will make you grateful for three things: Zion, our liberty, and that there's still time to fight for both!"
—R. C. HANCOCK, author of *An Uncommon Blue*

"In *Call to Arms: Nations Fall*, Lindsay steps up the tension and deepens the drama of families and individuals thrust headlong into the coming last days. Written with a sense of emotional drive and cutting-edge realism, Lindsay's narrative is a chapter in time torn from the pages of scripture, the warnings of the prophets—and the inevitable headlines of tomorrow."
—STEPHEN J. STIRLING, author of *Shedding Light on the Dark Side* and *Persona Non Grata*

"It is one thing to talk about the end of the world in impersonal terms, but another altogether to see the impending demise through the eyes of various characters experiencing it. Randy Lindsay takes a catastrophic event anticipated by the Christian world for centuries and puts a personal face on it. *Call to Arms: Nations Fall* thrust me into a world of increasing chaos in an intimate and intriguing way that echoed in my head and kept me pondering long after I turned the last page."
—BROCK BOOHER, author of *Healing Stone* and *The Charity Chip*

CALL TO ARMS

TO

ARMS

NATIONS FALL

ALSO BY RANDY LINDSAY

End's Beginning: The Gathering

CALL TO ARMS

NATIONS FALL

RANDY LINDSAY

BONNEVILLE BOOKS ™

AN IMPRINT OF CEDAR FORT, INC.
SPRINGVILLE, UTAH

This is a work of fiction. The characters, names, incidents, places, and dialogue are products of the author's imagination and are not to be construed as real. The opinions and views expressed herein belong solely to the author and do not necessarily represent the opinions or views of Cedar Fort, Inc. Permission for the use of sources, graphics, and photos is also solely the responsibility of the author.

ISBN 13: 978-1-4621-1688-1

Published by Bonneville Books, an imprint of Cedar Fort, Inc.
2373 W. 700 S., Springville, UT 84663
Distributed by Cedar Fort, Inc., www.cedarfort.com

LIBRARY OF CONGRESS CATALOGING-IN-PUBLICATION DATA

  Lindsay, Randy, 1959-
  Call to arms : nations fall / by Randy Lindsay
     pages ; cm
  ISBN 978-1-4621-1688-1 (softcover : acid-free paper)
  1. Rapture (Christian eschatology)--Fiction. 2. Families--Religious life--Fiction. 3. Christians--Fiction. I. Title.
  PS3612.I5353C35 2015
  813'.6--dc23
                        2015008622

Cover design by Michelle May
Cover design © 2015 by Lyle Mortimer
Edited and typeset by Melissa J. Caldwell

Printed in the United States of America

10 9 8 7 6 5 4 3 2 1

I dedicate this book to the person who made it possible for me to pursue my dream of becoming an author. She is the rock that steadies me during emotional storms. She is the sunshine that brightens my days. She is my best friend. She is my wife. Thanks, LuAnn, for all that you do. This book is for you.

1

Private Robert Williams woke suddenly, his head rebounding off the roll bar of the Humvee. The vehicle must have hit another pothole in the road—if it could even be called a road. The route the Turkish government had insisted his unit take to the embassy was as poorly maintained as it was unnecessarily long.

His eyes closed, and he started to drift off to sleep. If six months in the army had taught him anything, it was how to fall asleep on command. Any concerns about the assignment, how the family was doing back home, or when he might receive the next letter from his girlfriend, Sierra, could all wait until he caught up on his rest.

Bam. Another pothole.

Private Gutierrez looked back at Robert and laughed. The driver's tobacco-stained teeth showed through his sadistic smile, which drooped on one side. For some reason, he took pleasure in making Robert's life more difficult. Even though there was an entire vehicle full of soldiers, Gutierrez timed his pothole encounters specifically for him. "Having problems sleeping, recruit?"

If Robert hadn't been wearing his helmet, the head-bump could have really hurt. As it was, it annoyed him more than anything. He rubbed his eyes and gave up on getting any more shut-eye.

"Sleep is overrated. Thanks for reminding me that I should be doing something important with my valuable transport time."

"Glad to be of assistance, recruit." He laughed and then plastered that lopsided grin back on his face. His eyes flicked from the road to the rearview mirror.

Unwilling to satisfy Gutierrez with a reply, Robert pulled out his latest letter from Sierra. A quick glance toward the front of the vehicle confirmed that the driver had lost his smile now that the game of potholes was over.

Robert,

I'm still having problems adjusting to the move. Living with Mom and Dad again isn't so bad because I know I'm here to help them out, but I haven't made any friends, my new boss is a complete jerk, and worst of all, they don't have a good barbecue place like the Slab Factory. Thinking about our date there is one of the few bright moments I have in the middle of dealing with the necessities of life. If the two of us were a little less sensible, we could be together right now.

Dad finally took my advice and put security screens on the windows and installed two security doors. I went with him to pick them out. Being in the store reminded me of our meeting at Handy Hal's. I wonder if things might have worked out a little differently if Hal had hired you. You wouldn't have gotten a security job and might never have had the crazy idea to join the military. Now we're half a world apart, and we're both trying to help our families make ends meet.

Argghhh! What am I doing? You're in Turkey, probably being shot at even while I'm writing this, and all I can do is complain about my life. I hope you get the mess at the embassy cleaned up quick and they send you back home. I'm worried about you. Guys with an innate sense for finding good restaurants are hard to find. Please stay safe. And write to me soon.

—Sierra

Weird. Robert wasn't worried about getting shot at or blown up or mobbed by fanatics; instead, his mind kept asking how long it would be before Sierra found someone else to take her for barbecue.

When he was dating before his mission for The Church of Jesus Christ of Latter-day Saints, his parents had always told him not to worry about whether the girls he liked would wait for him to return. They said if it was meant to be, it would happen. And even though Sierra wasn't a member of the Church and the two of them had not had many dates together, he still hoped Sierra would wait for him to get home from the war.

"That girlfriend of yours finally decide to dump you?" Gutierrez slapped the steering wheel and laughed loudly.

The dig from Gutierrez elicited a few chuckles from the rest of the guys in the vehicle, but Robert ignored them.

Bam. The Humvee bounced along the road.

"Man," said Gutierrez. "That was one big dip. Sort of like you, recruit."

Robert folded up the letter and tucked it back inside his shirt pocket. Through the window he could see that they were approaching the Ankara city limits. Portions of it looked like any modern city: tall buildings covered with reflective-tint windows; parks with fountains; people sitting on benches talking on cell phones; and well-maintained roads—finally.

Right alongside the modern structures were mosques with Ottoman-style minarets reaching into the sky. The blend of the Old and New World cultures reminded him of the time he had spent in Italy. Not for the first time, he wondered how the people he had met there were doing. His church mission felt unfinished. Even though he had been given an honorable release as a missionary, he couldn't get rid of the feeling that there was still something he needed to do.

Then all thoughts of Italy fled. Among the rows of red-ceramic-roofed homes that flanked the road stood a pair of men with an American flag. The Stars and Stripes had "Death to the US" written on it in black paint. Robert thought he spotted assault rifles strapped to their backs. But the Humvee rolled past, and he was left to wonder if their convoy was about to be ambushed.

"Did you see those men?" Robert asked. He peered out the back window to see if they had stepped out into the road, but there were too many bodies in the vehicle blocking his view.

Gutierrez sneered. "Protestors got you spooked, recruit?"

"I think they had guns."

Gutierrez checked the rearview mirror, his expression of contempt gone for a moment. As the brick-hued homes receded in the distance, he shook his head. "You're probably just imagining things, but keep an eye out anyway."

An image flashed in Robert's peripheral vision: a head peering down at them from on top of a roof. Then it was gone, too fast to be certain that he'd seen it at all. He continued to watch the building but saw no other sign of a possible assailant.

They passed more Turks. None seemed to have guns. None had defaced American flags. None of them even had protest signs. Just normal people wearing normal clothes, walking on the sidewalks.

The Humvee drove through a dozen more neighborhoods before it slowed. The buildings in this section of Ankara looked no different from the buildings in any major city. The number of women wearing shawls, the number of men wearing beards, and the occasional ancient ruin nestled between the skyscrapers was all that prevented this from resembling home.

Robert looked out his window at the remains of the US Embassy, which had been bombed six weeks ago. Most of the front had collapsed, leaving a cross-section view of the building. He could see into rooms on each floor. Some of them still had furniture. It looked like a giant dollhouse waiting for an enormous toddler to come and play with it. A huge pile of blackened debris had been stacked out front, created during the rescue effort that immediately followed the terrorist bombing. Light glinted off shards of glass scattered across the embassy compound, looking a bit like the sun as it reflected off Green Lake back home.

Nearby buildings still sported scars from the blast. Holes in the walls had been patched but not yet painted over. Many of the windows remained boarded up or covered with plastic sheets that puffed out from the rooms that they tried to protect from the elements.

Two other American embassies had been bombed during the last few months. In each case, the host country seemed unconcerned about finding the responsible parties. It left Robert with the impression that the United States was unwelcome in at least part of Europe.

Concern lay heavy in the pit of his stomach. Robert didn't mind the physically demanding work that lay ahead, but he did worry about what he might find amid the rubble—human parts, or even whole bodies. He scratched his jaw, wondering how he would react when he did.

The Humvee braked hard and came to a sudden stop, causing Robert to bang his head on the roll bar once again. Gutierrez snickered. "Oops. Guess I should have warned you that the brakes are touchy. Huh, recruit?"

Robert nodded. He briefly considered a number of ways to repay the favor. They all seemed appropriately funny but would only escalate the problem. He shrugged off the rookie hazing as part of the wonderful experience that was the military.

The rest of the team piled out of the vehicle, expressing a wide range of vulgar thanks for having reached their destination.

First in. Last out. Life as the newbie was a cornucopia of little tortures. Robert ached from sitting so long in the cramped confines of the Humvee. Slowly, he crawled out of the vehicle, stretching each leg as it reached for the ground. Once he was fully out, he extended his arms high above his head. It felt good to be unfolded at last and away from the concentrated smells of oil, dust, and sweat.

The radio squawked inside the Humvee.

Gutierrez groaned. "Probably the captain checking to make sure the recruit didn't run out on his first deployment."

"More likely," said Robert, "HQ is wondering if you got lost."

"In your dreams, recruit." Gutierrez reached inside the vehicle and grabbed the microphone.

A small and demanding feeling stopped Robert mid-step. The expectation of bad news sent a chill sliding down his back. This herald of dread told him to stop and listen.

He did.

"All units be advised. All units be advised. Condition Redcon-2 initiated. The Russians have invaded Germany. All units in the Mediterranean and Middle East are hereby on full alert. Individual unit orders will follow."

Had he heard that correctly?

For a moment Gutierrez stood there—speechless. His face whitened. Then he turned and faced the rest of the squad. He licked his lips and said, "Well, I'll be. Did you get that, rookie? We're at war!"

War?

Maybe it was joke. A horrible joke like yelling "fire" in a movie theater. Or maybe it was just a misunderstanding, a few Russian vehicles accidentally crossing the border. If no shots had been fired and no one had died, then it wasn't too late to stop it. Because it *had* to be stopped. A war between Russia and the NATO allies would tear the world apart.

Robert stared at the mic in Gutierrez's hand, the surreal quality of the moment preventing him from doing anything more than wondering if the Russians had really just started World War III.

2

The phone rang on Calvin's desk. Massaging the bridge of his nose with two fingers, he picked up the receiver with his other hand. The office of Vice President of the United States involved too much paperwork for his liking. "McCord here."

"The Russians just crossed the German border." The voice belonged to Kyle Dalton, a long-time friend of Calvin's who worked as a CIA analyst. "It looks like the entire 6th Army invaded."

The news wrenched Calvin's insides into a tight knot of dread. What the world didn't need right now was another massive war that dragged in nation after nation and slaughtered millions. "Russia and Germany don't have a common border. How did the Russian 6th Army get there?"

"Based on the early data, I'd say Slovakia let them through. Anything else you're going to have to get through your people. I have satellite images to study, and then I have to report whatever I find to my superiors. Man, this is *bad*."

"Thanks, Kyle." Calvin disconnected the call and dialed Ms. Wilks, the President's personal secretary. "This is McCord," he said when she answered. "Let me talk to Boggs, please."

"I'm sorry." Her husky voice sounded anything but sorry.

7

"President Boggs is unavailable at the moment. He's preparing for an important cabinet meeting."

"Why haven't I been notified?" Calvin's voice rose more than he intended.

"I'm sure that I don't know, Mr. McCord. Would you like to leave a message?"

Calvin suspected that Ms. Wilks took more than a little pleasure in frustrating his efforts to get anything done around the executive wing. She wielded protocol and schedules like twin samurai swords. He knew from past experience that further argument would be worse than useless; it would make her even more difficult to work with in the future.

"Don't bother. I'll come over and give him my message in person." Calvin hung up the receiver, taking a little pleasure of his own in cutting off the old biddy before she had a chance to protest his impending visit.

Calvin placed the classified files he had been looking at back into their folder and locked them in the safe under his desk. Standing to leave, he looked at the filing cabinet where he kept a bottle of Jack Daniels. He felt like taking a good shot of the whiskey to take the edge off the news of another war in Europe but decided against it.

As he left the office, a pair of Secret Service agents fell in behind him. Calvin referred to them as Curly and Moe because they were a couple of stooges. He suspected that they reported every step he made to Boggs.

"I'm off to see the President," Calvin told his secretary, Gwen, as he passed through the outer office. Gwen had auburn hair with a slight curl that tended to frizz at the ends. The rectangular-framed glasses she wore gave visual confirmation of the no-nonsense attitude she brought to work. A red blazer over a white sweater made her green eyes stand out while maintaining a professional look.

"Do you think that's wise considering what happened last week?" Gwen asked.

"Probably not, but I have to at least try to convince him to honor the treaty with our NATO allies. The Russians pose a serious threat to all of Europe and could eventually decide to focus their military might on us." Calvin steamed down the hallway like a runaway train. If anything, Boggs had arranged for Calvin to have even less power as Vice President than he had when he had served as Secretary of State.

Curly whispered something into his cuff mic, most likely a warning to Boggs's security detail that the Vice President was on his way. Both of the agents who had been assigned to Calvin were burly and thick through the neck. They hadn't been placed as guardians to protect Calvin—they were enforcers meant to keep him in line.

As Calvin came within sight of the President's usual briefing room, he spotted two Secret Service agents blocking the hallway, hands folded in front of them, looking cool and casual in their sunglasses and dark suits. One shook his head before Calvin closed the distance between them. Both moved sideways to block him.

"Out of the way," said Calvin, without slowing down.

"Can't do that, sir," said the shorter of the two agents. "We have specific orders to make sure you don't interrupt the President."

"What do you plan to do to stop me from seeing the President?" Calvin asked with as much menace in his voice as he could muster.

"If necessary," said the taller agent, "we will physically take you down and then escort you back to your office."

"Are you willing to do that in front of whatever witnesses might be present?" Calvin pointed to a pair of interns who were watching the event.

Both agents looked at one another and shrugged.

Calvin pushed his way past, making a mental note that at some point that ploy wasn't going to work. He had no doubt Boggs would order the agents to remove him if he got out of line—away from the public eye, of course.

Two more agents stood outside the conference room door. They spotted Calvin bearing down on their position, and their expressions turned to looks of surprise. One spoke into his cuff mic while the other turned to face Calvin, the unsteady movement betraying the agent's hesitation.

Calvin didn't give the third set of agents time to coordinate with the others. He blew past them and into the conference room. Conversation among Boggs's trusted panel of advisors stopped and all heads whipped up as Calvin entered.

Boggs, as usual, recovered first. "Calvin, your presence is not required at this meeting. I will be happy to have my secretary forward you the minutes once they have been typed up."

"The Russians have just started World War III," said Calvin. "I'd say that's an important enough event to have me contributing to America's political and military response to the situation."

"Gentlemen, if everyone would excuse us, I would like to have a brief discussion with the Vice President." Boggs stood up and straightened his suit jacket. "I'm sure everyone could use a break. Please, meet back here in fifteen minutes."

Both he and Calvin waited until the room emptied out.

"You can't—" Calvin said.

"No." Boggs pointed an accusing finger at Calvin, his face flush with anger. "You can't just barge in here. I'm in charge of the country and I decide who needs to be involved in finding a solution to our problems. The heroics you pulled off last year won you a spot as the Vice President in my administration. Everyone was impressed with the way you risked your life to stop a terrorist bombing and save half of the Washington elite. Or at least that's how it played out in the press.

"The country needed a hero and they needed to feel that both political parties were working together for the benefit of the people. Your appointment as Vice President did exactly that. Sit back and enjoy your time as a hero, but do not mistake it as an invitation to influence the politics of this country."

Politics! The country is falling apart and all Boggs can think about is politics, Calvin thought. It infuriated him that Boggs couldn't forget their political affiliations and work together for a solution. Calvin's important connections in Russia had made it necessary for Boggs to keep him around when the tides of political power had changed. That need had turned into a powerful resentment.

"This is a serious situation," said Calvin. "We need everyone involved. Stop this partisan hogwash and let me help."

"First of all," said Boggs, regaining his composure, his politician's face back in place, "this is not World War III. Russia is involved in another border dispute. I am already drafting a stern response condemning this act of aggression. Several of our NATO allies have agreed to consider sanctions if the Russians are not willing to pursue diplomatic means in resolving the matter."

"You've got to be kidding." Of all the things Boggs might have said, a bold-faced denial of war took Calvin by surprise.

"No matter what you call it," Boggs continued without missing a beat, "this is not something that the United States needs to be involved with. The United States has had three embassies attacked in as many months. Before that, terrorists bombed the campaign headquarters of Governor Ross in the hope of sparking another civil war. We are a nation under siege. Troops will be redeployed in a manner that best allows us to protect our own interests around the world. Europe will have to deal with the problem on its own. I have faith that working together the EU has more than enough resources to repel the Russian aggression."

"That sounds an awful lot like war to me."

"You'll just have to trust me, Calvin. This is nothing more than a small border dispute. Keep in mind I have access to a greater level of information about the situation than you do. If I thought this squabble threatened the country, I would not hesitate to involve you in finding a solution."

Does he really expect me to believe that load of baloney?

"Russia cannot take on the world by itself," said Boggs. "End of discussion."

Calvin slammed his fist down on the conference table, ignoring the pain and doing his best to ignore his mounting blood pressure. "Regardless of how you spin Russia's armed incursion into another country, I need to be involved. I *am* the Vice President."

"I'm glad you brought that up." Boggs offered one of his slick political smiles and leaned back in his padded swivel chair. With his thin lips, the smile gave him a slight resemblance to a snake gloating over his meal. "Your threats to go to the media anytime you don't get your way need to stop. I will not allow you to continue to use the heroics of last year as a means to blackmail me. The fact that you risked life and limb to foil a terrorist plot is old news. I have given the Secret Service strict orders that no leeway is to be given to you. Any agents who have a problem with the order will be reassigned."

Calvin understood the real meaning of that message; Boggs intended to surround the Vice President with men loyal to him. Step out of line and who could tell what the agents might do to enforce the President's will.

Not only that, but American troops were being moved away from the conflict in Europe. Calvin had to find a way to force Boggs's hand.

"We are done here." Boggs picked up the phone on the table in front of him. "I have recently recruited a couple of uniquely qualified Secret Service agents. Their names are Bowers and Hancock."

"We've met already," said Calvin.

"Good, that saves me an introduction. Now, are you willing to leave on your own or should I call them in here to escort you to your office?" Boggs's hand hovered above the keypad.

"I can find my way out."

A knock sounded at the door. Perhaps Boggs had already alerted Bowers and Hancock. Instead, a tiny frail-looking aide stepped inside. "Something important came up and I thought you should know about it." The aide looked ready to duck out of the room at the first sign of presidential displeasure.

"What is it, Riley?" Boggs asked.

"Italy has been hit by a massive earthquake. We should probably respond to the event as quickly as possible. I took the liberty of putting together a couple of quick sound bites for you to give the media."

"Excellent," said Boggs. "Leave them so I can look them over."

Riley scuttled across the room to deposit the notes on the table and then blitzed out of the room twice as fast as he entered it.

The brief interruption gave Calvin time enough to devise the beginning of a plan, an end-run solution for the Russian invasion. "Be reasonable. I have to do something productive. If you won't let me address the conflict in Europe, at least let me work on helping Italy."

Boggs tilted his head and narrowed his eyes, obviously suspicious of the new direction Calvin had taken their discussion. "You want to head up the relief effort?"

"I'll do the hard work and you get the credit. It makes you look like the bipartisan hero you claim to be."

"And what do you get out of it?" asked Boggs.

"I get the opportunity to help out the people in an allied country."

"Come up with a plan, and I'll look it over when you're done."

Calvin spun around and marched smartly out of the room. All he had to do now was find a way to disguise a military deployment as a rescue mission.

3

I t's time for the Saints to gather," said John. He kept his voice calm, hoping the example would convince his daughter to adopt a similar, reasonable tone.

"I'm not going!" Sarah shouted. She paced the living room in front of her parents, her feet stomping the brown shag carpet in muffled protest. "How can you even consider giving up this house to go live in the wilderness? For one thing, you're just handing the house over to the Church. At least sell the place and put the money in the bank in case you finally come to your senses. And then there's this whole matter of living in what amounts to a modern-day pioneer village. We don't have to do that. This is not the end of the world."

"Look around you," said John, placing an arm around his wife, Becky. "The signs of the apocalypse are everywhere. World War III just started in Europe, and your brother Robert may find himself right smack in the middle of the fighting. Isn't that proof enough that we have entered the last days before the Savior's return?"

"It isn't World War III." Sarah faced her parents and used both hands to emphasize her words. "The President announced on the news that there's no need to worry. This is just a small dispute between Russia and Germany."

John closed his eyes and took a deep breath. He had found that helped him keep his cool whenever the President's latest antics were mentioned. It amazed him how one man could be so wrong so much of the time. At nineteen, Sarah still had a lot to learn about how the world really worked. "President Boggs doesn't know what he's talking about. There is no doubt that an armed conflict between Russia and Germany is just the beginning of another major war."

Becky moved forward and took Sarah's hands in hers. "Besides, the prophet has said we need to do this."

"He did not." Sarah shook her head hard enough to send her hair whipping around her head. "The bishop and the stake president told you to do this. Have you considered the possibility that this is a scam?"

John hated to admit it, but he had thought the same thing when he'd been asked to move his family permanently out to Camp Valiant. This was no small decision. It took real faith to leave behind a comfortable home, prized possessions, and a modestly successful career as an architect to move over two hundred miles away for a future that promised to be hard and demanding. He wondered how many of the Saints would heed the call and how many, like Sarah, found the situation unbelievable or even unacceptable? How many of the members would refuse to believe that the call to gather really came from the Lord rather than from the local leaders?

For the moment, the decisions others made about accepting or rejecting the call was not his concern. Getting his family to go along with the plan had proven a monumental task in itself.

"I know this may seem extreme," said John. "And the idea that we might have to live in a communal home, or even in tents, scares me a little too. Keep in mind that if a struggle to survive is what's in store for the faithful, just imagine the pain and suffering the rest of the world will experience as the Second Coming approaches. But most important, I know that this is what our Heavenly Father wants us to do."

Some of the fury left Sarah's eyes. "This isn't easy for me, Dad. I just don't believe moving away from the city is what God wants me to do. I can't go with you. I'm an adult and I want to find my own place in the world. I have a friend who has invited me to move in with her."

"Oh, Sarah." Becky wrapped her arms around her daughter. The two of them hugged each other in silence, tears rolling down Becky's face.

As tough as it was to accept, John understood why an individual needed a personal testimony that the call to gather had indeed come from God. It was a confirmation of the divine call that would give them the strength they required to survive and prosper when everything around them fell apart.

"All right then," said John, trying not to sound as worried and disappointed as he felt. "I'll support your decision. Let me know what day you plan to move in with your friend and I'll make sure to block out enough time to help."

Sarah, locked into an even tighter embrace, looked over her mother's shoulder and smiled. "Thank you, Daddy."

⸻

John pulled his dented red toolbox from inside the mobile storage pod and walked over to the small pile of items going to Camp Valiant. "This needs to go with us."

Packing proved to be even more stressful than John had imagined. He and Becky had fought more in the last week than they had all the rest of the time they'd been married. Both had firm notions about what items were essential and should go with them, what needed to be placed in the storage pod, and what to give away.

Even as John reached for a pair of shoeboxes, each secured with a thick rubber band, Becky came out of the house, waving her finger at him. "Don't you dare touch the family pictures. They are going."

"We don't have enough room for them."

"But you can take your tools?" Becky asked, her voice shrill and fists on her hips.

The stance surprised John. His wife had never spoken to him like that before. "I know the pictures mean a lot to you, but my hand tools are necessary for the construction work I'll be doing. Once we build a few more houses, we'll have room for the family mementos. Until then, they can stay in storage. It's not as if we're going to spend our evenings looking at vacation pictures."

Becky's stance remained just as resolute. "What if something happens to the storage pod? Or if we never have a chance to come back to the city and get our stuff out of it? The pictures and letters in this box represent our family. We have to bring them for the sake of our grandchildren and great-grandchildren. Church leaders haven't had us doing family history all these years just so we can leave it behind."

"Okay." John held his hands up in surrender. "We take both and find something else to place in storage."

Easier said than done. The instructions passed on to him from Salt Lake placed an extreme limit on the amount of personal items that could be taken. That allotted space had to be shared with the four children still living at home. During the first few passes through their stuff, the family merely selected the items they had little use for but had never gotten around to tossing out. When only the treasured possessions remained, the selection process turned into emotional agony.

Even limiting himself to the items he actually used during the last six months, John far exceeded his allotment of personal items: the set of antique hand tools his grandfather had given him for his sixteenth birthday, his collection of Tom Clancy books, and the set of Dutch ovens he had carefully acquired over the years. Undecided as to what he could afford to live without, he looked up to find Becky still watching him.

"I promise to leave your pictures alone."

Becky relaxed. "Why don't you come in and let me fix you a sandwich? You look like you can use a rest, and maybe you'll think of a solution while you eat."

"Continue to agonize over what to leave behind or share a few tasty morsels with a beautiful woman?" John winked at Becky. "That's the easiest decision I've had to make all day."

John got as far as washing his hands and sitting down at the kitchen table before a knock sounded at the front door. Hoping that it might be a buyer for the stuff Becky had advertised in the paper, he got up and answered it. Carl Poston and Tom Hale stood out front.

"Looks like you're moving," said Carl.

John already didn't like the sound of this. Carl and Tom both attended his ward and vocally opposed the move to Camp Valiant. All John wanted to do was eat a sandwich and get back to packing. He nodded rather than risk revealing his mood with the tone of his voice.

"We've been friends a long time," said Carl.

"Thanks," said John. "I appreciate you coming over and telling me that."

"What Carl means," said Tom as he stepped forward, "is that we hope you haven't fallen for this whole 'gathering' baloney."

"Considering that the direction comes straight from Salt Lake," said John, "I hardly think this is a joke, a scam, or a mistake. If the two of you don't approve, then by all means stay behind."

John tried to remain calm, but the trial of faith involved in accepting the call to gather was difficult enough without friends and neighbors criticizing him. And it wasn't as if the ranks of the doubters were void of influential members either; more than a few bishops and stake presidents chose to stay in their homes and pray for deliverance.

This marked the first great hurdle for the modern Saints; a purification process which would ultimately determine who was righteous enough to greet the Savior when He returned. Carl and Tom had fallen to the subtle whisperings of comfort and ease and had chosen to stay in their homes rather than heed the call of the prophet.

John wondered what would happen to those who stayed behind when they eventually faced truly harsh opposition.

"What are you going to do when you find out this isn't the end of the world?" Tom asked. "How would that affect your family?"

"I think the question you should worry about is what you'll do when it turns out that the prophet was right," said John. A nagging sensation told him that rather than bickering with his friends, he should be attempting to convince them to join those who were going to Camp Valiant. "You're right that this isn't the end of the world. It's just the end of the world as we know it. When the Savior returns, the wicked will literally be burned and the righteous will remain to finish the Lord's work during the Millennium. But between now and the Millennium, it's sure going to look like the end of the world."

Carl laid a hand on Tom's shoulder. "There's no need to get upset. John, we just want you to consider both sides of the issue. It'd be a lot safer if all of us stayed together."

"Not to mention how it's going to look for the rest of us when half of our members run off like a bunch of crazy preppers," said Tom.

"You've been in the ward for a long time," said Carl. "People look up to you. They'll listen to what you have to say. With everything falling apart, we really need your leadership."

"I think the obvious solution is for you to come with us," said John.

"We can't," said Carl. "The house market has tanked. Word got out that the Mormons were moving out and the buyers are looking to pick up bargains because of it. Even if that weren't a problem, I just got promoted at work."

"Does any of that really matter?" asked John. "You can't take it with you when you die. It's just—*stuff*. Are you actually going to cleave to material things of the world instead of heeding the Spirit? Can you honestly tell me that a voice inside you isn't telling you to go with us?"

Carl crossed his arms and broke eye contact with John.

Tom seemed more angry than moved by the Spirit.

"I need to get back to my packing," said John. "Let me know if you change your minds. We have plenty of room for you and your families at the camp."

Tom and Carl turned and left without saying another word. John watched them until they crossed to the far side of the street. The argument had strengthened his resolve to go, but he felt as if he had failed. What else could he have said?

So many groups in the past had predicted the end of the world and had been wrong. If this was another false prediction, then in a year the members who had gathered would be broke and the subject of cruel jokes by the rest of the world.

What if I'm wrong?

4

Captain Mayo had decided against letting a Redcon-2 situation disrupt the job at hand. Full alert just meant that his troops needed to labor with their Berretta M9 pistols strapped onto their sides and a cache of locked and loaded M4 carbines located nearby.

It might work that way in John Wayne movies, but Robert had a hard time focusing on clearing debris with a pistol on his hip. His unit's assignment entailed hauling around a lot of construction materials that used to be homes or businesses or, in this case, embassies. The army called it "Debris Management." It sure sounded more important than calling it what it really was—a clean-up detail.

Back home, joining the US Army Corps of Engineers had seemed like a reasonable step to reach his career. Robert could work in the engineering field and the government paid for any related education. But the reality of the situation was that he had been shipped overseas to do unskilled labor, close to where all the fighting was going on. That couldn't be good. Could it?

What am I doing here?

"Hey, recruit!" Gutierrez bellowed as he crossed the rubble-strewn floor that had been the embassy's front lobby. Beside him walked a soldier with an assault rifle and a unit insignia, marking him as regular army—not an engineer.

With brown eyes, dark hair, and a cleft chin, the soldier looked a little older than Robert. If the soldier stood more than five foot five, it'd be a miracle. And yet, marching toward Robert, he appeared taller. His stiff, upright gait seemed to add height to the numbers that a tape measure would surely confirm. He moved like a matador facing a red-eyed, steam-snorting bull.

Wondering where the new guy had come from, Robert glanced out toward the street. Several additional Humvees had joined those that belonged to his unit. By his quick estimation, it looked to be a platoon's worth of troops—a mere forty soldiers.

Only a platoon?

The appearance of reinforcements should have given him some comfort, but it had the opposite effect. Cleaning up the target of a terrorist bombing with the distant threat of the Russian invasion in the back of the mind was unnerving and had everyone on edge. Assigning an armed unit to help meant that the engineers themselves were in danger. Robert hoped that a platoon would be enough to deal with any hostile forces in the area.

Gutierrez stopped in front of Robert and pointed at the soldier with him. "This here is Feldstein. You and him have something in common. You're both snot-nosed recruits."

"Is that what passes for sophisticated humor in this unit?" Feldstein asked.

Gutierrez's lopsided grin faded. His lips tightened. "Smart guy, eh?"

"Smart enough to know that I don't have to put up with crap from another private," said Feldstein. "Seems to me you've been in the military too long to still be at the bottom."

"Watch your mouth," Gutierrez growled. He took a step toward Feldstein, his hands balled into fists.

Robert stepped between the two. "I imagine you didn't walk Feldstein all the way over here just to tell me he's a noob. Why is he here?"

Hostility burned in Gutierrez's eyes as he continued to scowl at Feldstein. "Command has raised the threat level in this region. They've reinforced us with one lousy platoon. I hear there's fighting in Kars and Erzincan. Until ordered otherwise, the two of you are going to be pals. Whatever garbage job we find for you to do, Shorty here will be posted at your side. Who knows, maybe if he gets on his tippy-toes he can see over the tops of his boots."

"Is he going to be helping me?" Robert asked.

"Are you kidding?" Gutierrez snorted. "Regular army doesn't know how to do anything except stand around and get shot."

Feldstein didn't miss a beat. "And yet the engineers still need us to protect them."

"And what about me?" Robert asked. "What am I supposed to be doing?"

The grin returned to Gutierrez's face. "I made sure to find the worst, most disgusting job available for you and your girlfriend here."

"Thanks," said Robert.

"Now I feel bad," said Feldstein. "You went to all that trouble for me and I didn't get anything for you." Fishing through his pants pockets, he pulled out a quarter. "Take this. It should be enough to buy an upgrade for your personality."

Gutierrez raised a scarred fist, his face flush with rage.

"What did you find for us to do?" Robert asked, hoping to distract Gutierrez from the insult and steer him back to his gloating. "What wonderful and highly skilled job can we look forward to doing?"

It worked. Gutierrez lowered his fist and faced Robert. "Latrine detail, of course. All of the porta-potties need to be emptied and sanitized. And when you finish with that, do it again."

"I'll need the keys for the sanitation truck," said Robert.

"Are you kidding?" Gutierrez stared straight at Robert and laughed. "Sanitation trucks can only be driven by a specialist, and you are—"

"—a recruit," said Robert. "I got it."

"Sergeant Wojcik will meet you over there," said Gutierrez. "He'll sit in the truck and monitor your efforts. And make sure you keep in mind that Captain Mayo likes the latrines in his unit spotless."

Gutierrez favored Feldstein with one of his nastier sneers and then turned and strutted off toward the rear of the embassy. That probably meant a long walk around the building that would keep the Private First Class safe from doing any real work.

"Like the man said, I'm Feldstein. Gilbert Feldstein. My friends call me Gil."

Robert extended his hand. "My name's Robert Williams. I guess we'll be enjoying the worst that the military has to offer together."

Gil grasped and shook Robert's hand. "Since you put it that way, how can I not look forward to it?"

Leading the way, Robert wove through mounds of rubble to where Sergeant Wojcik and the sanitation truck waited. The sergeant had an X-Men graphic novel in his hands and gave them the briefest of nods, not bothering to look up as they arrived.

"Do you always let that jerk hassle you?" asked Gil.

"Who? Wojcik?" Robert whispered, not wanting to offend the sergeant.

"No. That loudmouth, Gutierrez."

Robert shrugged. "I'm new to the unit. That's just the way they treat the 'new meat.' Besides, I figure if I ignore him, he'll get bored and find some other way to amuse himself."

"While I find the idea of a pacifist in the army rather novel, you really have to learn to stand up for yourself. No one has the right to mistreat you just because you're new. Be more assertive."

Robert chuckled.

"What's so funny?" Gil asked.

"You know," Robert said as he pulled a long hose out of the utility compartment of the truck and attached it to the pump, "you're the new guy now. And here you are giving me advice on what the new guy should do."

"Then I must be onto something."

In the distance, a stream of automatic gunfire rattled.

The noise jolted Robert, leaving him a bit shaky inside.

The two of them stood still for a moment and listened for more shots, but there were none. Just the haunting whisper of the wind.

"You're pretty jumpy," said Gil.

"What can I say? I grew up in a pretty peaceful neighborhood. Not all of us can be calm, cool, and collected like you."

"Good point," said Gil, but his attention was focused in the direction of the gunshots. His eyes scanned the streets and buildings beyond the compound.

Robert approached the truck and tugged on a long, thick hose that draped across several storage mounts. "Can you give me a hand here? These are heavy."

"Not a chance," said Gil. "My orders are to keep an eye out for any hostiles in the area and protect the debris-clearing effort. If they caught me without my rifle in hand, there would be all sorts of grief and misery sent my way."

The response brought back the seriousness of the situation. This wasn't like a construction job back home. He and the rest of the American soldiers were targets for the disaffected citizens of this country and those who considered themselves allies of Russia. At any moment, they could find themselves under fire and would have to kill or be killed.

How was his family back home handling the news of the invasion? They had to be worried about him. Sierra too. Did that improve his chances that she'd wait for him to get back to the States? Or would it hurt his chances? For a moment, he imagined a reunion where Sierra met him at the airport and threw her arms around him as soon as he exited the plane.

The warm feeling of that scene was suddenly doused. What about the people in Italy? Were the people he had met and had come to love on his mission in danger? When Russia finished chewing up Germany, was Italy next?

Robert lugged the hose over to the first latrine and lowered the nozzle into the holding tank. Then he returned to the truck and turned on the pump. Stirring up the waste material permitted a sewage stench-storm. It didn't seem to bother Gil, but Robert covered his nose with his arm to block out the worst of the olfactory assault.

"Hiding from the problem won't make it go away," said Gil.

"Which one? Gutierrez or the smell?"

"Both."

Robert didn't bother to respond. The reminder of the danger that existed had dampened his mood, and he didn't feel like being lectured on how to be more assertive in his dealings with the rest of the unit. He worked his way through all four latrines, emptying the contents of each before disconnecting the hose and reattaching it to the chemical tank on the truck. This time, when he threw the switch, a blue liquid flowed through the hose and into the holding tank. Traces of the sewage odor remained as a new and nearly as pungent chemical smell took its place.

During the process, the hose seemed to get heavier and heavier. As Robert pulled to stretch it far enough to reach the last latrine he stepped on a brick fragment. His ankle rolled to the outside, causing him to lose his balance and pitch over sideways.

Gil propped his rifle against the truck and rushed over to help Robert stand up. "You okay? Sergeant Wojcik took off while you were still emptying the latrines. Do you want me to find him and get permission for you to see the medic?"

"No, I'm all right," said Robert. "Just embarrassed."

Ping!

Something ricocheted off the metal chemical tank, barely missing Robert's head.

The sound reminded him of the near misses in the movies as bullets flew fast and furiously in the midst of a gun battle. A bit delayed, he dove to the ground as another couple of misses rang off the vehicle. His hand fumbled for the pistol at his hip. On the third try, he finally unsnapped the case and pulled out his Berretta M9. By then, the attack had become a series of pings followed by the thud of broken bricks falling on the pavement.

Rocks.

"What are you doing on the ground?" asked Gil from a safe spot behind one of the latrines.

"We're under attack!" Robert shouted. Only then did he look for his attackers.

About a dozen boys stood at the edge of the embassy grounds, near a pile of debris. They wore dirty sweaters that had once been bright reds, yellows, and blues. Their slacks were tattered, and they had no shoes. But they all had one thing in common: expressions of hatred. The clenched mouths, knitted brows, and glaring eyes all were intended for the American soldiers.

"Yeah, we're under attack by a bunch of kids hurling rocks at us. That's no reason to panic and flop on the ground." Gil had concealed himself behind one of the latrines, keeping him safe from the continuing volley of stones.

"Excuse me," said Robert. "I guess I should be hiding behind the potty, like you."

"What'd you expect? I'm not going to just stand there and get pelted."

One of the rocks skipped off the pavement in front of Robert and smacked him in the mouth. Already, he could taste blood and feel his lips starting to swell. The pain motivated him to act, and he rolled under the truck, temporarily a bit safer from the hail of stones.

All he had to do now was figure out how to handle a mob of rock-wielding children without the situation getting out of control.

5

A strange sense of disorientation hit Sarah when she opened her eyes. The bedroom window wasn't where it was supposed to be. The pictures, awards, and various mementos of her life were nowhere to be seen. She felt . . . displaced.

Sitting up in bed, she looked around the room and spotted her desk against the opposite wall. Stacks of cardboard boxes littered the floor and reminded her that she had moved out of her parents' house. This was her new bedroom. Not just a new bedroom, but a new life as well.

A thrill passed through her as she thought about finally living away from the cramped quarters of her parents' home and the rigid rules and high expectations they had forced on her. For the last four years, her parents had woken her up at 4:00 a.m. so she would have enough time for prayer and scripture study before heading off to seminary for more of the same. Three hours of meetings on Sunday. Weekly personal interviews with Dad. Would the world suddenly end if you took a day off?

After living in the same house for nineteen years and having to share the same bedroom with her sister for nearly as long, she expected it might take a while to get used to her new living arrangements. Not that sharing an apartment with her best friend was a problem. Two years ago, when Brooke was a senior and Sarah a mere sophomore, the two had formed a friendship at school. Sarah had occasionally helped Brooke with her studies and Brooke had introduced Sarah to a more popular crowd of people.

When Sarah's parents announced that the family would be moving to Camp Valiant, Brooke had been more than eager to help Sarah with both a place to stay and a job. It looked as if Sarah's life was finally going somewhere. The lessons her parents had taught her about choosing the right and developing worthy traits were fine if you wanted to live a safe and boring life, but Sarah dreamed of having some fun while she screamed down the road to success.

Tossing back her paisley covers and rolling out of bed, Sarah knelt for morning prayer. The routine had been drummed into her head by her parents for so long that it had become habit. She paused for a moment, wondering what she should pray for now that she had moved out.

Don't be silly. Just pray for the same stuff as always.

Even with that thought in mind, it took several minutes for her to focus on the actual prayer. She offered thanks for Brooke's timely help and started in on her usual list of requests for God to look after her family when a knock sounded on her bedroom door.

"Wake up!" Brooke called through the door. "You don't want to be late for your first day of work."

Sarah sprang to her feet, afraid that her friend would walk in and see her kneeling next to her bed. Maybe she could finish the prayer later. Surely Heavenly Father understood that she needed to hurry and get ready.

With her bathroom kit in hand, she sped down the hall and hit the shower. In record time, she washed, dressed, fixed her hair, and applied makeup. Ready for the day ahead, she waltzed into the kitchen.

"Good morning," said Brooke. "You want some coffee?"

"No thanks. I'm not really a coffee drinker."

Sarah watched for any sign that her refusal had upset Brooke and silently released the breath she'd been holding when her new friend continued on with the task of making breakfast, which consisted of a large steaming cup of coffee and a peanut-butter granola bar.

Life as a Mormon had its advantages, she supposed, but Sarah just didn't have the passion for it that her parents did. As long as she stayed away from drugs, alcohol, and people sporting gang tattoos, what could it hurt to enjoy herself a little? Since Brooke seemed to know how to do that without going too far, Sarah hoped to follow in her footsteps.

"Help yourself to anything in the fridge or cupboards," said Brooke. "I don't do a lot of cooking here, but you're welcome to whatever you find."

Sarah settled for a glass of orange juice and a couple pieces of toast, lightly buttered, no jam—because there was none. She studied the apartment as she ate. Compared to this place, her parents' home seemed more like a run-down shack.

In the living room, a trio of white bookshelves stood out against the sapphire-blue wall behind them. Two padded wooden chairs and a white couch occupied the room, forming a U that allowed anyone sitting there to easily see others as they visited. In the center of the U stood a wood-framed table with a glass top, holding a crystal bowl filled with ornamental stones.

The effect, as a whole, was like the pictures Sarah had seen of homes owned by the rich and famous. During her first visit to the apartment, she had commented on the lavish lifestyle her friend lived, but Brooke claimed that it hadn't been expensive at all. It just took a little effort and a sensibility for style.

A talent that Sarah's parents had never acquired.

With Brooke as her mentor, Sarah hoped to create a home of her own every bit as breathtaking as this one. She knew that money wasn't the key to happiness, but certainly it wasn't sinful to want to live in a nice home.

The two of them finished eating and then carpooled to work in Brooke's silver Acura TLX. Brooke tuned the radio to the Roderick Dorgan show. As usual, the anti-Christian radio personality was ranting about how people of faith were the real problem in America today. Today's rant dealt with the Mormons.

When Sarah's parents had announced they were selling their home and most of their possessions so they could prepare for the Second Coming, she had thought them insane. That was the kind of talk you expected from cults, the kinds that involved crazy rituals and drinking Kool-Aid without question. She had no plans to join them in their voluntary exile into poverty.

But it sounded different when Dorgan got worked up about the topic. Sarah knew these people. The Mormons, especially her parents, weren't wild-eyed fanatics. They were kind people, however unrealistic at times, who wanted to help others. Dorgan had convinced a good number of people in the country, including President Boggs, that the Mormons represented a threat to the nation, that the food hoarding and the decision to gather the Saints were the first steps by a bunch of gun-toting survivalist to overthrow the government.

"Would you mind if we turned the radio off and just talked?" Sarah asked.

"Not at all." Brooke tapped the power button. "What do you want to talk about?"

"How about work? What's everyone else going to think when they find out that I don't have any experience in marketing?"

Brooke glanced over at Sarah, one eyebrow cocked. "First of all, they don't need to know that little detail. And really what does it matter? I convinced Joel to bring you on because you are bright, friendly, and have a knack for connecting with others. The rest you learn as you go."

"I'll do my best."

"You'd better." Brooke smiled as she said it, but there was an underlying menace in her tone. She turned the car into the Third Street, parking garage and pulled into a reserved spot on the ground level.

Brooke checked her makeup in the mirror. It was perfect—of course. Bright red lipstick and a beauty mark made her look like a brunette Marilyn Monroe. She wore a scarf around her neck like an oversized tie with a zebra-pattern that matched the frames of her sunglasses. A tight white business dress and a black designer-original jacket gave her a smart and sexy look.

"Loosen up," Brooke said as they walked into the Media Slick offices. "You have it easy today. All you have to do is follow me around and watch what I do. However, I expect you to know who everyone is by the end of the day. Not only their name, but what they do for the company."

"I should be able to handle that." Mentally, Sarah did a palm slap against her forehead. Here she stood, embarking on a career in the glamorous field of maximum-exposure marketing and that was the best she could come up with as a response?

Learning who everyone was turned out to be an easier task than she imagined.

Joel owned the company and served as the market researcher and brand manager that matched rising stars in the entertainment industry with companies wanting to maximize the impact of their advertising dollar. He set the stage for the success of everyone else. Brooke kidded that he had hired plastic surgeons to fix a smile permanently in place because no one ever saw him without one.

Olivia pulled in the high-end clients. A sultry voice and a wicked smile combined with bountiful amounts of bright red hair formed a dynamo that didn't understand the concept of "no sale."

Ethan and Ashley handled all of the art needs for the company. He was short and sharply dressed while she was tall, slender, and even better dressed. Together, they represented a living, breathing art exhibit of the human form.

Logan was the talent coordinator. He worked with gifted artists, actors, and bands looking for a breakout opportunity that would catapult them into stardom. But what really stood out about him were his soft brown eyes that drew people in and promised them the world.

And Chloe sat at the front desk, greeted visitors, and answered the phone.

A few freelancers worked with them on specific projects, but

Brooke explained that they didn't really register on the corporate radar. Sarah was exempt from having to know who they were or what they did, at least for now.

Joel called an end to the workday at 5:30 p.m. "Company meeting at the Firehouse. I think I can pop for one of their appetizer platters, but you're on the hook for anything else. Make sure to bring news of something good that I can take home with me."

"Are we really having a company meeting after work?" Sarah asked.

Brooke flashed her a don't-be-naive look. "That's just what Joel calls them. He does it to give everyone an excuse to get together and socialize a little bit before they head home. The employees don't have to go, but it probably isn't a good idea to skip all of them."

"Isn't the Firehouse a bar?" Sarah asked.

"It serves food and you can watch sports there, so I don't know that I would call it a bar. I hope that isn't going to be a problem for you."

6

A short blast of a siren sounded, and John looked up to see red-and-blue flashing lights in his rearview mirror. He gave Becky and the kids a quick look before pulling over and rolling down his window.

"You want to step out of that car?"

John recognized the voice of Sheriff McKinney. The sheriff kept the peace in the little town of Greenville, about twenty miles from Camp Valiant. The last time he saw McKinney, things were good between them. Noticing a snarl on the sheriff's face, John wondered if anything had happened to change their relationship. John climbed out of the Suburban.

"Good to see you again. I see you brought the family with you this time," said the sheriff as he removed his sunglasses and slid them into his shirt pocket. "Thought you might want to know that we've had quite a few people in town asking about you folks. They strike me as a bunch of yahoos wanting to cause trouble with the Mormons. I ask them to move on whenever I run across one, but they're starting to show up more often of late. They haven't done anything illegal yet, but I don't trust them. You might want to watch out."

"I can't say I'm surprised," John said. "Roderick Dorgan is still blasting the airwaves with propaganda about us. He's asked his listeners to take a more active stance in preventing the Mormons from bringing ruin to the nation. I'm sorry if that's causing problems for you and the town."

Sheriff McKinney flicked a hand as if brushing off the comment. "Not to worry. My job is to make sure people behave while they're in Greenville, and that responsibility extends all the way out to Camp Valiant."

"Thanks, Sheriff." John shook hands with McKinney. "Is there anything we can do to help you?"

McKinney pulled his sunglasses back out and put them on. "Just make sure all of your people stay out of trouble, and I'll handle the rest."

John opened the door and slid into the driver seat.

"Problem?" Becky asked.

"Probably. I'm not going to worry about it today though."

"Who was that, Dad?" asked Cody, the eight year old.

"That was Sheriff McKinney. He wasn't real happy about a bunch of Mormons moving in next to his town. We had some problems with him when we first started building Camp Valiant, but he's turned out to be a good friend. All it took was a disaster to tear up Greenville and our willingness to come in and help afterward."

"Cool," said Cody. "It's good to have friends when you move into a new neighborhood."

John pulled onto the road and drove through Greenville, making sure to follow the posted speed limit. He waved to people on the sidewalk, even recognizing a couple of them.

"Is this the nearest town?" asked eighteen-year-old Lucas.

"Yes, it is," said John. "For a while, Greenville may be our only contact with civilization, but I think you'll like it. The people are friendly."

"Do they have a theater?" asked Jesse, the older of the fourteen-year-old twins.

"This place is small," said the younger twin, Elizabeth. "I don't see a shoe store anywhere."

"I hope they have a McDonald's," said Cody.

"No theater," said John. "No shoe store. They don't have a McDonald's either, but they do have a Dairy Queen on the far side of town. That and Mama Pearson's Diner are the only options for dining out."

Lucas, Jesse, and Elizabeth all groaned.

"Great," said Cody. "I love Dairy Queen. Can we go there now?"

"This stinks," said Jesse. "No television. No radio. No video games. How pathetic is it that a trip to Dairy Queen will be the exciting event in our lives? I don't even like Dairy Queen."

"Let's not get into this again," said Becky. "We know this is tough on all of you. It's tough on us as well. But this is what the Lord has asked us to do. I think that it won't be so bad once you get used to it."

"Yee-haw," said Lucas, crossing his arms and staring out the windows. "I can't wait for the first community hoedown."

"Trust me," said John. "There will be plenty of positives that come from this move. I guarantee that in a few years, you are going to be so happy that we did this."

At the edge of town, John turned onto the dirt road that led to Camp Valiant. The area around the camp was mostly flat and full of grayish-green sagebrush. A few cottonwood trees broke up the otherwise barren landscape. John stopped at a gate, which marked the edge of the property owned by the Church. A sign read, "Private Property: No Trespassing."

John got out of the Suburban and opened the gate, drove the vehicle through, and then shut the gate behind them. It took another fifteen minutes before they rolled within sight of the few buildings that currently composed Camp Valiant.

In the few months John had been absent, the camp had changed. The mobile trailer had been moved close to the entrance gate, facing the sturdy fence that surrounded Camp Valiant and the dirt road approaching it. Construction on the dorm, workshop, and warehouse had been completed, their exteriors painted barn-red. The skeletons of four more buildings stood opposite the warehouse, their placement forming Camp Valiant's first street. To either side of the gate, acres and acres of fields had been cleared for cultivation, the naked dirt ready to receive seeds once planting season arrived.

Those details only briefly caught John's attention. Past the buildings, in fields still green with grass and flowers, stood dozens of white tents—sturdy tents large enough to house an entire family if they weren't too concerned about privacy.

"Where are all the houses?" asked Elizabeth.

Becky cast John a concerned look but didn't say anything.

"We might have to camp for a while," said John, "until our house is finished."

"How long will that be?" asked Jesse.

"At least a couple of months." John stopped the Suburban in front of the gate and honked the horn.

Bill Summers, the leader of the work crews at Camp Valiant, walked out of the trailer a few moments later, raising a hand above his eyes to block the sun. A grin spread across his face as he spotted John. He sprinted to the gate and opened it wide, waving the family through.

"Right on time," Bill said when John pulled his aching body out of the car.

"Actually," said John, "I'm two hours behind schedule."

"Not the way I figure it." Bill cleared his throat. "We have a few situations that I think could use your attention."

"I thought we should probably get settled first," said John.

"There will be plenty of time to do that later."

"Go ahead, John," said Becky. "It'll give the rest of us some time to stretch our legs and look around the place."

"Well, if you don't mind, then I guess that'll be okay," said John. "There's nothing like jumping right in and working to make you feel at home."

Bill laughed. "That-a-boy." He turned to face Becky and the children. "By the way, my name is Bill. I'm responsible for all of the construction at the site. You must be the Williams family."

"Where are my manners?" asked John. "This is my wife, Becky, and my four youngest children: Lucas, Elizabeth, Jesse, and Cody."

"As much as John talked about all of you," said Bill, "I feel like I know you already."

John waited until everyone in the family had shaken hands with Bill. "Now that we have the introductions out of the way, let's go take a look at these . . . situations."

Bill led John over to the warehouse, a large single-story building with enough room to store supplies for thousands of people. When he opened the door, John found it filled with boxes, plastic ten-gallon buckets, and large square cans. Only a quick sidestep kept John from tripping over the food containers.

"Maybe we could move some of these into the workshop," said John.

"We did. In fact, I'm having a hard time getting any work done over there it's so crowded. And before you even ask, the dorm and the trailer are full as well. There just isn't room to keep all the food storage and still function."

Keeping in mind the gas and food shortages the rest of the country had to deal with, John was happy to tackle this problem. Crop failures across the nation, weather-related disruption of the transportation industry, and the reduction of foreign oil supplies had all created a situation that required the Church to create a series of camps for the much anticipated gathering of the Saints.

John had initially been called to oversee the construction of the camp, but he was now the director of defense, a new calling in which he was responsible for the safety and welfare of everyone at Camp Valiant. It worried John that a calling like that should even exist. As much as he hoped the calling, or at least the title of the calling, was an unnecessary precaution, he doubted that the Brethren would have made this move without good reason.

He considered calling President Drollinger to authorize the rental of a refrigerated semitrailer. Or even two. As the stake president for this area, Drollinger had the authority to allocate resources to the camp, but John decided against the idea. Camp Valiant was intended to be largely self-sufficient. The sooner John adapted to that way of thinking, the more prepared the camp would be when the events of the world made it necessary for them to function on their own.

"How about putting them in tents?" John asked.

"I thought about that, but it's still too warm. Some of the food might spoil. Give it another month, and I think the weather will be cool enough for that to work. What do we do about it until then?"

John looked around the camp, hoping that a solution might spring up. If he put the whole construction crew on one of the unfinished buildings, it should only take a couple of days to attach the walls. They could slap some plastic over the windows and attach a swamp cooler to the building right away. That would solve the immediate problem, but at the expense of hindering the workers as they tried to finish construction on the new building.

"Let me think on that one," said John. Roughly translated, it meant give him some time to pray for inspiration because he was stumped. "Unless you have something else that needs my immediate attention, I might as well get situated."

The two of them strolled back toward John's Suburban. They had almost reached the car when a shouting match erupted among the tents. John picked up the pace, with Bill right behind him. A teenage boy and a man who looked to be his father stood next to a tent, glaring at one another. The older man, arms across his chest, ignored John's arrival.

"What's going on, Steve?" asked Bill.

"Just a little family dispute," said Steve Knoll. "Nothing that concerns you two."

"I'm afraid that it does concern me," said John.

"How do you figure that?" asked Steve.

John wondered if it really did concern him. So much of what the Saints would experience from here on out would be new. Did his calling give him the authority to intervene in an argument between parent and child?

"As the director of defense for Camp Valiant, it falls to me to make sure everyone is safe," said John. "I guess you could consider me the camp sheriff."

"And until other arrangements are made," said Bill, "he is the ranking authority for the camp. I'm in charge of the construction crews and the work that needs to be done, but John is responsible for everyone here."

Steve nodded. "My son, Roger, wants to leave."

"How old is he?" asked John.

"I'm eighteen," said Roger. "That makes me an adult, and I can leave if I want."

"No matter how old you get," said Steve, "you're still my son. As your father, I believe I know what's good for you and for the rest of the family. It's my responsibility to keep all of you safe, and that is exactly what I'm trying to do here. If I didn't love you, I wouldn't care what you did."

President Drollinger hadn't said anything about this. John had no real power here. His control of the people in the camp extended only to the level which the individuals chose to listen to him.

"This is still America," said John. "According to the laws of our country, a person has the right to make their own choices once he or she turns eighteen. If you want, I can ask Sheriff McKinney to come out here and settle the matter."

"No," said Steve. His shoulders sagged. "I'm just worried about him."

"Great," said Roger. "That means I can leave. Can you make my dad give me a ride back home?" he asked John.

"That will be up to him," said John. "Along with the right to decide whether you stay or go comes the responsibility for your actions. As an adult, if you want to return to the city, then it's up to you to find your own way. I can probably arrange to have someone take you to Greenville the next time they go, but if you're in a hurry, you might want to ask your father for a ride."

Neither father nor son spoke. John stood there long enough to make sure another fight wasn't going to break out, and then turned and headed for his family once again.

Bill gave John a friendly slap on the back. "Boy, I'm glad I don't have your job."

John just snorted and shook his head.

When he reached the Suburban, John found Becky talking with Paul Young, who sat in one of the four-wheelers the camp used to check the fences and run other errands. Paul was part of the original work crew who had come out to build Camp Valiant. With any luck he'd be here to help John unpack.

"I have something I think you need to see," said Paul.

"Right now?" After getting up extra early this morning to finish the last of the sorting and packing and then driving for two hours to get here, all John wanted to do was move into his new home and rest.

"It's probably best if you do." Paul patted the seat behind him.

"Find me when you get back, and I'll show you where you're staying," said Bill.

John grabbed a helmet sitting on the backseat and put it on. Then he mounted the four-wheeler, and Paul turned it around. They followed the fence south for about five minutes until they reached a hillside close to the edge of the property. Then they traveled along the rocky base of the hill and came across a gully.

"We walk from here," Paul announced as he stopped the vehicle.

Paul hopped down into the shallow gully and climbed up on the far side. About two hundred meters past the gully, a cave penetrated the hill.

"It looks like an old mine."

"Why didn't anyone tell me about this before?" asked John.

"Because nobody knew about it. This is a large property, and when we fenced the perimeter we never came close enough to the cave to spot it. The only reason I found it is because some of those Dorgan kooks have been sneaking around the area, and I thought they might be camping here."

John's mind was reeling. The popular radio talk show host Roderick Dorgan had created all sort of problems for the Saints with his anti-Mormon rants. According to him, the Saints were gathering so they could keep the vast stores of food they had hoarded out of the hands of the hungry American citizens who needed it. If the Dorganites were out here, then it meant problems for Camp Valiant.

On the other hand, he could have a team check out the mine. If they found it safe and stable, then this could be the cold-solution to their storage problem. John patted Paul on the back. "You've done good."

"I told you that you'd want to see it."

By the time John and Paul returned to camp, it was nearly dark. John wasted no time getting Bill to show him where the Williams family would be living. A short walk brought them to the first row of tents. Bill stopped to the right of the tent flap. "I took the liberty of selecting this one for you. It's closest to the buildings and the front gate. That makes you easy to find and places you near where most of the action is likely to take place."

A tent!

Becky and the kids stood at the entrance of the tent, luggage still in hand, and frowns dominating their faces.

"This is going to suck," said Jesse.

"Can we go back home?" asked Elizabeth.

"It's a lot less space than what I pictured in my mind," said Becky.

During the initial construction phase, he and the other men had stayed in the warehouse, and for some reason that had stuck in his mind. Even though he knew they would be living in a tent, the reality of the situation hadn't struck him until now. John enjoyed camping as much as anyone, but what was it going to be like to have the whole family live out of a tent for the next six months, or even longer?

7

"Are you planning to shoot them?" Gil asked.

Robert looked to where his companion had taken refuge behind the latrine and gave him a you-have-got-to-be-kidding scowl. "Don't be ridiculous."

"Then you should probably put the pistol away."

For a moment, Robert considered using it to scare the stone-hurling children. The sight of an unholstered weapon being waved wildly in the air had to have some intimidation value.

Or would it?

It might not scare the little monsters, but it certainly had the potential to bring a whole world of trouble down on Robert's head. His mind played out a scene where a photo of him pointing a weapon at a group of kids got displayed on every news station around the world. Even worse, what if he accidentally fired a shot and started a chain reaction of events that eventually resulted in the deaths of several innocent people?

And that was only what had popped into his head in the first few seconds. How many ways were there for this situation to go wrong? Too many. Robert slid his Berretta M9 back into its holster and secured it. "Any ideas on how to handle this situation?"

"We could call for Gutierrez and let the brats throw rocks at him instead." Gil dodged back behind the latrine as a pair of rocks flew past. "I'd rate that high on the positive-outcome scale."

"Not a chance. For the rest of my enlistment, I'd have to hear about how we were defeated in combat by a bunch of unarmed kids."

"Good point. Still, it might be worth it to see him get beaned in the head."

Robert peeked out from under the truck and waved a hand at the children. "Hey. Why are you throwing rocks at us? We're the good guys."

"Oh yeah," said Gil. "That's going to work."

The rain of stone stopped for a moment. One of the boys, the tallest, stepped forward. "Shut up, you stupid American. Go back home to your mansions and leave us honest people alone. My papa has no work because of you. Go home."

All of the children started chanting, "Go home. Go home. Go home."

Then the torrent of rocks resumed, thudding like hail on a roof.

"I think you ticked them off even more," said Gil.

"Wait!" Robert hollered. "Can't we just talk about this for a minute?"

The barrage stopped.

Robert crawled forward so he could get a good look at the children while letting them see his friendly, smiling face. "Why do you think we're responsible for your papa not having any work?"

"My papa has none of the gasoline," shouted the child. "He cannot drive his truck to the market to sell our figs. Now we will all starve so that you greedy Americans can buy fancy cars and eat at McDonald's."

"The Americans don't control the oil and gas resources here," said Robert.

"You lie. Our friends, the Russians, have told us that this is because of you."

A stone pinged off the truck and a couple more of the children cocked their arms back to throw. Robert was in danger of losing his audience.

"Of course the Russians are going to tell you that. They control the—"

A stone skipped past, just to the left of Robert's elbow. More banged against the truck. One shattered a window, showering the ground around him with glass.

Robert wiggled back to his position of safety, under the truck.

All of a sudden, the attack ceased. Robert waited a few seconds to make sure this wasn't a trick to get him to poke his head out and then he risked a quick look. The children had turned and fled. Their leader stopped once to pick up a stone and sent a last defiant message to the US Army. The missile fell way short of Robert and the truck, but the child seemed to take courage from the act anyway.

"What is going on here?" the voice of Sergeant Wojcik barked. "I step away for a minute and the two of you are hip-deep into inciting an incident with the locals."

Wojcik wasn't alone. He had brought an entire squad along with him, including Gutierrez, who sported a smirk big enough to be seen from space.

"Robert was wearing them out." Gil stepped out from behind the latrine. "Any second and they would have run home, arms aching from all the rock throwing they did."

"Shut up, Feldstein." Sergeant Wojcik picked up Gil's rifle from where it leaned against the truck and gave a look that dared him to explain. "Look at the damage to the truck. And not just any truck—my truck!"

"Sorry," said Robert. Several explanations and excuses came to mind, but he discarded each of them in quick succession. Finally, an idea popped into his mind. "I was looking for a diplomatic solution to the problem. These children are upset because their lives have been disrupted. Their families might be facing the prospect of little to no food because of the gas shortage."

"A gas shortage." Wojcik's tone had gone from angry to confused. "What gas shortage?"

"I don't know exactly, but the boy I was talking to insisted it was the reason his father was out of work. The point is I didn't want to make things worse by yelling at those kids or running them off with a stick. Who knows how that would have ended?"

"You thought all of that up on your own?" asked the sergeant, but he didn't wait for a reply. "I suppose that's a better plan than getting into a fight with a bunch of delinquents. You still screwed up, though. You should have called for help. Anytime a situation like this develops, you alert someone in the chain of command. Got it?"

"I will," said Robert. "I mean, I got it."

Wojcik studied his truck, his expression like a young boy who lost his dog.

"Couldn't we help them?" Robert asked Wojcik. "Give them some of our gas."

"No way." Wojcik shook his head emphatically. "We're short on fuel as it is. And then there's the matter of getting that gas tossed back to us as a batch of Molotov cocktails. I appreciate that you want to help these people, but we can't compromise our position. Besides, our situation here has changed."

It hadn't occurred to Robert that the children might take whatever aid the soldiers gave them and use it to attack them. Thinking about it left him with a weird feeling like the moment when you close your car door and realize that your keys are locked inside.

Wojcik glanced once more in the direction the children had fled and then dismissed the men who had followed him. He signaled Robert to follow him. "I have a new assignment for you."

That didn't sound good, but Robert couldn't think of any task worse than latrine detail. Whatever it was had to be bad. Really bad.

Gil fell into step behind Robert.

"Not you, Feldstein." Wojcik tossed Gil's rifle at him. "You get to clean up this mess. Glass, rocks, and anything else that doesn't belong here. Then when you're finished with that, you can give my baby a bath. Make sure she shines by the time you're done."

"Why me?" asked Gil.

"Williams may be a clueless recruit, but at least he tried to do something. He didn't hide behind a latrine and wait for the problem to go away."

"That's not—"

"I don't want to hear it." Sergeant Wojcik raised his voice, halting whatever Gil had been about to say. "Just do what I said and then you can report back to your unit."

Robert almost allowed himself to smile. Even if for just a moment, Gil rather than Robert was in the pit of disfavor. Then guilt replaced that small sense of relief. He refused to embrace a better-him-than-me attitude. Everyone lost with that one.

Sergeant Wojcik marched over to a Humvee that had a pair of NCOs standing at the back. They had the rear hatch open, working on something inside.

"Williams," said Wojcik. "This is Sergeant Shaw."

A stocky black man turned around and looked Robert over. Shaw had deep creases in his forehead from the intense scowl he wore. He crossed his arms over his chest like a tollgate barring entrance to his soul.

"And this is Corporal Cohen." Sergeant Wojcik nodded in the direction of a man who was average looking in every way except his eyes. They were the lightest blue he had ever seen and held a dangerous impression of crazy within them.

"Gentlemen, this here know-nothing private is Williams," Wojcik said, indicating Robert. "If you have anything dangerous that needs to be done—use him. There are plenty more like him, but we would have to pull a lot of strings to replace either one of you."

"Understood," said Shaw, with a deep voice that sounded a bit like someone gargling with boulders.

The two NCOs glanced at Robert and then gave one another a what-are-we-going-to-do-with-him look.

As Robert stood there, nervously waiting as the NCOs conferred with one another, he examined the equipment in the back of the Humvee. Blocks of what appeared to be clay had wires coming out of them. Then it dawned on Robert that these were explosives. "You're the demolition experts."

"That we are," Shaw rumbled.

Cohen gave a single nod, his creepy eyes remaining fixed on Robert.

"What am I going to be doing?" Robert asked.

Both of them laughed.

"You're going to help us blow up an embassy," said Shaw.

"Ours?" Robert asked.

"Yep," said Shaw.

"I thought we were going to clear out the debris so we could rebuild it."

"Change of plans," said Shaw, loading explosives into a backpack. "This is the second time terrorists have attacked this embassy in the last decade, and with Russia on the offensive, the region isn't safe. Washington wants us to pack up anything worth keeping and then blow the whole thing. The Turkish government can worry about cleaning up the mess."

That didn't make any sense to Robert. Turkey was an ally. They should be helping secure the embassy. Instead, it seemed like both sides were anxious to evacuate the US soldiers.

"Okay," said Robert, "but what am I doing with you guys?"

"We blew up our last assistant," said Cohen. "We need a new one."

Robert hoped the corporal was kidding, but with those eyes, he couldn't be sure.

Now that he'd talked, Cohen sounded like a cartoon character from the movies. A maniacal, death-dealing cartoon character. Robert wasn't sure which bothered him more, the silent Corporal Cohen or the weasel-voiced Corporal Cohen.

Sergeant Shaw laughed again. "We're just yanking your chain, Williams. Our last assistant transferred out. He said that the constant threat of being blown to bits made it hard to sleep at night."

That response didn't make him feel any better about the situation. Robert had gone from menial tasks in a semi-dangerous area to having death placed directly in his hands. If there was any good that could come out of this, it was that the Corps of Engineers had finally placed him in a spot where he could learn an actual engineering skill.

"Look on the bright side," said Shaw. "If you screw up, you won't be around long enough to worry about it."

And yet, as dangerous as his new placement sounded and as hard as the two NCOs worked to tease Robert, it didn't bother him. In fact, it felt right to be with these two men, as insane as they might seem.

"You do know that I don't have any demolitions training," said Robert.

Shaw shrugged. "That just means we don't have to unlearn you all the junk they teach in demolitions school. Instead, you will be getting the very finest education available—on-the-job training with Cohen and me."

Cohen offered a wicked grin.

"What do I do?" Robert asked.

"Carry this." Shaw handed him a large concrete drill.

Robert lifted it and then set it back down. It was heavy. Getting a better hold on the drill, he lifted it again and hefted it onto his shoulder. He hoped they were taking a direct route to whatever part of the building needed to be drilled. Picking up the drill repeatedly could definitely wear a person out.

Shaw and Cohen each grabbed a bag of gear, and then the sergeant led the way. They marched into the section of the building that still remained standing. Dust covered the white marble tile and anti-American graffiti adorned the walls. They took the stairs up to the second floor.

Halfway up, Robert understood why the previous assistant had chosen to transfer. He stopped to rest and to get a better grip on the drill. Luckily, the embassy was only three stories tall—he could imagine what it would be like with a taller building. The two demolition experts didn't blow up their assistants—they wore them out.

When they reached the second floor, Shaw pulled out a set of blueprints and studied them. After a moment, he set them down and started marking spots on the floor. He turned to Robert. "Drill wherever I mark the building. Sink the holes the full length of the bit."

Assault-rifle fire crackled in the distance.

Shaw seemed to take no interest in it until a series of bursts followed. He glanced in the direction of the sound and then returned to his work, his expression more serious than before. "We better get a move on this."

"Yep." Cohen cupped a hand to his ear. "Nothing like the festive sounds of AKs and M-16s exchanging greetings with one another. Must be a party."

"Not my kind of party, though," said Shaw.

"You can tell what kind of guns those are from the sound?" asked Robert.

"Yep," said Cohen.

"That's the easy part," said Shaw. "The AK-74 is an updated version of the assault weapon the Russians normally supply to their second-rate allies. What I don't know is who brought them into Turkey and whether they're shooting at the Turks—or our guys. In either case, you better get a move on it."

Robert nodded and then dashed down the steps to the unit's compressor parked in front of the building. He grabbed a coiled air-hose, checked to make sure it was plugged in, and returned as fast as he could uncoil the line.

Before he reached the building, Robert spotted Gutierrez heading straight at him.

"Tell the amazing exploding duo they need to hurry up," said Gutierrez. "Captain Mayo has orders to pull out as soon as we can."

"Gotcha," said Robert.

"No, I don't think you do." Gutierrez put a restraining hand on Robert's shoulder. "That popping sound you hear isn't fireworks celebrating our presence in the city. The word is that Russia has armed Turkish dissidents and they're headed our way. If the three of you don't get done before they arrive, we may just leave you behind."

"Then shouldn't you let me get back to work?" Robert asked, unable to avoid sneaking in a liberal amount of sarcasm into his voice.

"Listen, recruit . . ." Gutierrez had a finger ready to jab into Robert's chest. But Shaw called out from a window above. "Just get it done. Fast!"

49

Robert ascended the stairs two steps at a time, paying out the air-hose as he went. He plugged in the drill and set immediately to sinking holes in the concrete floor, the smell of stone dust filling his nose. Sometimes when he stopped to move the drill to a new location, he heard gunfire in the distance. And in the not-so-distant streets nearby.

As Robert drilled holes in the floor, Shaw marked spots on the columns, placing big red Xs with a circle at the center. Cohen had brought up the explosive charges and started inserting them into the holes.

Even though Robert had started boring holes before Cohen had moved the explosives to the second floor, the corporal was quickly catching up. To make matters worse, Shaw finished marking columns and was now helping Cohen set the charges.

Robert drilled the last two holes with Shaw and Cohen watching him, arms crossed and faces scowling. He backed the drill out of the hole in the floor and set it down. Only now did he permit himself an opportunity to stretch his aching muscles.

"What are you doing?" asked Shaw.

Robert scanned the floor to see if he had missed a spot. "I'm done. I drilled all of the locations you marked on the floor."

"The columns need to be drilled," said Cohen, without looking up from his efforts to place the explosives in place.

"How am I going to do that?" asked Robert. "I can't lift this drill up and use it on those columns."

"Get the baby drill," said Shaw. "It should be next to where you found Big Al."

The trip down to the engineer vehicle took longer this time. Fatigue had worked its way into Robert's bones. He wasn't sure how he was going to manage to drill another twenty holes into the thick support columns. Then a fierce exchange of gunfire sounded only a few blocks away.

He pictured a scene of Shaw, Cohen, and himself working frantically amid a pelting rain of bullets. With renewed energy, he snagged the baby drill and sprinted back to the first column. He had four columns completely prepped for demolitions before his fear-inspired strength faded.

This time when he moved to a new spot, he heard no gunfire. That bothered Robert even more than the constant reminder of the hostile forces working their way closer to the American soldiers. A sense nagged at him that whatever forces had been opposing the AK-74-wielding fanatics had given up, leaving the unknown enemy to move unopposed against the embassy.

Gutierrez appeared at the top of the stairs. "Captain Mayo says you have thirty minutes to finish this up. It will take the rest of us that long to get everything loaded and ready for transport."

Then he retreated from view, the sound of rapid steps descending the stairs serving as his good-bye.

Robert lifted the baby drill . . . or at least he tried. He raised it to about chest level before his arms shook from the strain. Not willing to give up, he grunted for added strength and lifted it another couple of inches before his arms gave out.

How am I going to drill another two dozen holes?

"Williams!" a cartoon-weasel voice yelled next to Robert's ear.

Robert jumped. His heart stayed up in the air as the rest of his body returned to earth. Cohen was insane. Any moment now they could start taking fire from hostiles in the city and the corporal found this to be the appropriate time to scare the insides out of the new assistant.

"What?" Robert shouted, the response coming out louder and sharper than he intended.

"Give me the drill." Cohen laughed. "You're too slow. In case you hadn't heard, we have to get out of here. Go help Sergeant Shaw."

Cohen didn't wait for a response; he took the drill out of Robert's hands, bored the necessary holes in record time, and then moved on to the next column.

If Shaw was feeling any pressure, it didn't show. Slowly, methodically, he worked on wiring the explosives, each of his moves deliberate and precise.

"Congratulations on passing Explosives 101," said Shaw. "Are you ready for the next stage of your engineering education?"

Education? People with guns were on their way even as they spoke and the sergeant chatted like it was a lesson in school. He wanted to scream at Shaw to hurry it up, but what came out of his mouth was, "What do you need me to do?"

"Watch."

Oh, sure!

If he hadn't been certain before, he was now. Shaw and Cohen were certifiable. That made sense when you considered that they handled explosives on a regular basis and a single mistake could send them home in body bags small enough to hold your lunch.

"Pull. Secure. Insert. Check. Double check."

The words brought Robert's attention back to Shaw and the explosives.

"You pull the next detonation wire from the harness," said Shaw, emphasizing his actions as he spoke. "Secure the explosives in place. Then insert the detonator into the C4. When you've done that, go back and check it. And then check it again. Got it?"

"Sure," said Robert. "Pull. Secure. Insert. Check and double check."

For the first time during the instruction Shaw looked up at Robert. "Make sure you don't forget those last two steps."

"I won't," said Robert.

Pull. Secure. Insert. Check. Double check.

Pull. Secure. Insert. Check. Double check.

Once Shaw started, he moved like a machine. They finished the floor quicker than Robert expected, but still not fast enough.

"Ten minutes," Gutierrez shouted from below.

Cohen had just finished drilling the columns. He switched tasks and placed explosives in the holes with Shaw following right behind him. In a way, it looked like a strange masculine dance of death. But one that was too slow for Robert's liking.

They moved to the last column.

Pull. Secure. Insert. Check. Double check.

Pull. Secure. Insert. Check.

Shaw folded up his toolkit and turned to face Robert. "Ready?"

Robert hesitated. He had paid close attention to every charge that Shaw had readied. The sergeant had followed the exact same procedure for each on of them—except the last. Did he dare tell Shaw that he missed a step? Or maybe Robert had just missed it.

"Um . . . ," Robert started.

"What is it?" Shaw demanded, staring straight into Robert's eyes.

"Double check. Sir."

"Do you have a problem with the sergeant's work, Private?" Cohen wheezed from his position behind Robert.

"I . . . I don't have a problem with his work. It's just that he didn't double check the last charge."

The faintest hint of a smile crept across Shaw's face. "Is that so?"

"Yes." Robert wanted to say more, but nothing came to mind.

"Do you know what that means, Corporal?" asked Shaw.

"It sounds like he passed the next test," said Cohen.

"I guess that's what it means," said Shaw, smiling.

The sound of the unit's Humvees being started interrupted the moment. It was followed almost immediately by Gutierrez's announcement, "Mount up. Let's get out of here."

"We can celebrate later," said Shaw. "Williams, you grab the airhose and the baby drill. The corporal can take Big Al. And I'll grab our tools. Move it, gents."

The three of them double-timed it downstairs. Robert and Cohen loaded the equipment into the engineering Humvee while Shaw rolled the detonation wire down the street to a point safely around the neighboring building.

Assault weapons discharged their deadly loads a couple of blocks away. A quick exchange between two unseen forces and then there was silence again.

That signaled the rest of the unit to mobilize. Except for the demolition vehicle, all of the Humvees executed an orderly withdraw in the opposite direction of the gunfire.

Cohen sat in the driver's seat, with the engine running.

Shaw connected the wires to the detonator.

Robert hunkered down behind the sergeant.

Shaw signaled Cohen with a thumbs-up and then moved his hand over the detonation switch.

The ground shook. Buildings shook. A low rumble rose up from the ground. The noise and shaking lasted almost half a minute and then subsided.

"Can we get out of here now?" asked Robert.

"Not yet," said Shaw. "I still have to blow up the embassy."

"Then what was all that ground shaking?"

"You tell me," said Shaw, "and then we'll both know."

8

In war, timing is vital to the success of any campaign. That rang even truer in the kind of war Calvin waged against partisan politics, which threatened to allow Russia to stomp all over Europe.

Calvin checked his watch. He knew from experience that Boggs tended to run long on his speeches. If he left his office now, there would be just enough time to ditch Curly and Moe and still make it over to where a potpourri of politicians and the press had gathered to hear Boggs wax eloquently about his plans to solve the growing civil unrest in the country.

An intern who owed Calvin a favor had had the chance to look at the speaking notes for the event. Somewhere in the middle, Boggs would mention the disaster in Italy as part of the hype, demonstrating his great compassion for the unfortunate.

Right at that point, Calvin planned to present the solution, ready for Boggs to endorse. Surrounded by press and members of his own political party, who had been taking a beating in the recent approval polls, the President would have no choice but to sign.

Calvin tucked the document into his jacket pocket and casually walked out the door of his office. He traded a couple of pleasantries with his secretary, Gwen, and announced his intention to visit the restroom.

Curly and Moe fell right into step behind him.

"Boys . . ." Calvin placed a palm on each of their chests and stopped them. "I think I can manage this on my own, and this is one of those times that I *really* don't want an audience."

"Mr. McCord," said Curly, "it's our job to stay with you wherever you go and make sure you're safe. Restrooms are the most likely spot for an assassination attempt."

"You can't seriously be worried that anyone other than Boggs, wants me killed. I think this is just an opportunity for you to spy on me. What could I possibly do in the bathroom that Boggs needs to know?"

The comment seemed to set the agents back on their heels. Moe shifted uneasily from one foot to the other. "I don't have an answer for that, Mr. McCord, but I have explicit orders to stay with you."

Calvin hadn't reckoned on this sort of reaction from his security detail. He had almost decided to order them away when an idea struck. "If the bathroom is so dangerous, then perhaps the two of you better go ahead of me. When you give me the all-clear signal, I can come in and conduct my business. Make it quick, though. I'm under a lot of pressure at the moment."

The agents hurried inside the bathroom. Before the door had finished closing, Calvin dashed down the hall in the opposite direction. With any luck, he could move out of sight before the agents had finished their security sweep of the bathroom.

A couple of hallways and a flight of stairs later, he switched to a more leisurely pace. He whistled "The Army Goes Rolling Along" as he walked, fighting the urge to look back to see if they were following him.

As soon as he turned the corner, he sprinted through the building. Political decorum dictated that VIPs never move faster than a brisk walk. Calvin's jog through the hallowed halls of power raised more than a few eyebrows. However, his only concern at the moment was avoiding the Secret Service, who upon seeing him would wonder where the Vice President's escort was and call in an alert.

He dropped in behind a couple of aides who were too busy

bragging about their latest hot dates to notice him and followed them through the corridors, feigning interest in their discussion. That allowed him to keep his head turned away from most of the people they encountered without attracting attention.

The tactic worked until he reached the checkpoint. Nobody passed through without being identified and searched.

"Mr. McCord," said the security guard, "I didn't recognize you at first. You normally have your security detail with you. Do you want me to find out where they are?"

"That won't be necessary," said Calvin. "I'm sure they'll be along any moment now. If you could just hurry this along, I'm late for a meeting."

The guard waved him through, and Calvin strode away from the checkpoint with a determined stride, hoping it was slow enough to avoid extra attention and fast enough to move him out of the area before the Secret Service had a chance to track him down.

Calvin slipped into the conference room and joined the crowd in the back, keeping low to prevent anyone from spotting him. He stood behind a pair of photographers and pretended to admire the gold curtains next to him. The room was too warm from the unusually large number of reporters packed tightly into the limited space.

All attention was on the President, reporters furiously scribbling notes on paper. The soft clicks of cameras echoed in the room as reporters snapped a continuous stream of pictures. Calvin waited for Boggs to mention Italy and hoped that Curly and Moe hadn't put out an all-points bulletin on him already.

The President's self-administered pats on the back went on longer than Calvin had anticipated. Across the room, a door opened, and Agents Bowers and Hancock stepped inside. They scanned the gathered dignitaries and then briefly looked out across the crowd. Agent Bowers shook his head at Agent Hancock, and then they exited the room.

"A few of you have been asking me what plans are in the works to help our allied nation of Italy after the horrendous disaster that befell them yesterday." Boggs puffed up his chest and beamed his best "aren't I grand?" smile at the crowd. "And I am happy to inform all of you that—"

"I have a solution for the problem!" Calvin shouted from across the room, the documents held high above his head. He elbowed his way through the mass of people standing at the back of the room and moved to the front, avoiding the Secret Service agents who moved tentatively to intercept him.

Boggs stiffened at the sound of Calvin's voice. His eyes flicked from side to side, locating the agents in the room and their progress toward the Vice President. For a moment, he seemed to have forgotten the television cameras and the horde of reporters standing before him as his face reddened and his fist clenched the podium. Then he broke out one of his practiced smiles and stepped forward to greet Calvin.

"We could all use a bit of good news." Boggs took Calvin's hand and shook it. The grip was firm, almost crushing. "Please, tell us what you have in mind."

"A unit of the United States Army Corp of Engineers is currently stationed in Turkey. All you need to do is give the word and sign this document. They can be mobilized within the hour and on their way to relieve the suffering of the good people of Italy."

"Is sending our soldiers to the area really the best solution to this problem?" Boggs asked. "A disaster relief program seems more in line with their needs."

"Engineers, Mr. President," Calvin jumped right in with his response. "The Army Corp of Engineers. They handle matters of disaster relief on a daily basis. In fact, there is probably nobody better suited to the task. Any other solution will take time to organize— time that our allies, the Italians, don't have."

An uncomfortable silence filled the room, broken only by the soft whir of cameras. All eyes focused on Calvin and Boggs.

Calvin made a show of placing the documents on the table in front of the President and handed him a pen.

The President kept a rigid smile on his face and snatched the pen. As he leaned forward to sign the papers, he whispered to Calvin,

"You will not get away with this blatant public blackmail. I guarantee that this is the last time you use the media to force my hand. This will not end well for you."

Placing his arm around Boggs's shoulder, Calvin faced him toward the crowd. "I hope you appreciate the decisive leadership that President Boggs has shown here today. Everyone, stand up and give him the recognition he deserves."

If anything, the Washington crowd knew how to applaud on demand. Calvin hated the theatrics he had just performed, but gut instinct told him that if they didn't do something to stop Russia, the United States might very well find an angry bear growling at its doorstep in a few months.

The crowd stood to give Boggs their adorations.

Calvin took that as his cue to retreat from the conference room. He spotted Agents Bowers and Hancock making their way through the throng of people. Holding the document high over his head, he waded toward the exit, waving people to the side. The mass of humanity before him parted to either side, as if letting an Olympic torchbearer through. Then they closed ranks, preventing Bowers and Hancock from catching him.

After breaking free from the crowd, Calvin sprinted out of the room and took the closest elevator he could find. Changing levels would put him out of the line of sight of the two pursuing Secret Service agents. After that, it was a matter of weaving his way through the halls until he reached the parking garage.

He took the stairs down to the garage level, sneaking a quick peek to make sure no agents were in the vicinity, and then he quickstepped it to his Mercedes. Ten minutes later, he walked into the office of a friend at the Pentagon.

"I have authorization to send troops into Italy"—Calvin pulled out the documents—"signed by the President himself."

General Ken Condie cocked an eyebrow. He leaned forward in his chair and accepted the documents across his large mahogany desk. "You must've gotten an early start on Happy Hour, Calvin. The President has been shutting down the military whenever he can and withdrawing our troops from key strategic points when that doesn't work. Moving our forces into Europe will be seen as a sign of opposition to the Russians."

"That's what I had in mind, except we're deploying the U.S.A.C.E. and calling them an organized and ready-to-function disaster relief group. Once we have them in place, if there's any movement by the Russians in their direction, we can force Boggs to support our people with a larger military force."

"There is no way that President Boggs agreed to this." General Condie scrutinized the document. "Looks like his signature all right. Did you forge it?"

"I have a room full of witnesses that saw Boggs sign off on this action less than twenty minutes ago. If we act fast, we can get this into motion before he finishes his conference and has a chance to stall the deployment."

"Where are the engineers now?" Condie asked.

Calvin walked over to a world map that hung on one of the walls and pointed to Turkey. "Ankara. Almost right next door to where we want to send them."

General Condie rubbed his chin while examining the documents.

"We have to do this," said Calvin. "Boggs is planning to slap the Russians on the wrist and then tell them to play nice with the other nations. He thinks this will preserve the US image in the world community without having to commit any actual combat troops to the war."

"But in reality," said Condie, "we're placing these engineers in harm's way just so we have an excuse to act against the Russians when they threaten to attack the unit."

"They're soldiers first and engineers second. Besides, it's the only way I can think of to get some troops on the ground before Russia tramples over all of Europe. We both know they're not going to stop in Germany."

"A single company of engineers isn't going to be much help against a couple of reinforced armor divisions," said General Condie. "The Russians wouldn't even have to slow down to grind our guys into the ground."

"They would be working with NATO troops until reinforcements arrived. Still, it might be a good idea to assign an infantry company to the mission. Who can complain about attaching a small contingent of soldiers to defend our own people on a mission of mercy?"

"President Boggs has made it clear that he will in no way support military action of any kind in Europe. If he finds out what you're really up to, then both of us could be tried for treason."

"It's the right thing to do," said Calvin.

"Maybe." Condie picked up the documents. "I'll send the troops, but I'm going to hold onto these orders. Hopefully, they will be enough to keep my career from flushing down the toilet."

"Thanks, Ken."

"I hope it's worth it." Condie opened a wall safe and stored the documents inside.

———

Calvin decided against making it any easier for Boggs to stop the deployment. Without access to the exact details of the mission, it would be harder to counter the orders. He drove to a small bed and breakfast he frequented whenever he wanted to escape the political madness of Washington and checked in under an alias. Calvin requested to have lunch and dinner delivered to his room.

Around midnight, a text came in from an unidentified sender. It said, "On the way."

Calvin slept better than he had in a long while knowing that General Condie had succeeded in deploying the company of army engineers. He woke up late, ordered a big breakfast, and took his time eating it. Bacon. Eggs. Pancakes. His doctor wouldn't approve, but Calvin didn't care. He savored every salty bite of bacon and each sweet mouthful of pancakes.

Full and well-rested, he made the trip back to the political jungle.

As he rode the elevator up from the parking garage, Calvin turned on his cell phone. Almost double the usual number of messages vied for his attention, most of them marked urgent. He read through the senders' names and listened only to those people he was waiting to hear from.

When he walked into his office, Calvin noticed that Gwen seemed unnaturally stiff. He looked around and noticed that Agents Bowers and Hancock stood on either side of the door behind him. Hancock grinned a wicked little grin.

"Where are Curly and . . . where are the men the agency assigned to protect me?" asked Calvin.

"They have been reassigned," said Bowers. "Agent Hancock and myself are now part of your new security detail."

"And because of a threat the agency received overnight," said Hancock, "we have been instructed to not let you out of our sight. Not to worry, Mr. McCord. We promised President Boggs that we would take good care of you."

9

"Has the military gone out of its tiny, narrow, war-happy mind?" Gil asked for the sixth time in the last hour. "Russia is storming through Europe, and they want to put us directly in the path of the entire Russkie Army. I'd like to get my hands on the genius who thought up this wonderful piece of strategic planning."

Gutierrez turned around in the driver's seat of the Humvee. "I'm sure the brass at the Pentagon are waiting to hear what Private Know-Everything has to say on the matter." There was a greater-than-usual level of snarkiness in his voice.

"Get them on the phone and make sure to tell them to run any further ideas they have past me before they put them into action," said Gil. "Right, Robert?"

Robert grunted. He had participated in the first round of discussion about the unit's deployment to Italy in response to the earthquake that hit the region. Two days of arguments over the sanity of whoever made that decision had worn thin. Gil and Gutierrez could continue this latest reincarnation of the issue without him. He planned to finish his latest letter from Sierra. It still carried the floral scent of her perfume.

Dear Robert,

The networks just announced that Russia invaded Germany. That'll be old information by the time this letter reaches you. I doubt that I have anything to say about it that hasn't already gone through your mind.

I walked through the living room the other day while my dad was watching an old war movie. It's strange comparing the black-and-white film about WWII to the war in Europe today. They feel so different. Maybe that's because the war there now has the chance of impacting the lives of the people I know. The other one is just history. I wonder if my grandchildren will feel the same way in fifty years.

When they announced the invasion yesterday, the people here went crazy. I called in sick today because I didn't feel safe driving to work. In a way, it feels like we're at war here as well.

At least you aren't close to the fighting.

Like they said in the movie, "Keep your head down and your socks dry."

—Sierra

While he was reading the letter, Robert felt as if he were with Sierra. She had included a picture of herself sitting on the hood of her red Toyota Corolla with her legs kicked out in front of her. She had a quirky expression that was part smile and part smirk. The distance at which the picture had been taken prevented her freckles from showing. Her brown hair hung down on one side in a braid.

But it was her eyes that always caught his attention.

Blue. Like a beautiful spring day. Although on any day—spring, summer, fall, or winter—those eyes caused her to stand out in a crowd.

That's how Robert felt.

"What are you looking at, recruit?" asked Gutierrez.

"A picture of my girlfriend," said Robert. "At least, I think she's my girlfriend."

"You must have left some impression on her if you don't know. Let me see." Gutierrez reached for the picture but couldn't stretch his arm far enough back to grab it.

Robert folded up the letter with the intent of stowing it and the picture into his shirt pocket, safe from Gutierrez. His hand hesitated. He wanted to read it again. Read it for the twentieth time. Read it for the hundredth time. Because as long as he kept reading, he wouldn't have to look out the window and see the damage the series of earthquakes had inflicted on his beloved Italy. As long as Sierra's captivating eyes gazed at him from the picture, he could ignore the devastation.

"What was the Army thinking when they sent us here?" Gil complained again.

"They were thinking that the people need our help." The response burst out of Robert. "They were thinking that earthquakes don't pick convenient times and places to strike, and we have to go *when* and *where* we are needed."

His comments silenced Gil and Gutierrez, who both had their mouths still open in mid-argument. Good! That meant he had their attention. Maybe something he said would sink in.

"They were thinking that we're the good guys." Robert's voice had dropped to its normal level, the angry edge of a moment ago gone. "And that America is not afraid to risk the lives of its soldiers to save others."

Gil shut his mouth and nodded.

The rest of the soldiers in the vehicle seemed content to stare out the windows at the disrupted countryside. For once, Robert had silenced them.

Then Gutierrez spoke. "Why are you even riding with us? Shouldn't you be with Shaw and Cohen?"

"Their vehicle is filled with demolition gear," said Robert.

"In other words," said Gutierrez, "they only had room for the important stuff."

That triggered a round of laughs from the men in the vehicle.

Sooner or later, Robert was going to have to face the aftermath of the earthquake. Maybe if he focused on what he could do to help the people here it might dull some of his fear of being so close to the Russian front. For the first time since they had left the landing field, Robert looked out the window of the Humvee.

The homes he spotted along the road didn't look as bad as those around the airport where their C23 Sherpa had landed. Based on the few reports that Command had bothered to pass along to them, he knew that most of the damage in Italy had occurred in the southern portion of the country.

Why were they headed north when they were needed so badly in the south? It didn't make sense. They were moving away from the area that needed the most help. And without all of the equipment they normally took with them.

"I still don't understand how Russia was able to hit Germany without any warning," said Gil.

"They might have rolled through Poland," said Gutierrez.

"You mean over Poland, like Germany did in '39," said one of the soldiers at the back of the Humvee.

"Too bad HQ is blocking all of our media access," said Gutierrez. "Otherwise we could turn on CNN and know everything we wanted to know about the war."

"I guess it was going to happen sooner or later," said Robert. He kept his voice low enough that he hoped only Gil, sitting next to him, could hear it.

"What was going to happen?" asked Gil.

"Armageddon," said Robert. "The prophets have warned us that there would be 'wars and rumors of wars' in the last days. These are the events that are foretold to happen prior to the Second Coming."

"Are you kidding?" Gutierrez snorted.

There went Robert's hope for keeping this part of the conversation between him and Gil.

"I hate to admit it, but I have to agree with Mr. Dim," Gil said with a nod toward Gutierrez. "War is war. Russia deciding to give Germany a little payback for WWII has nothing to do with religion or the return of God. War is just the natural state of man."

"You're not going to start preaching to us?" asked Gutierrez. "Because I don't think I can take that. I'll just surrender to the Russians right now, even if I have to drive through half of Europe to do it."

Robert considered shutting up. But the damage was done. Regardless of what he said now, Gutierrez was going to heckle him over what he had already heard. "Don't you believe that the Savior will return and rule the earth?"

"I'm Jewish," said Gil. "I don't believe Jesus has the power to return from the dead, or save the earth, or bring peace and harmony to the misguided masses that live here."

"Well, I'm not Jewish," said Gutierrez, "and it still sounds like a bunch of crazy Mormon talk to me. Why don't you go back to staring at the picture of your girlfriend?"

Robert fidgeted with the letter in his hand and fell silent. He hadn't considered what the civil unrest back home, the increase in disasters, and now the war in Europe might mean to someone who believed differently than he did. For him, all of this was a means for God to humble His children. How were unbelievers to turn to Jesus for help if they didn't even believe He existed?

The Saints.

A voice inside his head gave Robert the answer. It reminded him of the lessons in Church that discussed how it was the responsibility of the faithful to spread the word to everyone else.

Was that why he was here? Did he need to get Gil to understand that Jesus was the Messiah, and that they were in the midst of the End-Times?

Maybe Gutierrez was right. It did sound like crazy Mormon talk.

Their vehicle rolled past buildings that had partially collapsed. People near the road paused from clearing debris and watched as the Americans continued along the road, a sad and defeated look in the Italians' eyes.

Robert's heart ached to help the dirty and ragged individuals he saw, but the fear he felt threatened to overpower all else. He didn't want to die. And he certainly didn't want to kill anyone, even if they were an invading army. The possibility that he would be involved in a kill-or-be-killed situation weighed on his shoulders like a lead jacket.

The vehicle stopped just before a town square. At the center stood a fountain with a statue of some important historical figure on top and nearly a dozen smaller statues surrounding the base. Streams of water arced out of the cherubic statuettes.

White, gray, and yellow buildings surrounded the square, all of them showing damage of one sort or another. In a couple of cases, walls had partially crumbled, the bricks still occupying the street where they had fallen. A tall, square clock tower that stood a silent vigil over the town had lost most of its parapets, giving it the look of a beheaded giant.

Robert's mood darkened even further upon seeing an architectural artifact wounded like this. Ancient and noble like the town around it, it should have been spared. His eyes moved from damaged building to damaged building as he crawled out of the Humvee.

The people in the square looked up from the jagged piles of stone they were bent over and then straightened up, stretching their back and resting their arms. Dust coated their clothes and skin except where sweat had turned it into mud. As they watched the Americans, a flicker of hope registered in their eyes.

An elderly woman stepped out from the middle of the crowd and walked straight toward Robert. She wore a simple brown-on-green floral print, a heavy dark-brown sweater over the top of it, and a dark-green headscarf. Curls of white hair strayed out from under the scarf. Deep wrinkles creased her browned skin. But her eyes shone with the brightness of youth. Within them, a twinkle of joy greeted Robert.

"*Sono lieto che l'abbia finalmente arrivato.*" She may have said it in Italian, but Robert understood it as well as if it had been spoken in English. Then she smiled and gave him a matronly hug. "God told me you would come."

10

The Firehouse bar was different than how Sarah had pictured it in her head. No dark, dusty corners to cloak the nefarious activities of creepy underworld thugs. No hunched-over forms of drunks lined along a bar, mumbling about the lost opportunities of their youth. No looming threats of ill consequences that her parents had always warned her about in places like this.

She felt a little uneasy being in a place that primarily served alcohol but shrugged that off as the conditioned response her parents had worked so hard to instill in their children. The Firehouse itself turned out to be fairly charming. Wooden ladders, fire extinguishers, and fireman uniforms adorned the red-brick walls. A large faux fireman pole occupied the center of the room. And several Dalmatian statues, bearing adorable expressions of curiosity, watched over the customers.

The smell of steaks cooking over a wood-flame grill and the muted sounds of jazz playing in the background made the place feel more like a themed restaurant than a nightclub.

Sarah forced herself to relax. She wanted to fit in with her coworkers. With her family gone, she *needed* to fit in with these people. Besides, how could one visit to a place like this be spiritually dangerous?

A waitress seated them in one of the corners next to a yellow fire hydrant that had "New York, Fire Dept. 1904" printed on the side and a sign that promised relief if the situation got too hot during the evening.

Joel ordered a Firestorm appetizer platter. The waitress went around the table taking drink orders. Everyone except Logan ordered drinks that Sarah had never heard of before. Logan asked for a beer.

Then the waitress stood there, looking at Sarah, waiting for her to decide.

Sarah didn't want any alcohol, even though her new friends probably expected her to drink with them. The problem was that she didn't know what else to order. Did they even serve non-alcoholic beverages here?

"Can I have a soda, please?" she asked.

"Coke okay?"

She gave a half-nod, half-shrug gesture, unsure if the choice was all right or not, but said, "Sure."

The response hadn't drawn any surprised or disapproving looks from the others. That might not have been the case if she adhered to the strict no-caffeine policy many of her Mormon friends had adopted.

Joel looked Sarah in the eyes. "How did you like your first day on the job?"

"I thought it was amazing. Who wouldn't? All of you . . ." Sarah blushed at being the center of attention in a group that routinely worked with the rich and famous. "I mean all of us have the opportunity to shape the attitudes of society. We have the chance to look at the world in a new way and share that vision with everyone else. I can't wait to start contributing to the process."

"What'd I tell you?" Brooke asked Joel. "Sarah is perfect for us."

"I never doubted it for a moment." Joel flashed an even bigger and toothier smile than normal. He grabbed a drink from the tray the waitress carried over and held it in the air. "Here's to our new office assistant Sarah and to a long, profitable career with Media Slick."

The rest of the group took their drinks and joined in the toast.

Sarah tingled inside. Under the table, she bounced her legs in joyous celebration, but she kept her upper half calm and poised. She had found a place to fit in.

"New outfit?" Olivia asked when Sarah walked into the office.

"Yes, it is." Sarah swirled in place to show it off. "Logan is taking me along for a meeting between the CEO of Second Chance Looks and the actor who will be starring in their commercials. I wanted to make sure I look good for the occasion."

"That's the third one this week. We must be paying you well."

Sarah giggled. "My first-ever credit card came on Monday. I decided to buy some new clothes, and some jewelry and shoes to help accessorize them."

"Smart choice," said Olivia as Sarah walked past the front desk and headed toward the central portion of the building.

Only a month at Media Slick and already Sarah felt as if the company and the lifestyle had always been a part of her life. Photo shoots, celebrity interviews, and the creation of online ads were almost daily occurrences. All of them produced a heart-pumping rush within her whenever she was involved.

This is living.

"Sarah," Brooke called out from her office. "I have a task for you."

That translated into: I have something for you to do that I consider too trivial or too labor-intensive to do myself. The trip with Logan promised to be ever so much more interesting. If she was lucky, this new task might be something that could be done later in the day.

Sarah stopped and leaned back to where she could peek into the room and find out what Brooke wanted. "What totally amazing and exotic assignment do you have for me today?"

"Keep up that attitude and there will be no stopping you in this industry." Brooke waved for Sarah to enter the office. She smiled and held up a black flash drive with an image of a green skull. "This contains the names and phone numbers of people who have registered as fans of Stinking Death. The band got in trouble on their last tour and offered to help out the community in exchange for having the charges against them dropped."

"Okay. What do you need me to do?"

"The band's lead singer, Grim, wants to do a food drive for the homeless. The grocery stores we normally work with claim that because of the gasoline shortages, increases in beef prices, and some other ridiculous excuses that they won't be able to donate the food we need."

"I heard them talking about all of that on the news and—"

"Oh, pul-eeze." Brooke raised her hands in mock surrender and rolled her eyes. "You can't trust the news. They're just marketing companies without the guts to admit that they spin the events of the world to their liking. Listen, the cost for food and gas is the same for me as it is for everyone else. If people are having problems making ends meet, it's their own fault."

Sarah doubted that. She knew that Brooke, as the event organizer for Media Slick, made more money than many families who had both parents working full-time jobs, but she didn't plan to argue the point. "Did you want me to call the people on the list and ask them to donate food?"

"It wouldn't really be a food drive then. Grim wants to send out a photographer and catch the action as people go from door to door."

"That sounds more like a PR campaign than marketing," said Sarah.

"It is. Joel thinks these guys are on the verge of hitting it big, and he wants them to owe him a favor when they do. Anyway, I need you to call the fans and ask if they'd be willing to participate in the food drive."

"Could I do it this afternoon? Logan asked me to go along with him this morning and help convince Harvey Thiele to upsize the marketing package he has with us."

Brooke tapped her polished neon-red nails on the desk and gave Sarah one of her trademarked don't-try-my-patience smiles that she usually reserved for the contract staff Media Slick used on special projects. "There will be plenty of chances for you to mingle with the clients on our high-priority list in the future. Right now, though, this is the task that you need to concern yourself with."

The subtext came across loud and clear to Sarah—you are still a peon and should stick to your peon assignments.

"I'll get right on it." Sarah offered one of the practiced smiles she had learned from working at Media Slick and did her best to hide her disappointment.

She still had an hour before Logan planned to leave. That left enough time to make fifteen or twenty calls. Brooke hadn't indicated that everyone on the list needed to be contacted. After all, how many volunteers did you need to keep the photographers busy and Grim happy with the fan support of his food drive? A dozen should be plenty.

The first two phone numbers on the list had been disconnected, and the third belonged to an older lady who had never heard of the band. Four more went straight to voice mail. It took eight calls before she actually spoke with a fan.

"Stinking Death would like you to help them embrace the community where you live," said Sarah.

"Is this a joke?" asked the man on the other end of the line. "Am I being punked?"

Obviously, that hadn't been the right approach. Sarah decided to drop the gimmicky stuff and play it straight. "The band Stinking Death is interested in helping the community and has asked me to contact their fans about participating in a food drive to help the homeless."

"I'm out of work. If I helped out, do you think I could take some of that food home with me? I'd be willing to help if I could do that."

"Well . . ." That sounded reasonable to her, but Sarah wasn't actually in charge of the event. It seemed like too many people needed help these days and not enough people were around to provide it. "I don't think I can authorize that right now. However, this is a great chance to show your enthusiasm for Stinking Death."

"Here's the thing, I don't actually like the band," said the man. "I just signed up on the fan page for a chance to win tickets to Holly's Hard-Luck Harlots concert last summer. You can go ahead and take me off the list."

The connection was terminated.

Another dozen calls gave the same results: either a wrong number or the people were just not interested. Fifty minutes passed and Sarah had yet to find a single individual who was interested in helping to collect food for the homeless. Then an idea struck her.

She pulled up the phone number of her Young Women's leader and hit the send key. Not all of the Saints had gathered in the wilderness. Some of them had the sense to stay put. Kayla Jenkins picked up on the second ring.

"Sister Jenkins," said Sarah, "I'm really in a jam. Any chance that either the Young Men or the Young Women are looking for a service project that needs doing?"

Kayla laughed. "You must be psychic. We had a lesson last week about how service teaches us to love those whom we serve and also that helping the community in which we live has a ripple effect that improves the overall condition of our cities, states, countries, and even the world. The youth need a project that will help focus that lesson."

"That's great," Sarah nearly shouted. Why couldn't her family have been as smart as Kayla and stayed in the city to help out the many, many suffering people here. "I'm organizing a food drive for the homeless. I think that would fit with what you need."

"I think so too," said Kayla. "It should be pretty easy to tie that in to our lesson."

"I'll get back to you with all the details . . . and thank you so much." Sarah disconnected the call. Mission accomplished and in time to go with Logan. All she had to do was pop her head into Brooke's office and let her know.

Brooke looked up from a file on the desk, her arched eyebrows prodding Sarah to state her business.

"Just letting you know that I recruited about twenty people

for the food drive," said Sarah. "That should be enough for what we need."

Surprise registered on Brooke's face. "How did you get that many people to volunteer so quickly?"

"It's all who you know—you know."

"Well then, I suppose if you still want to go with Logan, I guess that's all right." Brooke hesitated, telegraphing that there was more to follow. "A little word of advice, just between the two of us, you might not want to get too involved with Logan."

"Why? Joel always talks about the great work Logan does."

"It's not his work that's the problem. It's his attitude."

"He seems—"

Brooke raised a hand to cut Sarah off. "Think it over. Enjoy the trip."

Sarah offered a quick wave and then hurried down the hall toward Logan's office. Brooke's warning didn't make any sense; Logan was friendly and upbeat most of the time. In fact, of all the people who worked at Media Slick he was the one that Sarah felt the most comfortable being around.

She made a mental note to watch for any signs of what the problem might be between those two and to see if it involved any of the other employees.

Logan was waiting for her at his desk. "I was beginning to think you had decided not to go with me."

"Not a chance," said Sarah. "This is my first opportunity to meet with one of our future celebrities. I've been dreaming about this since I started working here."

"Good. I think you're going to like Cruz."

"Cruz Martinez? I didn't know that's who you had lined up for the commercials."

"I guess you know him then?" Logan asked.

"Well, not personally, but he played the lead role in the production of *Pippen* that the Third Street Theater put on last year. I saw it twice, it was so good."

Logan laughed. "I watched it three times, but that's because I know him. Whatever you do, don't mention the play. If you do, he'll talk about all the bloopers that happened during the run of the production, and we won't get any work done."

"I promise. I won't bring it up."

—————

Sarah and Logan arrived at the Dine Mine a little before noon. Pickaxes, shovels, rusty iron rails, and other assorted mining gear adorned the walls. True to the mine image it was meant to portray, the place was dark, giving it a feeling closer to a bar that happened to serve food than an actual restaurant. It even smelled dank and musty like how Sarah imagined a mine might smell.

As the hostess walked them to their table, Sarah caught a glimpse of a weather report on a wall-mounted television. It showed storm icons with arrows pointed toward the city. A headline listed it as the "Worst Storm in a Decade."

For Sarah and the rest of the people in the city, that probably meant leaking roofs, flooded streets, and power outages, but what about her parents? What kind of danger did this storm mean for them? They and the rest of the Saints who had answered the call to gather would be facing the fury of this storm in tents.

And all for what?

The world hadn't come to an end. Not even close. Sarah had a great job, a fancy apartment, and a new wardrobe that her parents would never have approved of, but it made her look like one of the rich and famous people she interacted with at work. If all went well, she wouldn't just look like one of the well-to-do—she would *be* one of them.

Her parents had made a really bad choice. Maybe if Sarah did well enough with her job, she could help them get back on their feet when they finally came to their senses.

Logan introduced her to Cruz Martinez. The man was even more impressive up-close and in-person than he had been on the stage. He had dark hair that could have been molded in place (not a single strand was out of place), a dazzling white smile that nearly glowed in the dim light of the room, and gold rings on each of his fingers.

Cruz said hello to Sarah but then turned his attention to Logan. They discussed upcoming projects each of them were involved with until Harvey Thiele, CEO of Second Chance Looks, arrived. Then everyone around the table focused on the specifics of the commercial they planned to shoot later in the week.

Sarah could have been a fly on the wall for all of the input she had on the matter. That was absolutely fine with her. Sitting at the table and listening to what each of them contributed to the creative process was incredible. It was like observing the birth of a media campaign.

When it was all over, Thiele excused himself from the meeting while holding a cell phone to his ear with one hand and waving good-bye to everyone at the table with the other. Cruz stuck around a few minutes longer and talked with Logan.

"See you Sunday," Cruz said when, at last, he got up to leave. He shook hands with Sarah and then sauntered out of the restaurant.

"What's going on Sunday?" Sarah asked.

Logan shrugged and turned his attention to signing the credit card slip.

"Oh, come on," said Sarah. "You can tell me."

"It's nothing really. Cruz and I attend the same church."

That seemed odd. Logan drank, swore on occasion, and some of the slick lines he had thrown out during lunch bordered on the disingenuous—behavior that Sarah had a hard time reconciling with someone who attended church.

"I didn't know you were a Christian," said Sarah.

Logan seemed to flinch at the statement. "Do me a favor and keep that to yourself. In this company, it doesn't really pay to have everyone know you believe in God."

11

John woke stiff and sore from an uncomfortable night of sleeping on the hard ground. He wished his family had chosen to pack a few cots or mats with their personal belongings. They would have eased the discomfort of what amounted to a prolonged camping trip.

It was only going to get worse the closer it got to winter.

As soon as he stepped out of the tent, his gaze fell on the Suburban. His family was already tightly packed in the tent. There was no way they could fit all of the stuff they brought with them into the tent and still have room to sleep. The measures that had seemed like draconian restrictions of what the Saints could bring now looked more like excess.

The Suburban wasn't an ideal storage solution. John planned to use it for trips into Greenville whenever the need arose. Aside from that, how long would it take for a vehicle sitting in a field to develop serious mechanical problems? Then multiply that by a hundred. With everyone bringing vehicles it wouldn't take long before Camp Valiant turned into a massive dirt parking lot.

John massaged his temples. He hadn't solved the first problem yet and another one had already popped up. A sense of dread nipped at him. It reminded him of the story of Hercules fighting the hydra—for every obstacle John solved, two more took its place. Except that he had not solved any problems so far.

An idea pinged off John's head. They might get the construction crew to assemble an outdoor closet for each of the families. Nothing more than a big box with a few shelves that could be placed at the back of each tent. Even that wasn't an ideal solution. The work that went into making the storage closets took materials and manpower away from the construction of the other buildings the camp needed. How did the emotional comfort that the closets would provide compare to the completion of a medical center or a community kitchen?

He considered waking up the children for breakfast but decided they needed the extra sleep more. Adjusting to a new environment would be tough on all of them. A little extra rest could go a long way toward feeling more comfortable here. John glanced inside the tent and watched his family sleep for a moment, then headed for the trailer to get started on the day's work.

A pair of white Econoline vans approached along the dirt road leading to Camp Valiant. Most of the people who were part of Phase Two were scheduled to arrive today. That meant John needed to be near the gate in order to greet them. He poked his head back into tent. "Duty calls," he told Becky. "I'll try to grab some breakfast when I'm done."

As the vans got closer, John saw they were overpacked. People were jammed in among all their belongings. John wondered how the unfortunate family members in the back were able to breathe with all the personal items packed on top of them. These folks had not followed the guidelines on what they could bring. Even if they had one of the imagined outdoor closets, it wouldn't be enough to hold all of the items they had brought.

John opened the gate and strolled over to the vehicles, patiently waited for the drivers to extricate their families from inside the vans, and then introduced himself.

"I'm Derek Reidhead," said a tall, slender man. "Plumber by trade and poet by nature. This is my wife, Helena."

"We're the Jacksons," said the driver of the second van. He

pointed to himself and then the rest of his family as they walked about, obviously attempting to stretch their legs. "Scott, Karen, Jake, Luke, and Faith. What's next?"

"You're here kind of early," said John, not really sure what to do with them.

"The vans got dropped off last night," said Scott. The man had a lot of energy, especially for someone who probably had been up all night. "Derek and I are both from the same ward. We packed right away and decided not to wait until this morning to leave."

"Yeah, it felt weird just sitting in our homes—waiting," said Derek.

The looks that the wives and the children gave the two men stated their disagreement louder than words. All of them looked tired and worn. John suspected their moods would worsen once they found out about the living arrangements.

"We were just getting to breakfast," said John, hoping they might take the news better with some food in their stomachs. "Why not hold off on the unpacking until after you've had something to eat?"

That caught their attention. Most of them nodded.

John escorted the Jacksons and the Reidheads through the gate and around to where Bill Summers had set up an outdoor kitchen behind the trail, if you could really call a couple of grills under an awning a kitchen. Becky was among the kitchen crew, busy turning cans of powdered eggs and flour taken from the camp's food storage into a meal of scrambled eggs and pancakes. They smelled tasty, but John had his doubts about canned eggs.

Scott walked over and stood next to John. "Can you give me a better idea of what we should expect? I know that this is part of the literal gathering that has been prophesied for decades, but what does that really mean for us?"

"This is Phase Two," said John. He noticed everyone in the area turned their eyes toward him. "A large number of families will be moving into camp to work on construction of all the buildings we will need during our stay here. That includes a medical building, several workshops that will allow us to make goods necessary for our survival, and homes."

"I noticed that you mentioned 'during our stay,'" said Helena Reidhead, her voice hopeful. "Are we not permanently moving here?"

Obviously, John needed to be more careful with what he said. "The truth is that I don't know. These buildings will permit us to stay for an extended period of time, but the plan does not call for the construction of a whole new city. I think that means we will eventually return to where we came from. That's just a guess though. The truth is we don't know exactly what's going to happen over the next few years."

For a few minutes, only the blowing wind and the crackling of cooking eggs disturbed the silence. Finally, Karen Jackson spoke. "How many people will be here for Phase Two?"

"About sixty families," said John. "We plan to organize you into two wards that will be filled out once we transition into Phase Three and the bulk of the Saints arrive. That's a lot of what I'll be doing today: greeting the new arrivals and assigning them to one of the wards."

"What about us?" asked Shane Dawson.

Shane was part of the original construction crew who had stayed at camp while John returned home to gather his family and finish preparations for a permanent move.

The smell of cooking food had apparently attracted the rest of camp to the area, and John found himself at the center of their attention. "Pretty much the same. Everyone will be placed into one of the two wards. The actual decision will be based on the skill sets of the families. Ideally, each ward needs to function on its own."

"What if we want to be in a ward with someone else?" asked Scott Jackson.

"What if we don't want to be in a ward with someone?" asked Shane as he glanced toward another member of the construction crew.

"If you have any concerns about what ward you'll be placed in, you can bring those to me, and I'll do my best to address them," said John.

"Breakfast is ready," Becky announced loudly.

Two lines formed, a larger one for food and the other to speak with John. Shane stood at the front of the second line. During the first stage of the camp's construction, Shane had gotten into a doctrinal argument about the Second Coming, which had created hard feelings on both sides. As John suspected, Shane wanted to make sure he was not in the same ward with those members of the construction crew. A couple of men felt the same way about Shane.

John ended up last in line, and his food got cold before he could finish it. He grabbed Paul Young as the construction team member headed out to work. "Do you think you can investigate the cave you found yesterday without getting hurt or killed?"

"Worried about those Dorganites?" Paul asked, referring to the radio fanatic's followers.

"Not really. If the cave is stable, I think we can use it for storage. We should have some lanterns and rope in the warehouse, so take them and someone to go with you. Please, be careful."

Paul snapped his fingers and grimaced. "There you go, ruining a perfectly good opportunity to fall into a deep dark pit. I'll take Curtis Powell with me. See you later."

When John turned around, he found the Jacksons and the Reidheads waiting for him. None of them looked happy.

"I don't see any buildings for us to live in," said Scott, his arms folded across his chest. Karen nodded in agreement.

"That's what you are here to do," said John, an upbeat tone to his voice. He thought putting a positive spin on the situation would help lessen the impact of the blow. "We are going to ramp-up construction efforts at the camp to get ready for the big call to gather. For a little while, at least, all of us will be living out of tents."

"When can we expect to live inside a building?" asked Derek.

"Once the community structures are built, we can start work on housing units."

"I want to go home," said the Jackson girl, her lower lip trembling.

"We're all in the same situation," said John. "This is just as dirty, uncomfortable, and strange for me as it is for you, but it'll get better. I promise."

Unpacking turned out to be only a minor task, but rearranging the family possessions from the Suburban made up for it. The tent barely had room to accommodate his family, let alone their stuff. A few changes of clothes, personal hygiene kits, and a table just large enough to hold a lantern and a copy of their scriptures took up the rest of their available space.

John wondered how Sarah was doing back home. He hoped she was adapting to her new environment more easily than the rest of the family. No. Not the rest of the family, because that left out Robert, who most likely had it the roughest out of all of them. John closed his eyes and murmured a quick prayer for the safety of his two oldest children.

More of the Phase Two members arrived at the gate. John left Becky and the kids to finish turning their 18 × 20 tent into a home. With a few exceptions, the realization of what life was going to be like for the foreseeable future had hit the new families hard. He started telling them that he'd address the topic in a special camp meeting that night.

If only he knew what to tell them.

After the evening meal, everyone at Camp Valiant gathered around a large fire in a section of the compound that John called the Field of Serenity. Currently, several fallen trees occupied the spot, but he planned to turn those into benches in order to hold Church services and special meetings like this one.

The crackling of the fire and the smell of smoke reminded John of previous campouts with his family and the fond feelings he still had for the outings. He wondered briefly if this is what it had been like for the pioneers during their trek to the Salt Lake valley.

Becky led the group in the first verse of "Come, Come Ye Saints." The tension John had felt all day drained away with the music. He sensed the mood of the group change. They seemed calmer—ready for his message.

"Let me address all of you, my valiant ones," John raised his voice loud enough for everyone to hear him. "I call you that because you are valiant. It has never been easy to live as God wants us to live, but you have accepted the task to prepare the way for others. It is time for the Saints to stand taller, work harder, and open our minds to a better understanding of our grand mission. This is the season when our strength, spiritually and physically, must stay resolute. We have to forge ahead regardless of the consequences, just as the early members of the Church paved the way for all of us. In preparation for the return of the Savior, we must keep the commandments and extend a hand of kindness to those in distress. We must be considerate and decent to one another. It is the time to be more like Christ than we have ever been before."

John felt prompted to open the fireside up to anyone who wanted to stand before the others and share what drove them to accepting the call to gather. As the evening went on, the testimonies of their faith filled John with a new resolve to endure the challenges and discomforts they faced and to look forward to an era of peace and prosperity.

The glistening eyes and wet faces of the Saints assembled around the campfire bore witness to John that they felt the same way. They finished the evening with one more hymn and then went peacefully to their tents, full of faith and hope for the next day.

White, puffy clouds floated along a sky of deep vivid blue, pushed along by a warm breeze. Soft chords of organ music filled the rose-scented air. John put his hands behind his head and soaked in the perfection of the moment.

"It is time." A voice, though soft, caused the ground to vibrate. As soon as the vibrations stopped, the wind blew harder and colder while the clouds boiled, growing darker and changing shape. Within moments, the clouds had transformed into armor-clad angels with gray halos that spun like miniature tornados. In their hands, they held bolts of lightning. They called out to the forces of nature to hold back no longer, to rage against evil.

From a point high above a city, John watched as flood, storm, and earthquake destroyed buildings and tossed the inhabitants around like insects in a terrarium. Those who survived fought among themselves for scraps of food—until a great army assembled on the stony plains outside the city.

With a thunderous shout that shook the ground, the army charged across the plain. Men, women, children, and soldiers died. Blood flowed, staining the streets red with it. They killed one another until they were too tired to fight anymore and fell exhausted to the ground. Only the wailing sounds of mourning dared break the deathly silence.

One of the angels, face hidden behind a metal mask, streaked through the sky toward John. It stopped an arm's length away and hovered. Raising his arm, the angel pointed at John.

John bolted straight up. It took a moment to switch from dream to wakeful reality. Even then he wasn't sure that an angel hadn't been in the tent with him. He thought he smelled the fading scent of roses.

That was no dream.

In all of his years, John had never experienced anything like this vision. It felt completely different than a dream, more like a memory of something that hadn't happened yet. He couldn't shake the impression that this was a forewarning of the time of destruction.

"Are you okay, honey?" Becky mumbled from her sleeping bag.

"I'm fine," said John. "You should go back to sleep. I feel like taking a walk."

Becky was snoring again before John finished dressing.

As the Director of Defense, it fell upon him to ensure the safety of everyone in camp. Since his mind was too focused on the vision to sleep, he decided to walk the perimeter and check the fence. A stroll in the cool quiet of the early morning would give him a chance to mull over what he'd experienced.

He threw back the tent flap and stepped outside. All thoughts of the vision fled.

During the night, a cluster of small tents had been erected on the other side of the fence. People crowded the gate leading into Camp Valiant. A few sported white shirts and ties, but the majority wore sweaters with the American flag across the front. They held signs that sported anti-Mormon slogans like "Liars, Deceivers, Seducers," "Church of Latter-Day Lies," and "Jesus saves—Joseph enslaves."

The Dorganites had arrived.

12

"God told you the Americans were coming?" Robert asked the elderly lady in Italian.

"No." She smiled. "In my prayers, He answered that a young hero would come."

That hardly described him. Not only that, but what made this woman think that help was on the way and that he was it?

"He must've meant someone else, *signora*," said Robert.

"I am Cora Rossi," said the woman. "And I make no mistake about you."

"Robert Williams."

"Roberto." Cora raised her hands in the air as she said his name and then gripped him in a vigorous hug. "My oldest son, it is his name too."

"What a coincidence," said Robert, unsure what to say next. "He must be—"

"You speak Italian?" the coarse voice of Sergeant Shaw asked from behind Robert.

"*Si*," said Robert. "I mean, yes, I do."

"Good," said Shaw. "You stay here with the rest of the unit and help them with any translation needs they have. Cohen and I are going to take a look-see at the surrounding area."

"Damage assessment?" asked Robert.

Cohen chuckled.

"Yeah," said Shaw. "Let's call it that."

The two demolition experts left with a smile passing between them. They got into their vehicle and drove north, away from the town and away from the damage.

Robert turned back to speak with Cora and found himself facing a crowd. Up close, the haggard and forlorn faces bore testimony to the hardships they had suffered over the last couple of days. Each of them pleaded with their eyes for extra assistance in putting their lives back together.

He looked back toward the vehicles and spotted Sergeant Wojcik leaning against one of the Humvees, watching him. "Sergeant, what should we do?"

"I don't think there's much that we can do." Wojcik folded his arms and directed his stare away from the crowd and toward his feet. "Whoever planned this mission was an idiot. We don't have the equipment we need to do any heavy work. A few hand tools, but none of the big stuff. We won't be effective until the gear arrives that will let us do our job."

Robert scanned the crowd again. Men and women. Thin and heavy. Tall and short. The things all of them had in common were their dirty, torn clothing and expressions of exhaustion.

Then his gaze fell upon the children. Most of them stood silently in the crowd, looking up at him. The youngest ones clung to adults, wrapping their arms around legs, or necks, or whatever portion of a loved one they could reach. Tears had left smudged streaks in the dirt on their faces. Their expressions begged for help.

"These people can't wait," Robert said, with more force than he expected. "One of the great things about America is that we help others. We are taught the Golden Rule as children and are expected to be shining examples of it wherever we go. We *are* the good neighbor for the world."

Wojcik frowned at him. He studied the people gathered around the soldiers and then nodded. "I know. I want to help them too, but our orders state that we should establish a base and then wait for resupply. Any deviation from those orders needs to come from Captain Mayo."

"Right," said Gil, with a sly expression. "Do those orders specifically prohibit the men in the unit from offering help on their own? Like during our down-time between assigned duties?"

"That's a dangerous game, Private," said Wojcik, shaking his head. "I'll tell you that you *do not* want to go there. You start taking the initiative on matters like this, and the captain will come down on you like a ton of bricks. Take my advice and wait until Mayo gives us the order to help these people."

"They need help *now*," said Robert. When the sergeant didn't answer right away, he wondered if he'd stepped over the line.

"Okay." Wojcik held up his hands. "I think you're making a mistake. The captain will probably reach that same conclusion on his own, but if you're that fired up to help these people—now—then I won't stop you. I don't like standing here watching them suffer any more than you do. A good part of why most of us joined up was so that we could help those who need it. But I know enough to wait for the order to come down the pipeline. If you do this and the captain finds out, I am going to deny knowing anything about it. Is that clear?"

"Yeah," said Robert. His head told him to listen to Wojcik. He had followed orders all of his life. His parents had set rules for the home, and he had followed them. There had been rules on his mission, and he had followed them. And the army definitely had rules. In all of his experiences so far, it had been good to stay within the given guidelines.

But he knew there were times when a person had a moral obligation to refuse an order. Those sorts of situations seemed pretty unlikely to him. Would that change as the world drew nearer and nearer to the Second Coming?

Was this the time to ignore the rules, to exceed his authority, and to do what he felt was right?

Robert looked at the townspeople gathered around them and his heart said yes.

"What about you?" Robert asked Gil. "Want to give me a hand?"

"Were you paying attention to what the sergeant just told us?" asked Gil.

"So you're in," said Robert.

"Yeah, I'm in."

"That just confirms what the rest of us already knew," said Gutierrez. "The two of you combined don't have enough brains to fill a shot glass."

A few of the men looked as if they were wrestling with their consciences, but none of them spoke up or moved over to stand with Robert. All of them had more time in the military than he did, so it probably meant that he had made a pretty big mistake.

Wojcik turned his back and addressed the rest of the unit. "You know the drill. Johnson from the infantry platoon will prepare range cards for each approach to this central courtyard. Gutierrez, I want you to refill our water supply. The rest of you conduct preventative checks and service on your assigned weapons and equipment."

Several of the engineers hesitated, looking over at Robert—until Wojcik clapped his hands and shouted, "Let's get moving, people."

Gutierrez waited long enough for Robert to catch him smirking before he left.

After loading up with hammers, pry-bars, and shovels, Robert and Gil returned to the crowd of townsfolk and stopped in front of Cora.

"The rest of my unit needs to prepare our position, but the two of us will help you. Who has the most pressing need?" Robert asked in Italian.

All of them raised their hands and shouted for his attention. Robert considered asking Cora, with whom he already felt a connection, but he hesitated. This had to be his decision.

Everyone in the crowd showed expressions of desperation and need. How was he supposed to determine who they should help first by just looking at them?

Then his gaze fell on a trio of children standing toward the back of the gathering. They did not seem to be attached to any adults like the rest of the kids obviously were. A feeling inside Robert told him that this was where he should start his relief effort.

He gently pushed his way through the crowd until he stood in front of the children. "How can I help you?"

The smallest of the children was a girl of about six or seven years. Her hair had been pulled back into a ponytail, but now the dark strands bulged away from the dirty yellow band that had been used to keep it in place. She looked up at him, and her bottom lip trembled. A tear rolled down her cheek, following the muddy path made by previous teardrops.

"Our parents are still in our home," said the oldest child, a young teenaged boy wearing blue-and-white shorts and a faded blue polo shirt. His expression and his tone were subdued, even defeated. "We cannot reach them so they can be properly buried."

"Is there a chance that they are still alive?" Robert asked.

"No." The boy's head drooped forward, his chin resting on his chest. "You will see for yourself when we get there."

These children had lost their parents. Just the thought of it darkened Robert's mood, forcing him to think about how much worse it must be for the children. During last year's storm, his mother had been around to offer comfort and guidance. But these children didn't even have that. The recovery of their parents' bodies seemed insignificant to their needs.

"Lead the way," said Robert, placing a comforting hand on the boy's shoulder.

The boy led him through the streets to a pale-yellow, two-story house several blocks away. The roof and one of the outer walls had collapsed completely.

Robert noticed that an effort had already been made to clear away the debris that had once been the children's home. Loose bits of mortar, broken boards, and smaller sections of the crumbled wall had been tossed into the street in front of the building, leaving a small dent in the pile of rubble. A crisscross of heavy support beams blocked any further excavation by the children, and from between the beams protruded a woman's limp, lifeless hand.

Panic welled up inside Robert. This was the situation he had been dreading. Underneath the broken bricks and timbers of this home were the corpses of a man and a woman. Certainly the USACE didn't expect him to handle the mutilated and broken bodies of dead people. That responsibility had to fall on someone else.

He didn't mind the backbreaking work of hauling the remains of this building from one spot to another, but touching the dead . . . That was a whole different matter.

As he turned around, his gaze fell on the children.

The look of utter devastation on their faces reminded Robert that those were not a pair of dead bodies to these children. A loved mother and father lay in the ruins of their home. Even in death, the opportunity to see them again, or hold their hands one last time, had great importance. With the loss of everything that they had, it might be the *only* thing of importance.

Robert took a deep breath and faced the rubble. He imagined the hand he saw was that of his own mother. He felt a sting in his eyes as tears threatened to flow in reaction to his feelings. But it worked. He no longer feared touching the hand or the arm, or the body they were attached to. Instead, power surged within him. He moved forward, grasped a large section of cemented bricks, and pulled them away from the rest of the debris. Hobbling a few feet away, he tossed his load on the street and returned for more.

This time he didn't even flinch as the arm came into his view. His mind focused on the best way to move the rubble away from the children's parents without further damaging the bodies. He removed another grouping of bricks, revealing the shoulder and head of the mother.

That might have been a mistake.

The woman's face had been badly hurt. This should not be the last image these children had of their mother. They deserved to remember her whole, smiling, and pretty, as all mothers are in the sight of their children.

Determined to ask the kids to leave while he finished the work, Robert turned with the bricks still in hand and nearly tripped over a broken piece of cement. He tottered for a moment and only a timely intervention of the oldest child prevented him from falling underneath his load.

"Thanks," said Robert in English.

"*Si,*" came the response in Italian.

Robert looked past his armful of bricks to find the two oldest children helping him with his burden. Then he knew they should stay. The children needed to be a part of the recovery effort. They needed to be part of this last act of service to express the love they had for their parents.

Together Robert and the boy hauled out broken timber, tossed it on the street, and went back for another load. By then, the middle child, a girl of about eight with big soft eyes, had taken up a position beside the mother. She clasped her mother's hand in hers and sat there rocking back and forth. The first line of a song floated lightly in the air, barely audible to those who stood next to her.

"Be brave, Lucy," said the boy in Italian.

"I am, Enzo," said Lucy. "I am singing Mother a song to help her find heaven."

Enzo sang along with his sister as he and Robert hauled another support beam to the street. There, they found the youngest girl also singing as she dropped the single brick she carried onto the growing pile of debris. When the children repeated the song, Robert joined the growing choir. Even though he knew the language, he didn't know the verses. He did his best to follow along from his memory of the first time they sang it.

The song itself was about a woman teaching her daughter how to pray for the safety of the father who had gone off to war and how happy they both would be when he returned.

Gil used a crowbar to help them with the next beam, lifting a portion of the debris as Robert and Enzo pulled. "I don't have to sing, do I?" Gil asked.

Robert opened his mouth to respond, but the beam they were lifting groaned and cracked. The youngest girl had crawled under the crisscross mess of timbers to gather another brick. If the beam broke, the girl would be injured or even killed.

"Watch out!" he shouted. Then, with the speed of a diving hawk, he reached down and snatched the girl up with one hand, while still holding the beam with the other. He moved faster than he had ever moved in his life.

The beam snapped.

Timbers and bricks collapsed onto the spot where the girl had been only a second ago, and a cloud of dirt completely engulfed Robert and the girl.

"Gianna!" yelled Enzo in a panicked voice.

"I think she's okay," Robert called out, between coughs. He stepped away from the rubble and out of the dust cloud to find Enzo and Lucy waiting for their sister.

Other than a fine layer of dust that covered her, Gianna looked no worse for the incident. She rubbed her eyes and cried. "I can't see."

Robert stepped over the rubble and set the girl down on the street. He gently moved her hands away and examined her eyes. It appeared to be no more than a bit of dust that was causing the problem. He carefully pulled the top lid down and over the bottom lid and released it.

"Try opening your eye's now," he said.

Gianna blinked a couple of times and then opened her eyes fully. She smiled at Robert and said, "I can see."

"How did you do that?" asked Gil.

"My mom used to do that back home whenever we got dirt in our eyes."

"Not that," said Gil. "How did you save that girl? I mean, you were like superhero fast—and strong. That's the kind of stuff that only happens in movies."

Robert shrugged. He didn't know how he had done it, but now that Gil brought it up, he did feel strange—sort of jittery. His heart was racing and his limbs trembled. He felt full of energy. It had to be the aftermath of an adrenaline rush.

"It just happened," he said. "The beam cracked. I saw the girl. I grabbed her. She had dust in her eyes. I removed the dust."

The words flew out of Robert's mouth almost before he thought them. They streamed forth like an avalanche of water from a broken dam. He stopped and took a deep breath.

It didn't really help. He still wanted to babble. The shock of what he had done to save the girl was only now setting in. He had done something impossible. Maybe not so much him as the Lord. Robert just happened to be in the right place to act, and God had given him the ability to save Gianna.

An excess of energy still ran through Robert's body. He decided that he should put it to use before it ran out and possibly left him weak. Robert motioned for Gil to help him with the beam again, at least the half of it that stuck out of the rubble. This time, it pulled free with relative ease.

Enzo left Gianna on the sidewalk with Lucy and returned to work. This time they labored without song, only the sound of tumbling bricks and the scrape of wood against stone breaking the silence.

A couple of men from Robert's unit joined them after a while. They simply slid into the work without a word to anyone there. These were the same people who had hesitated earlier when Sergeant Wojcik had warned them against helping without the go-ahead from Captain Mayo.

Eventually, they removed enough of the rubble to permit Robert and Gil to pull the woman's body out from the remains of the building. Cora appeared with a sheet, and they wrapped the mother's body in it, laying it at the feet of a priest who stood with the children.

Robert took a moment to enlist the help of several of the villagers. Then he returned to the cavity from where the mother's body had been pulled and searched for the father. Without thinking about it, he directed the efforts of those around him, acting as the voice of organization. In a mix of Italian and English, he instructed his group of volunteers on what he wanted removed next and where it should go.

Only when the father had been located and hands had reached in to pull the body out of the ruin and from Robert's grasp did he notice that Gutierrez was among the volunteers.

Robert scrambled out from the cavity in the rubble and dusted off his uniform. He faced Gutierrez, surprised that the man had helped without being ordered to do so. That certainly warranted some sort of recognition. His mind searched for the right thing to say to the man who had made it his mission to bring Robert misery.

"Private Williams," the loud, angry voice of Captain Mayo sounded from behind Robert, "do you mind telling me who in the blazes put you in charge?"

13

Calvin knew something was wrong when the President's secretary greeted him in a friendly manner and immediately ushered him in to see Boggs. It felt like that moment of confusion after you've taken a hit during a football game and you're not really sure where you're at and what you're doing.

Agents Bowers and Hancock waited dutifully just outside the door. If their hearing was particularly good, the position should allow them to listen in on any conversation inside the office.

"Calvin." Boggs's smile of doom had returned. "I imagine this visit has something to do with the changes I made to your security detail. How is that working out for you so far?"

"Get rid of them."

"Why would you want me to do that? They are both highly trained agents that have received numerous commendations from their trainers, their superiors, and their peers. I doubt that more capable agents can be found anywhere in the Secret Service."

"They're goons," said Calvin.

"What I think you mean is they are individuals who are not intimidated by your position as Vice President or who are timid enough to be bullied by your brash military demeanor. In other words, they are just the kind of agents we need to keep you safe."

"I don't need the kind of protection they provide. In fact, I don't think I need protection at all. Consider this my formal request to remove the Secret Service from protecting me."

"That will not happen," said Boggs, sitting back in his chair as if he were enjoying a day at the beach. "You are the current Vice President of the United States. As long as you remain in that position, Secret Service protection is mandatory. We cannot leave you vulnerable to kidnapping attempts, where the safety of your person is then levied against US interests. I suggest you get friendly with them, because as long as you are in office, these are the agents who will be protecting you."

Calvin wondered if it could be as simple as Boggs wanting to force him out of office by assigning thuggish agents to dog his every move. Or did Bowers and Hancock represent a more hazardous threat? Had the politics of this country degenerated to a point where Boggs was willing to have Calvin encounter an untimely and fatal accident at the hands of his guardians?

All Calvin needed to do to answer his question was review the President's stance on the political bombing last year. The evidence suggested that Boggs could have been behind the order to attack the campaign headquarters of Texas Governor Arnold Ross, a man in Calvin's political party. At the very least, Boggs had turned a blind eye to the investigation that sought to find the responsible parties.

If the public found out that the President had ordered a terrorist attack on his political rivals, the news could send the United States into another civil war—with each side using violence to defend the actions of their own political party.

"Have you checked the early polls today?" Boggs asked. "Your little stunt yesterday resulted in a two point upward swing in my approval rating. If you meant to embarrass me—you failed. Anything else you had in mind will be discovered, and I will put a stop to it."

Calvin spun on his heels and marched out of the office with Bowers and Hancock falling right in step behind him. They felt like a pair of shadows, attached to him at the heel. If he was going to have to put up with the pair of muscle-bound agents, then the three of them might as well get the ground rules straight from the start.

Taking a nearby elevator to the bottom level, Calvin led the agents to an area of the White House less frequently used. Rumor had it that various Presidents in the past held clandestine meetings here, away from the public eye. Out of view from all but a privileged few.

Just as Calvin stopped to address the agents, he spotted a man strolling down the corridor. The man stood over six feet tall with slicked-back black hair; his bearing had a rigid military fashion. He wore a smartly cut suit that seemed out of place on his broad frame.

Something about this man bothered Calvin. "Do I know you from somewhere?"

"I doubt it," said the stranger. He kept walking.

Calvin thought he detected a trace of a Russian accent, but he needed to hear him speak a little more before he could be sure. "Maybe at the State dinner last week."

"You must have me mixed up with someone else." The man looked anxious to be on his way. He offered Calvin a mirthless smile and continued on.

The stranger had obviously worked hard to disguise his accent. Only the many years Calvin had worked in Russia and with the KGB allowed him to detect the slightest hint of it in the man's speech. With the war raging in Europe, Calvin wondered what a Russian envoy was doing down here.

Bowers and Hancock hovered close to Calvin, as agents did when they perceived a possible threat to their charge. That instinctive act on the agents' part told Calvin all he needed to know about them for the moment. They may have been assigned to keep Calvin in line, possibly even physically restrain him if necessary, but the instinct to protect him was still there.

Rather than force a confrontation with the Russian and risk

tipping him off to any suspicions, Calvin let the man retreat to the far end of the corridor, in the direction of the President's office.

If Boggs was involved in some secret negotiations with the Russians, any information Calvin uncovered in the presence of Bowers and Hancock would be reported straight to the President. Calvin settled on burning the image of the stranger's face in his mind and following up on his suspicions later.

══════

Kyle Dalton arrived at Calvin's office just before noon.

"Where do you want to go for lunch?" asked Kyle.

"I'm feeling adventurous," said Calvin. "Let's try someplace new."

"Like where?"

"Hmmm . . ." Calvin rubbed his chin. "I don't know. We can look online for a restaurant in the area, if you want."

Kyle followed Calvin into his office and shut the door behind him. "Do you really think all of that was necessary? It felt like my high school drama club all over again."

"Boggs has those two watching my every move," said Calvin, nodding toward Bowers and Hancock. "If the Russians are working with him under the table, I don't want them leaking it to him that I know. Just hop on my computer and pull up the program you need."

Kyle sat down at the desk and logged into the video security system for the White House. "You know I can get in trouble for this, don't you?"

"And if the President is dealing secretly with the Russians, all of us could be headed for a giant mound of trouble. Boggs has the best interest of Boggs in mind, not the people of the United States. With Mike Costa gone, you're the only one I can trust with an assignment like this."

Kyle accessed the camera footage for the White House, starting with the lower levels. Even fast forwarding through the video, it took ten minutes for Calvin to spot the Russian envoy as he passed through a security checkpoint. The stranger kept his head turned from the cameras so they didn't get a good shot of his face, but Kyle accessed the security logs to get the name of Doug Acero.

"That'll be an alias," said Calvin.

"Most likely," said Kyle. "It's a starting point, though. I can run the name to see if he has made any other visits in the last six months. Maybe I can also pull an image from one of the other cameras. Man, that's going to eat into my free time."

"As if you have a life anyway." Calvin patted his friend on the shoulder. "Close it up for now, and let's actually go to lunch before the guard dogs get suspicious."

"Too late for that," Kyle said, laughing. "I hope for all our sakes, Calvin, that you're wrong about this."

"So do I." But Calvin knew he wasn't.

14

sn't this lovely?" Gil leaned against one of the Humvees. He had
his M-16 in hand, the butt of the weapon resting on his right hip.

"I'm not any happier about the captain posting us on double
guard duty than you are," said Robert. His feet ached from standing
almost as much as the chafing from his rifle strap hurt from support-
ing the M-4 carbine that hung down his back.

It didn't seem fair to punish the two of them for helping out the
townsfolk. After all, that's what the USACE was supposed to do. But
Captain Mayo had made some excellent points during the dressing
down he gave Robert and Gil. Acting on their own, or ignoring the
orders they were given, unnecessarily risked the lives of everyone in
the unit. The captain had the big picture, and the soldiers had to
trust him to plan accordingly.

"You really ticked him off," said Gil. "My ear is still sore from
that chewing out he gave you. From now on, you can face the Wrath
of Mayo on your own."

In comparison to the reprimands he had received from his parents, the school teachers, and his mission president, this seemed
harsh, but by military standards, a dressing down and extra guard
duty were fairly mild consequences for upsetting the commanding

officer. "I think Captain Mayo really wanted to help these people too. I guess we should have waited until he gave us the go-ahead."

"Imagine that, an officer with a heart." Gil waved off the comment. "You've definitely been standing out in the sun too long."

Sounds of feet crunching on gravel and a pebble bouncing along the street alerted the two of them to someone's approach. Both of them bolted straight up and brought their weapons to attention.

An elderly man holding a maroon beret in both hands shuffled out from around a nearby Humvee. Wispy white hair ringed the lower half of an otherwise bald head. *"Mi scusi."*

"I'm going to have to ask you to step away from the vehicles," Gil announced in a stern voice.

"Cosa?" the man asked.

Gil rolled his eyes. "I guess you get to tell him to leave, Williams."

"Is there something that you need?" asked Robert in Italian.

"Yesterday, you helped the children."

"Yes," Robert said, "but today I must guard our vehicles. I cannot help anyone."

The man sighed and bowed his head.

"Why not ask some of your neighbors if they can assist you?" asked Robert.

"There is so much work to be done. They do not have the time to help me."

"You can speak to the leader of our unit." Robert lifted up on his toes to look over the top of the Humvees, hoping to spot Captain Mayo. "He might be able to assign a couple of men to help you out."

"Already the rest of the soldiers are working on tasks more important than mine. I hoped to convince you to help me since it would only take a few minutes of effort on your part. Thank you anyway."

Robert figured that a ten-minute break might be all he needed to solve this old man's problem, but he dared not leave his post. And even if he were allowed to take a break, the captain had been very specific that he should not even think about taking the initiative to help anyone else.

The old man offered a resigned that's-okay-you-did-your-best smile that made Robert feel even worse about the situation.

"Don't do it," said Gil.

"Don't do what?" asked Robert.

"Don't do anything except stand here and guard these vehicles. I can tell by the look on your face that you're contemplating something stupid. Just tell the old guy you can't help him and go back to the fun and excitement that is double duty."

Unable to look the man in the eye, Robert said, "I'm sorry. I can't help you."

The elderly gentleman closed his eyes and nodded. Then he turned around and returned from the direction he had arrived, his head hanging low.

A minute ago, Robert had thought he couldn't feel any lower. But he was wrong. A person as humble as this old man deserved to get the help he needed.

"Have a little faith," said Gil. "Someone will help him."

Robert repositioned himself so that he could close his eyes, bow his head, and offer a standing prayer, without Gil seeing him. It didn't do much to improve his mood, but it was the only thing that he could do to help the old man at the moment.

An hour later, his attitude hadn't improved and his feet and back hurt even more.

"Are you the American translator?" a woman asked in Italian.

The unexpected voice startled Robert. He had been so focused on the plight of the people in the town that he had not heard her approach. Robert spun around and found a thirty-ish woman with full lips and an even fuller bosom. Heavy mascara combined with dark, dark eyes gave her a decidedly ominous appearance.

She wore designer jeans and a form-fitting sweater that would have looked better on someone younger. The fashion clothes were an absurd contrast to their dirty and tattered condition. Robert couldn't decide if the combination of the two was tragic or funny.

"Yes, I am," he said.

Gil gave him a here-we-go-again shake of the head and resumed leaning against the Humvee he was standing next to.

"Wonderful." She flashed a toothy, fake smile at Robert. "I need some fuel for my car. Only three or four liters, a mere drop in the gas can for the American military."

"I'm sorry," said Robert. "I can't do that."

"That is no problem," she said. "If you don't know how to siphon gas from the vehicles, I can do that myself."

"It's not that," said Robert. "I just don't have the authority to give gas to anyone. If you want, I can contact my commander and you can ask him."

"No, that is not what I want. What is the big deal with giving me a tiny bit of fuel? No one has to know about it except for me and you and your friend here. I can even pay you for it." The woman reached into her purse and pulled out a wad of euros.

Gil stood up at the sight of the money being flashed at Robert. The situation had his attention, but he looked more interested in the event itself than the money.

"No, thank you." Robert held up his hands, warding off the black-market bribe.

The woman lowered the money but did not put it away. She studied Robert for a moment and then sniffed. Her lower lip trembled slightly. "It is just that my daughter is sick, and I need to drive her to the doctor in the next town. I am so worried about her."

"The doctor here in Trento has agreed to see patients for free as part of the disaster recovery effort."

"Yes." She paused again—for just a second. "He is too busy though. There are so many people waiting to be seen. I can't wait that long."

"Don't you mean that she can't wait that long?" asked Robert.

"Who?" asked the woman.

"Your daughter."

"Oh, yes. That is what I meant. My daughter can't wait that long."

"Then maybe our medic can take a look at her. Hold on, and I'll contact him."

"No. No-no." The woman changed position, blocking Robert's movement to where the rest of the unit was dealing with the aftermath of the earthquake.

"What's her name?" asked Robert.

"Who?" asked the woman.

"Your daughter."

"My daughter's name is . . . Sophie." The woman nodded her head as if the answer seemed reasonable to her.

"I can't help you," said Robert as he switched to a formal guard stance.

"Typical Americans," the woman said. "They care only for themselves. Their big-mouth politicians talk about how they want to help the people of the world, but when the time comes to lend a hand, they show their true colors. Selfish—"

She paused mid-rant. The anger on her face subsided. A sultry smile replaced the sneer. Taking a step closer, she laid a hand on Robert's chest, looked up into his eyes, and licked her lips. "I have other ways of paying for the gas I need. You and your friend must be lonely, being so far from home. I can show you a good time. Both of you." She turned her face in mock embarrassment. "Not both at once."

Gil stood up straight and strained his neck so that he could get a good view of Robert's face.

"I'm . . . you know . . . it's not . . . I mean, you are . . . here's the thing. . . . No." Robert's face burned from being placed in this awkward predicament. He glanced over to Gil for support, for some idea of what he should do next.

Gil chuckled and said, "I can't wait to hear this."

Taking a deep breath, Robert pushed the woman away from him. "I'm not going to give you any gas."

The woman hauled back and slapped Robert across the face. "I should tell your commander that you attempted to take advantage of me. The both of you harassed me as I was walking past, minding my own business."

His sisters hit him harder than that back home. The shock of the woman's sudden fury unleashed on him bothered Robert more than the sting of the slap. Anger welled up inside him and then slowly subsided. In the seconds it took for his emotions to return to their previously sullen state, he decided on what to do about the woman.

"Wait right here," said Robert. "I'll go get him."

"Forget it." The woman huffed once and then stomped off in the direction that she had come from.

"What was that all about?" Gil asked.

"She offered to have sex with both of us in exchange for three liters of gas."

"Boy," said Gil, "she picked the wrong person for that deal."

Robert cast a disapproving look in Gil's direction and then took up a position facing away from him. What was so funny about him doing the right thing? He expected that sort of response from Gutierrez or even Sergeant Wojcik, but not from Gil.

If Robert's cold shoulder bothered Gil any, he didn't show it. Gil whistled the Spider-Man theme for about ten minutes before he finally quieted down. It was almost an hour later when approaching footsteps broke the silence.

"Hey, Robert," said Gil.

"I got it," Robert snapped. "Tell them no and send them on their way. I got it."

"It's those kids we helped yesterday."

Robert looked in the direction Gil was pointing. Cora was leading the three now-orphaned children along the road. The dirt had been removed from their faces, and they all had on clean, ill-fitting clothes.

Already his mind wrestled with the best way to inform Cora and the children that he had been forbidden to help anyone else unless he was given direct orders from one of his superiors. He didn't know how he could refuse a plea for help from these kids who had lost everything. It tore him up just thinking about it.

"Roberto." Cora strolled up to Robert and placed her palms on his either side of his face. "My fine young hero. I have brought the children to see you."

"I have to stay here and guard our vehicles," said Robert.

"Yes. Yes. Yes." Cora's smile didn't fade in the least. "You must perform the duties assigned to you. If we did not do this, the world would be chaos."

That wasn't the response Robert expected. Not sure what else to say he continued with his explanation. "I got in trouble for helping the children yesterday."

Cora patted his cheeks and nodded. "That is so sad, Roberto. Still, I think this trouble is a little thing. You saved Gianna and have taught these little ones that even in our darkest moments, there is goodness and light around us. So what is a little trouble compared to that?"

Warmth filled Robert's heart. "Please, understand that I want to help."

"You have," said Cora. "The American soldiers continue the work that you started yesterday, and the townsfolk have more energy and enthusiasm today. Do not worry. Permit the Saints here in Italy to do what they can during this time of trouble."

"Saints?" asked Robert. "Are you LDS?"

"Don't act so surprised. Did you think there were no Mormons in Italy?"

"No. I served my mission here. I know that there are many wonderful members of the Church in Italy. That is one of the reasons I'm so sad about this disaster that has affected all of you."

Cora reached out and took one of Robert's hands. She covered it with both of hers, like his mother had done when he was young and troubled. "We are not the only land to have troubles. Look around you. All the world suffers."

Her comments reminded Robert of what had happened to his own family last year. His father had been out of town when a super storm swept through the western half of the United States. Their home had been damaged, the entire town without power, and the grocery stores without food. It had been tough, especially with him still hobbling around with a couple of broken ribs he had received during a riot at work. But it had turned out all right. The Lord had guided and helped them. Just like He would guide and help the Saints of Italy. Just like He would guide and help all of those who believed in Him, in whatever land they lived.

"Enough. Enough." Cora released Robert's hand and turned toward the children. "Enzo, Lucy, and Gianna have agreed to stay with me and help an old woman out until other arrangements can be made with their uncle in Ferrara. They have come to see you."

The youngest of the children, Gianna, stepped forward and handed Robert a family picture in a dark wood frame. In the photo, the family sat on top of a picnic blanket, taking a break from their meal to smile at the camera. And what beautiful smiles they had.

"Thank you for helping us get Mama and Papa," said Gianna.

"And for saving Gianna," said Lucy.

A sob caught at the back of Robert's throat. He dared not speak for fear of bursting into a full-out cry in front of the children—and Gil.

Robert rested his hand on top of Gianna's head and smiled at the other two.

Then the peaceful warmth of the moment was interrupted by a blaring blast of sound. Robert recognized the noise as a Humvee horn, and the roar of a racing engine accompanied it. Whoever was driving seemed to be in a hurry to get wherever they were going and it was closing in on his position.

At last, the vehicle careened into view. Sergeant Shaw was driving it.

It screeched to a stop a scant few feet away from where Robert and the others stood, kicking up dust and sending pebbles flying. Both Shaw and Cohen bailed out of the Humvee, wearing grim expressions.

Captain Mayo showed up from the direction of the main group with several NCOs in tow. "What's going on here, Sergeant?"

"The Russians are coming, sir."

15

Dozens of Dorganites, most of them men, camped near the front gate. As soon as they spotted John, the rabid fans of Roderick Dorgan grabbed their implements of protest, which looked suspiciously like baseball bats topped with anti-Mormon signs.

Not again.

Only a couple of months ago, citizens of nearby Greenville had protested outside that very gate. Along with the numerous Christian groups that assembled at the temple and ward buildings back home, it seemed as if everywhere the Saints went and everything they did drew organized protests and harsh criticism.

John detected a difference this time. The Dorganites didn't offer any witty chants. They clutched their baseball bat-protest signs as if they intended to swing them. These people weren't here to protest—they were here to fight.

"Looks like we have a problem," said Bill Summers as he walked up and stood next to John.

"I'd say that describes the situation pretty well." John expected the camp to have unwelcomed visitors from time to time, but he hadn't thought they would arrive so soon. As Director of Defense, his job was to protect the camp from aggressors, and the Dorganites definitely fit that description.

Even though he had spent many sleepless nights thinking about what to do when the angry mobs started showing up at the camp, he still didn't have an answer. He knew there would be times when the Saints had to defend themselves, possibly with lethal force. How would they know which situations required that level of response? How would he know when to ask the Saints to fight?

And when that time came, how would John ensure the safety of his wife and children? His teenaged sons, Luke and Jesse, could well be called to defend the camp. They would be placed in harm's way.

"Get the construction crew together," said John. "I don't want this to escalate into a conflict, so be discreet about it. Grab Paul and Curtis first. Both of them can handle themselves in any type of situation, and Paul has a cool head."

Bill marched toward the dorm where the construction crew slept.

Considering Paul Young had reported seeing Dorganites inside the fenced area, the time seemed right to organize the camp defenses. That meant a security detail who would act as guards. Paul was an obvious choice. Choosing another seven men would give him four teams of two—and himself, of course.

As Camp Valiant grew, assignments would have to be made for cooks, nurses, herders, messengers, and dozens of other vital positions that a community needed. John didn't envy the person who eventually would have to make those decisions.

Paul and Curtis joined John. So did Wayne Crawford, with a shotgun in hand.

"Whoa." John gently lifted the barrel of the shotgun so Wayne had it pointed straight up. "I don't think that'll be necessary. Why don't you put it away before things get out of hand?"

"They're armed," said Wayne. "And there are a lot of them."

John hadn't even considered the possibility that some of the Saints would bring weapons. Images of armed men patrolling the perimeter of camp flashed through his mind. A sickening feeling entered his stomach. He dreaded the possibility that the growing darkness in the world could lead to bloody conflict.

"Let's find another way," said John, his tone firm.

Wayne lowered the shotgun, barrel pointed at the ground, but he didn't leave.

"At least," said John, "go inside the workshop and keep an eye on us from there."

That produced a nod. Keeping his eyes on the Dorganites, Wayne walked slowly backward until he reached the building. He groped behind him for the doorknob and eventually found it. By then, Bill had returned with most of the construction crew and a few of the new arrivals.

"We need to contact the sheriff, and there isn't any cell phone service out this far," said John. "Any ideas?"

"Besides opening the gate and driving your Suburban straight through the mob out there?" asked Curtis.

"I was thinking we could try something a little more discreet," said John. "Like maybe using a four-wheeler to take an off-road trip to town. Are there any gaps in the fence?"

"There are a couple of posts loose enough that I could pull them out of the ground and lay down the fence," said Paul. "Then I can roll the quad over the top of the wire and put the fence back up when I'm done. These guys would never know I was gone."

"While you're doing that," said John, "I'll see about keeping their attention on the rest of us. If it looks like they might catch you, come on back here."

"Got it," said Paul, and he headed toward the back of the workshop where they kept Camp Valiant's two quads.

"Now, what do we do?" asked Scott Jackson.

Good question.

Then it occurred to John that the proper music was a solution to many of life's difficult moments—including this one. John took those who had gathered around him and formed two semicircles, facing away from the gate. Then he announced, "It seems to me that our guests are children when it comes to matters of the gospel.

So let's teach them like we would a child. Everyone should know 'I Am a Child of God,' and I want you to sing it with real, heartfelt meaning."

Most of the Saints looked at John as if he had sprouted a second head. Shane Dawson grinned and said, "I can't wait to see what our guests think about that."

Tom Gordon stepped up and offered to lead the music. John stood next to him and watched the reaction from the Dorganites as the Saints burst into song. Shocked didn't even begin to describe the looks on their faces. They were obviously lost as to what to do in this situation.

The Dorganites stood slack-jawed through the entire first song.

Members of the camp fared better. Though confused at the sight of the angry people gathered outside the gate, they readily joined the chorus, falling in line with the rest of the Saints. The sound of the music swelled on the breeze.

By the end of the second song, the Camp Valiant choir had tripled in size. Becky and the kids came and stood next to John. Tom stayed with Primary songs that everyone in camp knew. In addition to stumping the Dorganites, the music had brought more than a few smiles to the Saints.

The Dorganites huddled together during the third song and then actually joined in for the fourth one. They supplied their own foul lyrics and focused more on volume than musicality, singing as off-key as a pack of tone-deaf basset hounds.

The Saints sang "Popcorn Popping," "Book of Mormon Stories," and "I Love to See the Temple." Several of the parents had their children cover their ears as they sang, blocking out the profanity that came from the Dorganites.

As soon as the Saints finished the last song, the Dorganites advanced on the gate, shouting obscene threats. They banged their protest signs against fence posts, and a couple started climbing over.

Songs had helped as much as they were going to in this situation.

"Take the women and children into the workshop," John ordered Bill.

"They won't all fit in there," said Bill.

"Do your best, but get them out of here." When John turned around, he found that about half the work crew had armed themselves with hammers, wrenches, and even shovels. The rest of the new arrivals had responded to the noise and two of them held rifles in their hands. Things were about to get out seriously of hand.

"You boys stay close to your mother and protect her and your sisters if need be," John ordered Luke and Jesse.

John rushed ahead of the Saints and turned to face them. "Wait!" The Saints paused.

John spun about and shouted at the Dorganites, "What do you want?"

A large man stepped forward, thinned hair in front and arms as big as anacondas. He sneered. "We want to stop you Mormons."

"Stop us from what?" John asked. Not that he cared what these fanatics wanted, but at least, for the moment, they were talking and not fighting. None of the Dorganites appeared to have guns. If the two groups fought, the Saints were likely to win and, in doing so, create an even bigger problem for Camp Valiant. Dead protestors would become martyrs, demonstrating just how dangerous the Mormons really were. That's how John suspected the world would see it anyway.

"To stop you from spreading your propaganda and 'converting' more people into food-hoarding elitists," said the man. "All of you rich religious types are the same. Talk about helping others, but you really only help yourselves."

The man stepped forward, raising his bat to strike.

A gun blast silenced both groups.

John looked back to find Curtis standing in the doorway of the workshop, his shotgun pointed at the Dorganites climbing the fence.

"You might want to take a look down the road," said Curtis. He nodded his head toward Greenville. Everyone turned.

The sheriff's car sped along the dirt road toward camp with lights flashing and kicking up a cloud of dust behind it. Two trucks, an old Buick, and the camp's quad followed closely behind.

John wasn't sure if the appearance of local law enforcement convinced the Dorganites to hop back over the fence or whether it was Curtis and his gun that persuaded them. All he really cared was that it looked as if bloodshed had been avoided.

The Dorganites frantically grabbed for the signs they had pulled off their baseball bats and tossed on the ground. Stuffing them over the end of their bats, they worked to form a line before the sheriff arrived. Some were forced to hold torn signs in place with their hands because they no longer fit over the bats.

Sheriff McKinney bailed out of the cruiser as soon as it skidded to a stop. He moved his head from side to side as he scanned the crowd, his hand on the handle of his pistol. "I want all of you to stand down."

People piled out of the vehicles that had followed the sheriff. John recognized several of the townsfolk the construction crew had helped during the big storm a few months ago. None of them carried weapons, but they scurried into positions alongside the sheriff. The same look of menace that had been used against the Mormons not too long ago was now being directed at the Dorganites.

"Sheriff," said a big man, "our group—"

"You need to keep quiet if you want to avoid spending the night in my jail," said McKinney. "This is private property and these folks have asked me to explain to you, in no uncertain terms, that you are not welcome here. You *will* gather your belongings and leave immediately. Is that understood?"

Through clenched teeth, the big man said, "Enjoy your little power trip while you can. We have friends too. Powerful friends. Friends that are going to make you sorry you ever met us."

"Are you threatening me?" Sheriff McKinney leaned in until their faces were only inches apart. "I believe I will arrest you. Turn around and put your hands behind your back."

"You're making a big mistake, Sheriff."

"I'll just have to live with that," said McKinney as he cuffed the big man. "Anyone else want to press their luck?"

The Dorganites broke camp, casting withering glares at John and

Sheriff McKinney. They loaded their one-man tents into backpacks and then hiked along the dirt road away from camp with the protest signs resting on their shoulders.

Sheriff McKinney secured the big man in the back of the cruiser and then returned to talk with John. "You know they'll be back."

"Most likely."

"I don't know what kind of reinforcements they plan to bring next time," said the sheriff, "but you can rest assured I will do what I can to help out. The same is true for a lot of the people in town. You folks have been good neighbors. We take care of our own."

"Thank you, Sheriff," said John. "I appreciate the friendship that you and the people in Greenville have shown to us. The way things are going in the world today, I don't see how we can survive without working together."

John stood up with a groan, the bones in his back popping as he stretched from another night of sleeping on the ground, but at least one of the camp's problems had been solved. The cave Paul found turned out to be an abandoned mine that went about five hundred feet back in more or less a straight line. A couple of small side shafts branched off from it, but it had no pits or other dangerous excavations.

One of the new arrivals, an engineer with some mining experience, examined the stability of the mine support beams and had reinforced any area that looked dubious. When he was finished, John organized a work party to transport most of the food storage into the cool, underground facility.

A pair of guards were posted at the mine until they could install a door or gate of some kind. Not to keep out the members of the camp, but because John suspected the Dorganites might attempt to destroy the food or even poison it.

Even though they hadn't seen a Dorganite since the sheriff ran them off, John had no doubt that they would eventually return. When that happened, he expected real trouble.

"John!" someone shouted from outside the mine. A few seconds later, Bill ran inside, breathing heavy. "We need you at the gate."

"What's going on?" asked John.

"I think you'll need to see this for yourself."

John disconnected the small trailer he'd been using to haul food from the back of the quad, hopped on, and motioned Bill to take the seat behind him. He opened up the throttle and tore through the brush and scrub toward camp. As soon as he rounded the corner of the warehouse, he saw them—five large trucks colored military green and disgorging troops.

The National Guard.

Soldiers quickly exited the heavy vehicles and took up positions in front of the gate—guns pointed at the Saints.

16

Appetizers after work at The Firehouse. That was the daily ritual for the people who worked at Media Slick, although once in a while they frequented Steakensteins or Fun-Runners. Sarah continued to order Cokes while everyone else from the office selected alcoholic drinks. The novelty of an evening out on the town had worn a little thin. She still enjoyed the music and hanging out with her new friends, but it felt a little bit like wasted time.

As usual, Joel left once the appetizers had been washed down with the first round of drinks. Brooke claimed he did it to avoid accusations that he ran their social lives as much as he ran their work lives. All Sarah knew for sure was things got more spirited once he left.

"And the patient tells him, 'That's okay, I'll come back when you're sober.'"

Everyone at the table laughed at Ethan's joke. They always did, even though he seemed to only know three. Sarah had long ago memorized the punch line for each one. She supposed they were funnier once you had downed a few drinks, but she laughed along with the others, worried what they might think if she didn't.

I ought to go home. Maybe watch a movie.

Sarah leaned over and grabbed her purse. No excuse came to mind. She hoped one would by the time she fished out the money for her share of the tab.

It didn't.

Money in hand, she looked around the table. The others were oblivious to her as long as she sat there in silence. She knew that would change if she stood up and announced she planned to leave.

Ashley pointed over Sarah's shoulder. "Will you look at that?"

The television mounted on the wall behind Sarah depicted a virtual town made up of tents. At the forefront of the scene, being interviewed by a smug television reporter, stood her dad. A caption at the top of the screen read: "Doom Mormons."

"Now that's what I call a bunch of nut jobs," said Ethan.

Sarah flinched emotionally at hearing a coworker talk about her family in such an insulting manner. As much as she disagreed with the decision to give up everything and go live in tents with the rest of the faithful, Sarah knew they weren't the crazy fanatics the media so often depicted. Just misguided.

She clutched her purse, willing herself to get up and leave before she said something stupid in defense of her family. What did it really matter what any of these people thought about the Mormons?

It did matter, though. They were attacking her family and in a way they were attacking her. If this had happened a year ago she might be with the rest of the Saints in the camp. A part of her heart was with them anyway.

"They should do something about those people," said Chloe. "They're dangerous."

"I . . . I don't think they pose any real danger," said Sarah.

"That's not what Roderick Dorgan says." Ethan jabbed a forefinger toward the image of John Williams on the television. "According to him, the Mormons are the worst of the bunch. They think they can just do what they want and call it freedom of religion."

Sarah struggled to hold her tongue, biting her lip to strengthen her resolve.

"Dorgan isn't what I'd call a reliable source of information on the topic," said Logan. His voice held a trace of annoyance. "He campaigns against anyone who professes a belief in Christ."

"It's about time someone stood up to the Christian juggernaut," said Ashley. "They've been forcing their stupid beliefs on the rest of us for centuries. I'm glad that Dorgan has the moral strength to stand up to them finally."

The argument was quickly escalating out of control. Too bad Joel had already left for the night; his presence kept everyone playing nice, even when they disagreed over the topic of discussion.

Sarah piped in, her voice barely more than a whisper, hoping to sidetrack the discussion. "Anyone interested in catching a movie—"

"Moral strength?" Logan cut Sarah off, his face flush with anger. "Dorgan is a hypocrite and a bully, just like the rest of the lying snakes he represents. His listeners are the cesspool of society."

Logan stood up and looked around the table. The rest of the group sat in their seats, mouths hanging open, smoldering eyes locked on his. Slowly, his expression changed. He looked around the table as if realizing he had made a mistake with what he had said.

"I'm sorry," Logan said at last, his gaze directed at a spot in the center of the table. He avoided looking at any of his coworkers. "That's just what I've heard other people say about Dorgan. But, hey, this is America, and everyone has a right to his or her own opinion. The good old First Amendment and all that."

For a moment, that section of the restaurant seemed frozen in time. Nobody moved. Nobody spoke. An aura of awkwardness shrouded the group like a heavy fog as Sarah's coworkers waited for a breach of the cease-fire.

"Who wants to check out the new comedy club that opened last weekend?" asked Sarah. She tried to force a cheery tone into her words, but they sounded pretty nervous to her ears.

"Thanks." Logan offered the group a fake smile. "It's getting late. I really need to get some sleep. Stinking Death wants me to head over and listen to their latest batch of songs. Lots to do."

Logan laid a pair of twenties on the table and skulked away.

"Lucky for him he didn't spew all that garbage at work," said Ashley. "I'd report him to HR and make sure they fired him."

"Don't worry about it," said Brooke. "There are other options. It's all who you know—you know?"

17

"Williams," growled Captain Mayo, "you'll be accompanying me."

Robert jumped to attention and saluted. "Me, sir?"

Mayo stood next to the Humvee he used as a mobile command vehicle, his hands on his hips. "Do you see anyone else named Williams here?" The mirrored sunglasses the captain wore prevented Robert from telling what, or who, he was looking at. A strong chin and thin, tightly set lips gave Mayo the image of a man in perpetual disapproval of everything around him. There was more than a little bit of Hollywood theatrics to his command style.

"No, sir."

"Then it must be you." Mayo faced Robert as if he were reconsidering his decision and then sighed. "Stow your rifle in the back of the command vehicle and take the driver's seat. If I have to take you along, then I might as well get the most use out of you."

Robert saluted Captain Mayo and sat down behind the steering wheel. He started the engine and nearly put it into gear before deciding he should wait for Mayo to get in and tell him where they were going. The captain and two more soldiers climbed into the vehicle.

"Head north on the A22," ordered Mayo. "I want to take a look for myself at the approach the Russians are going to use to reach our position."

"Yes, sir."

"Then we'll swing down to Vicenza for a meeting with the combined NATO forces in the area. That should be a historic foul-up; the Italian military is calling the shots on this one."

Getting out of town proved more difficult than Robert expected. In addition to the debris that still littered most of the streets, people moved from building to building or chased vehicles in an attempt to climb inside in frantic anticipation of the Russian advance. Robert saw an old man clutching a small duffel bag to his chest as he hobbled along, a haggard expression on his face. The constant foot traffic made it almost impossible to navigate the streets without fear of running over someone.

The situation only worsened as they approached the A22. The Autostrada was choked with cars, trucks, and buses headed south. Vehicles with Italian, Austrian, and even German license plates occupied all of the lanes in their attempt to flee the Russian army that would likely barrel through the Adige Valley within a few more days.

"Find another route," ordered Mayo.

Robert worked his way to the eastern edge of town and took one of the smaller roads, but that had its problems too. Fewer vehicles. More people. They made slow progress through the street, crossing from Trento to Gardolo without a gap between the buildings or the traffic.

As they passed beyond the last of Gardolo's buildings, the number of roads going north was limited, and that meant heavy traffic filled the few routes that remained. For the most part, cars occupied the paved portion of the road, leaving the grassy shoulders open for people on foot. An occasional horse and wagon plodded along the road, slowing the traffic behind them.

Pedestrians included everyone from the elderly to entire families, in which even the children carried as heavy a load as they could manage. A woman herded three small children ahead of her while struggling with a backpack and a crying baby on her hip. Based on the clothing they wore, Robert guessed it was the poor who were advancing on foot.

Robert pulled over on the shoulder and looked for an open path.

"Private, I don't care how you do it, but find a way up north."

Robert unsuccessfully scanned the area ahead of him for a route through the countryside. Although there were some isolated dirt roads on the mountains a few miles away, getting to them would take too long and they were as likely as not to meander to the east. Beyond that, he had run out of options. What sort of solution did the army have for this situation?

"Go off-road," said Mayo.

Off-road meant barreling through carefully cultivated fields, crushing numerous grapevines, and destroying a few light fences that barred the way; nothing, of course, that would stop a Humvee. Robert cringed at the amount of property damage he would inflict on the unlucky farmers. He had joined the army to help people rebuild after disasters—not become a disaster himself.

"Won't that damage the crops, sir?" Robert asked. "Not to mention the fences and anything else we drive through?"

"Williams, once a couple hundred T-90 tanks roll over this spot, the locals won't even be able to tell that we crushed a few of their grapevines. What do you think?"

"I think you're right, sir."

Robert pushed down on the accelerator. The vehicle bumped over a curb and plowed through the first fence. He winced as light wooden posts snapped with the impact. They might have been Popsicle sticks for as much as they slowed down the Humvee.

Thump. Thump. Thump. The steady sound of destruction beat an image into Robert's mind of devastated farmers attempting to repair the damage he caused. Crops that he supposed had been carefully tended for years were mangled in less than a second.

Rows and rows of green vines with clusters of purple and white grapes peeking through the leaves were churned beneath the wheels of the Humvee. An occasional farmer in the field shook his fist at Robert, shouting curses.

Mangled crops, broken fences—if someone wanted to find them, all they'd have to do was follow the trail of destruction left behind. On the few occasions when traffic permitted, they traveled the road; otherwise, they tore up row after row of grapevines.

If this was the army's solution to the problem, it stunk.

Disregard for the property of others went against what Robert had always been taught. He could only imagine what his driver's ed teacher would say if she saw him now. As much as it bothered him, he realized that failing to locate the appropriate spot from which the NATO forces could defend would be much worse.

Beautiful mountain hamlets dotted the mountainsides in the area. They belonged in pictures that adorned the postcards you sent home while on vacation in Italy—they should not be used as targets for artillery, rockets, and whatever else the Russian army decided to bring with them.

Most of the buildings were gray stone with slate roofs, snuggled amongst trees, with a view of glaciers on the distant mountains. Elsewhere, homes and barns of unpainted wood bracketed the road north. Luscious green grass and even more trees made for a peaceful image of country life.

Captain Mayo studied the terrain on either side of the vehicle but seemed particularly interested in the mountains to the east. He recorded map coordinates in a black leather-bound notebook, nodding occasionally.

"Stop here," Mayo said a few miles north of San Michele. When the vehicle halted, he stepped out and surveyed the area with a pair of binoculars. He filled several pages with extensive notes. Then he climbed into the vehicle and pointed north.

He ordered three more stops and did the exact same thing. This area was not as wide as most of the Adige Valley they had traveled through already. The road followed the Adige River, which in turn followed the contour of the mountains. In spots, less than a hundred meters separated the road from the river to the east. A little ways beyond the eastern side of the river, the mountains rose. It seemed to Robert that an army on the road would be at a disadvantage if engaged by a force arrayed along the mountainside.

Their last stop was in Stazione. Captain Mayo finished his notes and snapped the notebook closed. "That's it. Now, let's see if we can make that meeting in Vicenza."

"How long do you think we have before the Russians arrive, sir?"

"Could be a couple of days," said Mayo. "Could be a week. It all depends on how well the Austrians hold out."

Even if the Austrians exceeded the captain's expectations, that didn't leave much time to prepare positions for defense, let alone time to build any emergency shelters for the ocean of refugees who were headed their way.

Robert turned the Humvee around and took the same route back that he'd used to get here, running over the same vines and zooming through the breaches in the fences that he'd made on the way up.

They caught a break as they exited the southern end of Trento. A military convoy was headed in the same direction. Robert pulled the Humvee in behind the last of the Italian vehicles and trailed them all the way to the main staging area for all NATO forces in the region.

The HQ for both the Southern Europe Task Force and the US 173rd Airborne Brigade was located just outside of Vicenza. Vehicles and men occupied the fields surrounding the actual base, tearing up the countryside much like Robert had done on the trip north.

Humvees were parked next to Puma-armored personnel carriers. Abraham tanks formed up alongside Dardo infantry-fighting vehicles and Centauro tank destroyers. Robert even spotted a handful of French Panhard light-armored vehicles. Uniforms of the soldiers varied from country to country and unit to unit, creating a kaleidoscope of khaki.

"Williams," Captain Mayo said when they slowed to a stop, "I understand that you speak Italian."

"Yes, sir," said Robert. "I served my mission in Italy."

"I'm not interested in how you learned Italian. What I am interested in is how to take advantage of your language skills in our current situation. While we are here, I have an assignment for you. I want you to find out what the Italian forces are really thinking."

"What?" Then it clicked that that wasn't the way you spoke to your commanding officer. "What I meant is, I don't understand the assignment—sir."

"You stay near me and listen to what the Italians have to say about the situation. Keep your mouth shut and don't let them know that you understand what they are saying. Got it?"

"Yes, sir." Robert tried to make sense of the instructions. Finally, he asked, "Aren't they on our side? We're all NATO and working together. Right?"

"That's what I want to confirm."

Robert pulled up to the guard post at the entrance of the base. The guards verified Captain Mayo's identity and waved them through.

The two soldiers who accompanied them on the trip stayed with the Humvee while Robert and the captain went inside the large building at the center of the base. There, once again, guards checked to make sure the two of them belonged in the big meeting that was going on.

"Stay close." Captain Mayo didn't even look in his direction. He spoke briefly to another officer and then waded into the logistics fray, leaving Robert at the door to the building.

For the first thirty minutes, Robert kept the captain in sight. The noise of hundreds of men and women attempting to talk over one another made it difficult to hear anything that wasn't being shouted. Even if Robert could have heard any private conversations in the room, the soldiers were either too busy contributing to the argument or they were running errands for one of the officers.

If he moved farther away from the confusion, he might be able to pick up more casual conversations from soldiers not directly involved in the defense planning. But that meant disobeying Captain Mayo.

Jumping into a rescue effort without permission was one thing. Going against specific instructions to stay close was another. Harsh penalties awaited soldiers who disobeyed their commanding officer in the middle of a war. And Robert liked to follow the rules.

The situation reminded him of the story about Adam and Eve. They were told not to eat the fruit from the tree of knowledge, but Eve disobeyed in order to obey the greater commandment God had given them and also that she might be made wise, like the gods. As long as man remained innocent, he could not fulfill his greater assignment to be fruitful and multiply. In this situation the captain had made it clear that Robert needed to find out what the Italian Army was thinking. Or at least what was on the minds of their lowly soldiers. And that couldn't be done in this room.

Robert glanced over at Captain Mayo with the impossible hope of finding the answer there, but the man was fully involved in defense planning. Why did Mayo even want him listening in on the allied troops? What was he really going to overhear other than a bunch of grumbling about how the officers were handling the situation?

His heart pounded harder and his stomach churned as he considered leaving the area in defiance of Captain Mayo's orders. Some part of him shouted to stay in the room and do his best to find out what information he could. That part was losing the argument.

This is insane.

With that thought firmly in mind, Robert marched out of the room.

As soon as he reached a spot in the building where the din of the battle room was muted enough to hear a conversation, he stopped and looked around. Three soldiers wearing the insignia of the Italian 3rd Army Corp Mechanized Brigade stood together talking rather loudly.

One of them glanced at Robert. "What unit are you with?"

"United States Army Corp of Engineers, Europe District," Robert answered automatically—in Italian. He recognized the mistake almost as soon as he spoke. "Sorry, I have business elsewhere."

Near the exit, he found another group of Italian soldiers, still from the 3rd Corp. This time, he didn't approach the group. Instead, he pretended to be bored and looked for a wall to lean against.

It worked. None of the soldiers paid him any attention.

"This must be some sort of joke." The name tag on the uniform read Moretti.

"If it is, then HQ should have issued a general order for all of us to laugh," said a soldier named Peluso. "How can they expect us to fend off the entire Russian army with reduced fuel supplies?"

"Perhaps," said another soldier with Confalone on his uniform, "they believe that with less fuel, we will have more reason to fight courageously because we cannot flee."

"We fight for our homes. There is no need for further encouragement." Moretti spat on the ground and glared at Confalone.

"He teases you." Peluso slapped Moretti on the shoulder. "Fuel is in short supply all over since the Russians took control of the pipeline."

"Except for the Americans," said Moretti. "They have enough to waste on sight-seeing trips and pleasure outings."

"They do not." Peluso laughed. "With the smaller force that the Americans have here, they are able to ship in most of what is needed. I've heard that they are rationing fuel as well. Just not to the extent we are."

Moretti snorted. "I think that we should take from them what fuel they have. Then they cannot run away when the fighting gets tough."

That silenced the others for a moment.

"Don't talk stupid," said Confalone. "If any of the American soldiers hear you spouting that nonsense, we could have even worse problems. It's not their country that's under attack. Be grateful they are helping."

The other two nodded in agreement.

Confalone scanned the immediate area around and spotted Robert looking at them. Their eyes locked. "Do you need help with something?" he asked in Italian.

Plenty of thoughts sped through Robert's mind—none of them helpful. "You . . . are . . . speaking Italian, right?" Robert asked. At least this time he managed to respond in English.

"Are you spying on us?" Confalone leveled a hard stare at Robert.

A knot formed in Robert's throat. His heart beat faster. "Could any of you translate that into English, please?"

Confalone turned back to his friends. "You call a person who speaks three languages trilingual. You call a person who speaks two languages bilingual. But what do you call a person who speaks just one language?"

"American," answered Peluso with a guffaw.

Confalone slapped Moretti on the shoulder again and then faced Robert. "I was telling you that you can get coffee over at the mess hall if you want. Do you know where that is?"

"I think I can find it," said Robert, still in English. He half-waved at Confalone and offered a weak smile before moving on, but his thoughts stayed with the group. How could any of the Italian soldiers think it was a good idea to steal fuel from their allies? Robert and his fellow Americans were risking their lives to help defend Italy. That wasn't the way you treated a friend.

It took a few minutes for Robert to calm down and focus on finding another group of soldiers to eavesdrop on. He made sure to move well out of sight of four soldiers who were now telling obscene jokes about the American army.

How funny would it be if we left you to face the Russians alone!

Robert found himself holding his breath. He had no doubt that his actions must have looked suspicious to the soldiers. A person standing barely a yard away and staring at them would set off alarms with anyone, let alone a group of men expecting to go into battle.

Was this the sort of information that Captain Mayo was looking for? It seemed trivial. Fuel rationing was a fact of life in the current situation. Unless the idea of taking the fuel from the Americans had any merit to it. Robert wasn't even sure if he should mention what he overheard to the captain.

Maybe his next attempt at covert ops would bear more fruit. He spotted a pair of soldiers. Based on their expressions, he guessed they were in the midst of a serious discussion. Both had lips thinned in concentration and their arms folded across their chest. A quick glance at the names on their uniforms listed them as Gallo and Agrussa. This time, he picked a spot close enough to overhear their conversation but faced away from them so it wouldn't be obvious that he was listening.

"Everything is a conspiracy with you," said the soldier named Gallo.

"When will you open your eyes to the truth?" asked the soldier named Agrussa.

"The truth? The truth is that the Americans are here helping us."

"Only a handful of the Americans are here, helping us defend against this invasion," said Agrussa. "The rest are in Germany. That's who they really want to help. Most of their forces in Europe mobilized to defend the Germans. Now the Russian army has them pinned down and can freely attack anywhere else they desire."

"You act as if the Russians planned it this way all along. Attack the Germans and once they and the Americans have dug-in, then move on to their real target. Do you really think that Italy was their target all along?"

"Yes." The response was firm and emotional.

"That doesn't make any sense," said Gallo. "Why would the Russians want to attack us?"

"They want to take out the Vatican," said Agrussa.

The Vatican?

It certainly sounded like a wacko conspiracy theory to Robert. But was it any different than the political attacks being made against the Saints back home? The few letters that he had received from his family indicated that a war against all of Christianity was being waged, and Mormons were the preferred target.

Agrussa raised his voice, snapping Robert out of his free-ranging thoughts. "The facts speak for themselves. Look at how few American troops are here. They are more than willing to allow Italy to fall."

"They will send more," said Gallo. "Like they have in every war."

"Not according to their president." Agrussa's voice rose in volume. "He has declared this a European matter. They are even considering withdrawing the troops that are already here. But I bet they leave the troops they have in Germany."

That was news. Did Captain Mayo know that the President didn't plan to send any more troops to Europe? And if that wasn't the case, did he know that the Italian troops thought they were being left on their own to face the mammoth Russian war machine? Either way, this was something the captain needed to know.

Another hour of covert bumbling failed to do anything more than add to Robert's concern about decreased levels of cooperation among the allies. Without knowing for certain how long Captain Mayo would take to offer his suggestions for defensible positions, it seemed like a good time to return to the war room.

He arrived in time to catch the captain looking for him. Fortunately, Mayo hadn't seen him enter the room, and Robert didn't plan to tell him that he had ever left. "Were you able to give your report, sir?"

Mayo didn't respond immediately. He studied Robert for a moment, his mouth set in a hard frown. "Williams, what makes you think you have the right to ask me questions? I'm in charge of the unit, and it is your job to follow my orders. Is that clear?"

"Yes, sir."

"Good. I expect I won't have to explain that to you again." Mayo arched his back and stretched his arms. "As it happens, I did give my report. Command will chew my suggestions over and contact me when they come to a decision. In the meantime, we need to get back to Trento. The Italian government has promised to supply us with the heavy equipment we'll need for whatever makeshift defensive measures we can put together before the Russians arrive."

The captain marched out of the building with a hasty step that Robert had never seen from him before. That alone testified to the seriousness of the situation and just how little time they had to prepare. They had just reached the command vehicle when four jets screamed over them.

Two F-16 Fighting Falcons bearing the markings of the 31st Fighter Wing rocketed toward the north, followed a moment later by a pair of Eurofighter Typhoons. The sound of their passing roared in Robert's ears, making him think of invincible dragons seeking villages to destroy. Or in this case, Russian planes and tanks.

The captain watched the planes fade from view, shaking his head. "So much for the hope of the Austrians holding out for another week."

18

John walked toward the gate. Slow. Cautious. He held his hands open and away from his body.

"What's going on?" Becky called out to John, clutching eight-year-old Cody close to her even though the boy struggled to move forward and get a better look.

"My guess is that these are the friends the Dorganites talked about when Sheriff McKinney ran them off."

A military officer stepped down from the cab of the lead truck, stern-faced with a touch of gray in his hair. His bottom lip was misaligned from a scar. He straightened his uniform and marched stiffly toward John. His gaze moved to scan the members of the camp and finally focused on John.

"I am Lieutenant Martin of the United States Army National Guard." His voice boomed through the otherwise still afternoon air. "You are hereby ordered to deliver to me all weapons in your possession, whether on your person or on the premises."

"Our weapons?" Becky asked in whispered tones as she moved up next to John, holding Cody protectively at her side. "Why would they be here to look for weapons?"

"Because we have enemies who disagree with our lifestyle," said

John. He gave Becky a little squeeze on her arm and stepped forward. Taking a big breath, he addressed Lieutenant Martin. "The Second Amendment gives us the right to bear arms. We have not broken any laws here. You have no business taking our personal property."

"Are you the leader of this group?" asked Martin.

"Yes. My name is John Williams."

"Mr. Williams, your group is suspected of terrorist activities. In the interest of the country's well-being I can, and I will, confiscate all weapons. I'll ask that your people approach the gate one at a time and carefully deposit any weapons they have on the ground. During that time, I recommend that none of you make any sudden and unexpected movements. Why don't we start with you?"

"I don't have any weapons," said John. He walked up to the gate and slowly turned around, giving the troops there a chance to see that he was unarmed.

Lieutenant Martin glared at John as if he expected some sort of trick. "What about inside the buildings? Do you have any weapons stored there?"

"Not me personally," said John. "I believe there are a couple of shotguns around camp somewhere. You know, to protect against snakes and stuff like that."

"Does anyone out here have a weapon on them?"

John looked around at the camp members that had assembled. All of them shook their heads. The only gun John remembered seeing was the shotgun that Curtis had pulled out during the Dorganite attack a few days ago.

"One at a time," said Martin, "I want you people to walk slowly to the gate and let Sergeant Crompton check you for weapons. Then you will stand outside the fenced area while we continue our weapon search."

John nodded in agreement. They didn't have much of a choice. Sixty mostly unarmed men and their families were no match for a unit of trained soldiers with automatic weapons.

Lieutenant Martin pointed at Becky. "You're next."

A shudder passed through Becky, causing her hand to shake in John's. She moved with the stiffness of fear, walking where directed, turning when directed, and finally standing as directed. When the soldiers finished searching her, she folded her arms and hunched over as if folding in on herself.

In quick order, Lieutenant Martin pointed to Lucas, Jesse, Elizabeth, and Cody, having them all follow the same routine. And just as quickly they were placed in a semi-circle of soldiers at gunpoint. As people woke up and wandered over to find out what was going on, they were added to the line waiting to be searched—children included.

The soldiers had processed about half the camp when Sheriff McKinney arrived. McKinney climbed out of his cruiser, adjusted his gun belt, and asked, "Do you mind telling me what you think you're doing?"

"Sheriff, this is not a criminal matter." Lieutenant Martin squared his shoulders. "You have no business here."

McKinney strode up to the officer, stopping a scant two feet from him. He removed his sunglasses and stared Martin straight in the eye. "These people are in my jurisdiction. That makes it my business. It's the army that has no business here."

"My orders come straight from Washington," said Martin. "I'm to quell any subversive activity that may exist here. These people have been reported as dangerous and ready to rebel against the government."

Sheriff McKinney busted out with foghorn laugh. "Washington thinks the Mormons are dangerous? Is this the same set of geniuses who told all of us that Russia wasn't going to start another world war?"

Martin's gaze drifted over to where the Saints were standing, his expression not quite as confident as it had been when he addressed John earlier. "I have my orders, Sheriff. You may think these people are harmless, but it's my job to make sure they don't pose a threat to national security. If they haven't done anything wrong, then they have nothing to worry about."

"I think I'll stick around and make sure you don't create a problem where one doesn't exist," said McKinney, putting his sunglasses back on. He strolled back to his cruiser and sat on the hood.

Lieutenant Martin turned his attention back to the weapons search. "Mr. Williams, you admitted there are weapons in camp. The fact that you have failed to bring any of them out here worries me."

The only person John knew for sure had a weapon was Curtis. John held up a finger, signaling Martin to hold on while he looked. Curtis hadn't been searched and wasn't with the rest of the Saints. John scanned the immediate area but didn't spot him.

Remembering to walk in a slow and nonthreatening manner, John checked the workshop. Bingo! Curtis stood just inside the door, holding the shotgun in his hands.

"I need you to come outside and surrender the gun," said John.

Curtis clutched the shotgun closer to his chest. "They can't take our weapons. The Second Amendment protects our right to bear arms. Isn't that what the prophets of the Church warned us about when they said that the Constitution would hang by a thread?"

"There's nothing we can do about it in this situation. A couple of shotguns are not enough to allow us to stand up against trained soldiers. Even if we did have enough weapons for everyone, resistance isn't the right course of action."

"So are we just going to turn the whole country over to the godless communists?" Curtis looked scared, not angry.

John wondered what the founding fathers would've done in this situation. Thomas Jefferson had said, "The tree of liberty must be refreshed from time to time with the blood of patriots and tyrants." Then again, Romans 13:1 indicated the Saints should be subject to the governing authorities. Both views seemed reasonable.

"Before the Berlin Wall came down, the Saints there were told to abide by the laws of that land," said John, "and look how that turned out. The twelfth article of faith states that we believe in being subject to kings, presidents, rulers, and magistrates, in obeying, honoring, and sustaining the law. As much as I don't like this situation, the right thing to do is surrender our weapons and find a way to legally appeal the action."

Curtis lowered the gun, his eyes no longer fiery with indignation.

"If we do the right thing," said John, "God will bless us."

Curtis unloaded the shotgun and then walked outside, barrel down.

The soldiers tensed at the sight of the gun and tracked Curtis with their own weapons all the way from the workshop to where Lieutenant Martin stood.

"It's unloaded," Curtis called out. He stopped a few feet in front of Martin and laid the shotgun on the ground, let the shells he held in his hand drop, and then stood there with his hands up.

Two soldiers approached him warily and checked for any more weapons. They nodded at Martin and then escorted Curtis to where the other Saints who had already been searched stood.

By the time they finished checking everyone in camp for weapons, they had netted three shotguns, a hunting rifle, two pistols, and a bow.

"Woo-wee," said Sheriff McKinney, "so that's what an arsenal of doom looks like. No wonder the United States government was worried about these folks inciting a rebellion. I can't tell you how much safer I feel knowing that the army has rendered this security threat inert."

Martin stood over the meager collection of weapons, thin-lipped and red-faced. "The buildings and tents will also need to be checked."

It took the rest of the day for the soldiers to examine every nook, cranny, box, crate, and pile of building materials on the property. They failed to turn up any more weapons inside the camp. With each passing hour, Lieutenant Martin looked less and less pleased about the situation.

While regular army units were fighting the Russians in Europe, Washington had sent Martin's unit out to harass the Mormons. That's what this basically amounted to. There had to be an amount of professional embarrassment over receiving an assignment like this. John only hoped that the lieutenant didn't take out his frustration on the Saints.

"We will retain possession of these weapons for the time being," said Martin, his eyes focused on the small pile of guns rather than looking at the Saints. "Until I receive further instructions from my superiors, I am going to request that you remain within the fenced area."

"You can't do that," said Sheriff McKinney. "These people are American citizens and they have the right to come and go as they please, until you can prove that they've broken some sort of law."

"At this point," said Martin, shoulders back and his chin thrust out, "all I have done is issued a strongly advised suggestion to these people in an effort to contain the situation. I believe that it is in the best interest of everyone involved if they agree to remain here."

"What if we have business in Greenville?" John asked.

"Then let me know and I'll have a squad of my men escort you there."

John bristled at the idea of an armed guard following him around, like he was a criminal who had to be watched at all times. Resisting Martin's suggestion would result in flared tempers and eventually an incident that gave the army a reason to clamp down hard on the Mormons. All of this seemed out of proportion for a people who had done nothing more than come together to grow food and avoid the worst of the disasters that lay ahead.

Martin signaled for a couple of his men to gather the weapons and secure them inside one of the trucks. Then he ordered his men to load up, leaving behind a security detail of about a dozen men. The rest of the trucks rolled down the dirt road for about a quarter of a mile and then pulled off to the side where they set up camp, far enough to give the Saints a little breathing room but close enough to keep an eye on them.

"Camp meeting tonight," John called out loud enough for everyone to hear. "Might as well get back to work until then."

═══════════

The meeting started unofficially outside the warehouse. Almost all of the adult members of the camp gathered around the entrance to the building and loudly discussed the matter before John called everyone to order.

"Can everyone go inside, please?" John shouted.

Camp Valiant residents crammed into the warehouse, many still engaged in heated arguments. Even with the removal of the food boxes and crates to the mine, the congregation barely fit inside the building. As uncomfortable as it might be, holding the meeting in the warehouse gave them a measure of privacy from the troops posted only a few meters from their front gate.

"Nobody said anything about having to fight the army," a voice rose above the terse rumblings of the crowd.

"Why are they bothering us?" asked Helena Reidhead. Only her presence at the front of the group had allowed John to hear her at all. "We haven't hurt anyone."

"This is not what I expected when I agreed to set up this community for the rest of the Saints," hollered Chad Carling. "I thought we were going to have buildings, and furniture, and *bathrooms*."

"It sounds like Salt Lake picked a lot of quitters to come out here and prepare for the Second Coming," barked Curtis. "If the pioneers had your attitudes, they wouldn't have made it out of Missouri, let alone all the way to Utah."

The entire room erupted in arguments. It was bad enough that all of them faced adversity in the form of primitive living conditions and aggression from groups with points of view different from the Saints, but fighting one another could only end badly.

John resisted the impulse to shout down the rest of the room. He needed to lead by example. Closing his eyes, he sang the first verse of "Come, Come, Ye Saints" in his head. Arguments raged all around him, but when he finished, his thoughts were more focused and his attitude improved.

Remembering how well singing hymns had worked in the past, John repeated the first verse, aloud this time. When he finished, he did it again. And again. It took five repetitions of the song before most everyone calmed down. Then he started the meeting with a prayer.

"Make no mistake about it," said John, after the prayer. "Things are tough right now. We are in the midst of the great and terrible days that have long been predicted. As much as I hate to think about it, our situation may get worse before it gets any better."

"Is that supposed to cheer us up?" asked Scott Jackson.

"Cheered? No!" John scanned the room, looking each of the other members of the camp in the eyes. "Resolved? Yes! Just as the pioneers were given a difficult task, so has the Lord asked us to prepare His way. I don't expect any of you to dance the 'happy dance' because the army is camped outside our gates. I'm just asking that you pay attention to the words of the song we just sang and see how they apply to you in this situation."

Bill Summers raised his hand to speak. "This song always choked me up whenever I sang it. I've always wondered what it must have been like for the pioneers to trek all day long and then sit around the camp-fires at night and sing like we just did. I wonder if it helped them find the courage to continue on in the face of sickness and death."

"It must have if they kept singing it," said Becky. "The stanza that I love the best is:

'And should we die,
Before our journey's through,
Happy day,
All is well.
We then are free,
From toil and sorrow too,
With the just,
We shall dwell.'

"That puts an eternal perspective on what the pioneers were asked to endure. The same thing applies to us. This is such a small moment in our lives. Heavenly Father has asked us to be brave and stalwart for this tiny period of time, for which we shall receive an eternal reward. We can be brave. I know we can."

John wrapped his arms around Becky. At the moment, he couldn't decide which of Becky's traits he appreciated more, her intelligence or her spiritual attunement. Fortunately, he didn't have to pick one over the other because they were part of the wonderful package that was his wife. He was eternally grateful for the opportunity to go through life side-by-side with her.

"What do you suggest we do?" asked Curtis. "Sing more songs?"

John ignored the sarcasm. "Sure, why not? We can even open the windows so that the soldiers can hear our beautiful voices. After a few songs to invite the Spirit here, I suggest we turn this into a testimony meeting. What experiences have you had in Camp Valiant that blessed you in some way? I think we may all be surprised at how richly we have been blessed during our stay so far."

Becky got up and led the group in singing several hymns and finished with the full version of "Come, Come, Ye Saints." She directed the music with her right hand and wiped away tears with her left.

John moved to take Becky's place and offer the first testimony, but she didn't move from the spot. Instead she spoke about how she appreciated the opportunity to grow closer to her pioneer ancestors through her experiences at Camp Valiant. She felt a new and stronger kinship with her great-great-grandmother, a woman she knew only through the journal entries she left behind.

Paul Young spoke after Becky.

Paul's wife spoke after him.

John considered stopping the testimonies after an hour but decided against it. This was exactly what all of them needed. Let the congregation continue to express their gratitude and maybe the Lord would accept their testimonies as petitions for help. They certainly needed a little divine intervention at this time.

One of the teenaged boys burst into the warehouse and announced, "They're back. The doofus-worshippers are back."

John and the other adults piled out of the building. Sure enough, the Dorganites had returned. They occupied a spot down the road on public land. If his eyes could be trusted, it looked to John as though they had doubled their number.

Tilting his head back, John mumbled a quick prayer to the heavens, "Dear Heavenly Father, we face two enemies now. Please help us."

As soon as John opened his eyes, a chill wind blew through camp and snowflakes tumbled from the sky.

19

Calvin added a new accessory to his wardrobe as he dressed: a nickel-plated M1911 pistol. He briefly wondered how the White House security would respond to him showing up to work with that holstered on his hip. The reaction from Agents Bowers and Hancock, as Calvin exited his home, gave him a pretty good idea.

"Mr. Vice President," said Bowers, "You can't carry a gun into the White House."

"Why not?" Calvin asked without breaking his stride.

"Only authorized military personnel and Secret Service agents are allowed to carry a weapon on the premises," said Hancock.

"I guess we'll find out if you're right when we reach the security checkpoint." Calvin climbed into the White House staff vehicle he had ordered for the day and waited for his security detail to join him. After instructing the driver to select a radio station that played country-western music, Calvin settled in and read through a report on the upswing in civil violence across the country. Fans from two rival football franchises had gone at one another in something close to a full-out battle, leaving thirty people dead and dozens hospitalized. In Missouri, residents on an entire city block had fought over a minor incident at a recent parent-teacher conference. Increased terrorist activity, the use of violence between the two political parties, and a general deterioration of the moral climate of the country had produced a mind-set that accepted violence among the people. It was grim morning reading, but he felt that he had to keep abreast of the escalating trend toward protest and rioting that currently gripped the country.

A reporter spotted Calvin—and the gun—as soon as he stepped out of the White House limo. More reporters joined the first until a small picture-snapping mob had formed by the time Calvin reached the front entrance.

"This isn't the way we normally go," said Bowers.

"For security reasons," said Hancock, laying a hand on Calvin's shoulder, "I strenuously suggest that we use the VIP entrance, Mr. McCord."

"I'm sure you do," said Calvin, "but then I'd miss out on the nation, and the world, seeing me walk into the Capitol exercising my Second Amendment rights."

Hancock's grip tightened on Calvin's shoulder with enough force to cause pain, but short of tackling the VP in public, there was nothing the frustrated agent could do to stop him.

The guard at the security checkpoint turned pale when he recognized the Vice President at the center of an excited gaggle of the press. His gaze traveled to the gun at Calvin's hip, and he immediately grabbed his radio and called for help.

"Mr. Vice President," a nervous security lead stuttered in front of a growing sea of cameras that were chronicling the event, "you can't bring a weapon into the White House, sir."

"I think you better double-check your regulations," said Calvin. "Handguns registered in Washington, DC, before 1977 are exempt from the weapons ban. As a citizen, I am entitled to carry a gun on my person. Not to mention, I am the Vice President of the United States. Should the President die, it falls upon me to take on the mantle of commander in chief."

The gathered media hounds broke into an excited roar of conversation. This sort of carnival sideshow stunt felt wrong to Calvin, but he was a lone soldier behind enemy lines in the political world. In order to ensure the safety of the people of the United States and to protect their constitutional rights, he needed to find a way to work around the partisan barriers Boggs had put in place.

Eventually, a full team of Secret Service agents arrived and took custody of the Vice President. They formed a ring around Calvin and escorted him, forcibly, to the President's office.

Boggs dismissed the Secret Service agents from the room. "Are you out of your mind, Calvin?"

"I'm legally within my rights," Calvin said, his tone calm and even.

"Does it really matter if you are technically allowed to carry a weapon into the White House or not? It will take an army of lawyers on both sides of the issue to shift through all the precedents and exceptions. And I think it sets a bad example."

"I don't feel safe with my security detail," said Calvin.

"Is that what this is all about? A temper tantrum because I changed the Secret Service agents assigned to protect you? How can you be so petty and self-absorbed?"

"Don't you dare turn this around on me!" Calvin shouted back at Boggs. "You have shut me out of every vital meeting concerning the fate of this country. You have assigned thugs to keep me prisoner and to prevent me from interacting with the rest of the political community, including members of my own party. We are on the brink of disaster, and you're still playing politics instead of working with me to find a solution."

Boggs took a deep breath. When he spoke again, a measured reserve returned to his voice. It was the same tone he used whenever dealing with members of the other political party—condescending. "The United States is besieged by dangerous militant cults who act to undermine the security of our great nation. I cannot allow that. Just as you feel that you must do whatever it takes to achieve your goals, so must I."

"You're talking about tossing aside the Constitution and forcing your own political beliefs on the nation, whether they want them or not."

"No. I am talking about taking the necessary steps to save this country." Boggs lowered his voice to slightly more than a whisper. "I hope you'll believe that I am taking what I think is the best course of action for everyone concerned."

Either Boggs had learned a new level of political talk or for the first time that Calvin could remember, the President actually meant it.

———————

The phone rang at Calvin's home.

He checked the clock by his bed. It read 1:32 a.m.

"McCord," Calvin croaked into the receiver.

"Just thought you'd want to know that the mystery guest shows up on the visitor list for 5:00 this morning," said Kyle.

"As in three and a half hours from now?'

"The very same. Hope that helps." Kyle disconnected the line.

Calvin reached over and adjusted his alarm. He wanted to be there in plenty of time to intercept the visitor who had been using the less-used hallways to meet with someone in the White House. Although he initially suspected the President might be the one playing host to the suspected Russian agent, 5:00 a.m. was too early for Boggs. Mr. Acero had to be meeting with someone else at the White House.

As hard as he tried to get back to sleep, Calvin's mind was racing. Another plot by the Russians. The United States may have won the Cold War, but it looked like we were left holding the bag on this one. Downsizing the military and covert agency operations had left America open to attack.

Since Boggs had declared that until the legal system could make a firm decision on the matter, Calvin was prohibited from carrying a weapon inside the White House, the Secret Service agents would come in handy for a change. They, at least, would be armed and within the vicinity of Mr. Acero when Calvin confronted him.

Calvin dressed, went downstairs to his kitchen, and made a

breakfast of coffee and toast with orange marmalade. He bided his time until 4:00 a.m. and then breezed out the door as if he headed to work every day at this time.

The Secret Service agents assigned to watch Calvin at night scrambled to catch up. One called into his cuff mic that the VP was on the move and to contact Bowers. A small sense of satisfaction came from the prospect of inconveniencing the two thuggish agents. Calvin could just picture them tossing on clothes in a whirlwind of activity and cursing his name.

Calvin ignored the security team's protest about his unscheduled visit to the White House, but apparently unlike Bowers and Hancock they didn't have orders to use physical force to detain him. All they could do was go along for the ride.

They arrived at 4:30 a.m. and Calvin headed straight for the corridor where he had last seen the Russian agent, close enough to the entrance to prevent Mr. Acero from escaping should the mysterious visitor decide to leave.

"Mr. McCord, what are we doing here?" asked one of the agents.

"Would you believe that I just like hanging out in this hall?"

"I find this behavior suspicious, Mr. McCord," said the agent. "This will have to go into a report to my supervisor."

"You mean Boggs."

Neither of the agents with him seemed happy with the response.

A couple of minutes before 5:00 a.m., the Russian entered the hall.

"Mr. Acero, isn't it?" asked Calvin, his voice firm.

Acero's eyes widened for a moment, looking like a rat caught in a trap.

Behind Calvin, a door opened. He glanced back to discover Agents Bowers and Hancock stalking down the corridor toward him. Their clothes were disarrayed, their hair messy. Red, sleepy eyes burned messages of hate into Calvin.

In the split second that Calvin looked away, the Russian spun about and reached for the door he had come through seconds earlier.

Calvin charged toward Mr. Acero, covering the distance with

surprising speed, closing to within a dozen feet before the Russian could flee through the door. Calvin extended his arms in preparation to grapple the suspicious visitor.

Wham!

Calvin pitched forward, his chin slamming against the floor. For a moment—it might have been a fraction of a second or it might have been more than a minute—clouds of darkness with points of sparkling light bounced around inside Calvin's head. By the time his vision had cleared, Mr. Acero had fled.

Rolling over, he spotted Agent Hancock getting up from his position after tackling Calvin to the ground, a satisfied smirk on his face.

The White House doctor had suggested Calvin go to the hospital for X-rays to make sure his jaw wasn't fractured. Enough punches in enough barroom brawls had given him a good sense of when any bones were broken. His jaw hurt, but not as badly as it hurt to have his only suspect in a possible espionage case get away.

He tossed the ice pack he'd been holding against his jaw into the garbage. All it had accomplished was to make his teeth ache from the cold.

Gwen walked into his office holding a folder. She looked nervous.

"Something wrong, Gwen?" Calvin asked.

"An intern just delivered your itinerary for the next three days." She handed Calvin the folder and then crossed her arms.

Calvin looked at the contents of the folder. A letter from Boggs sat at the top.

> *Calvin,*
>
> *In light of our recent conversation, it has occurred to me that you are in need of an assignment. And since you show a great deal of empathy for arming the populace at large, I have a problem that seems ideally suited to you. A religious group known as the Mormons have taken*

to setting up armed camps around the country. Reports have indicated that they pose a threat to both the harmony of the country and the security of the United States government.

I have made arrangements for you to travel to one of these sites and speak to the leader of this group. The Mormons have some eight million members in the country and could represent a serious threat if they are intent on mischief. Your assignment is to assess the level of threat they represent to the country and, if possible, broker an arrangement with them that will reduce the current environment of distrust that exists due to their anti-government gathering.

Of course, if you determine this to be too dangerous an assignment for the person of the Vice President, I completely understand and absolve you from any responsibility for resolving this situation.

—President Nelson Boggs

Calvin didn't know very much about the Mormons. The ones he'd met had always been polite, hard working, and patriotic. Did they really pose a threat to the United States? Or was this some wild-goose chase that Boggs had concocted to throw him off the trail of Mr. Acero?

20

The first bits of the broken Austrian army reached Robert's position around noon. At first only a trickle of troops flowed past the line of trenches that the engineers had dug the day before: an Ivecon utility vehicle filled with dirty and ragged troops, and a Dingo 2 infantry vehicle sporting scars of small-arms fire and shrapnel. As the day wore on, it became obvious that he was watching a full-fledged rout.

One Leopard 2A-4 tank limped down the road on clacking treads that seemed ready to fall apart at any moment. The hatch on top was open and an officer stood there, his right arm cradled in a bloody sling, his attention on the road behind him. For the smallest of moments, he glanced in Robert's direction but refused to meet his gaze.

They even smelled defeated. Oil from damaged engines and coolant from leaking radiators combined with the smell of gun smoke and dirt. Together, in this setting, they were the aromas of death and destruction.

"Stay focused," said Shaw.

The command brought Robert out of his fatigue-induced stupor. No one in the unit had slept since before the trip to Vicenza. Everyone was tired, but he knew he had to stay focused.

"You can't afford to make mistakes when you're dealing with explosives," growled Shaw. "Just keep in mind that demolition jocks are primed all the time. We don't get tired."

Robert searched for a snappy return, but his mind sat in neutral, refusing to budge. Instead, he gave a lame nod and then returned to the ordnance truck to grab another mine. Cohen worked fast and would be ready for another one by now. If Robert didn't hurry, he'd have to endure another one of the corporal's complaints based on some obscure demolitions reference. As tired as Robert was, he might even find it funny this time.

The anti-tank mines weighed about thirty pounds. Lifting one wasn't a problem. Lifting dozens of them over the course of twelve hours and hauling them to the waiting arms of the demo guys was another matter. He wished he had a wheelbarrow to carry them in. Even one of those little red wagons he'd had as a youth would help.

Artillery shells pounded the area to the north. That had been happening all day, but this time they sounded closer. Much closer. Maybe even as close as the next valley. The shock at hearing them explode only a short distance away caused Robert to fumble the mine. It tipped over.

His mind snapped into clarity. He snatched at the falling explosive—and caught it before it hit the ground. His heart beat heavy against his chest, and, at least for the moment, he forgot about his fatigue. To the best of his knowledge, dropping the mine wouldn't set it off, but he wasn't willing to bet his life on it.

He quickly walked over to where Cohen had cut a chunk of grass out of the turf and dug a hole for the mine. They had mined both sides of the A22 autostrada at the spot Captain Mayo had marked on the map. The plan was to strike the Russian units as they entered the area south of Stazione. NATO forces would have the high ground from which they could fire down on the invaders. Their first volley would take out tanks on the road, forcing the vehicles behind them to leave the pavement and enter the minefield.

The problem was that the Russians had a lot of tanks. Gilbert had complained earlier in the day that the only thing this could do was slow them down.

When Robert turned to head back to the demolitions vehicle, he spotted a man stomping through the vineyard toward him. Behind the man, the snow-capped Alps pierced the clouded sky. Even though more than one hundred meters separated Robert from the man, he could hear complaints about the military trespassing on his land. Robert continued to work as the man approached.

Was this for real?

In another couple of hours, the Russian Army would be rolling through this valley spewing out enough ordnance to level a good-sized town. And here this guy was not only going to stick it out, but apparently planned to also fight to protect his property.

"Please," said Robert in Italian, "pack up whatever you can take with you and find a safe place. It's not safe here."

Short and lean, the man barely came up to Robert's chin. The left side of his face drooped, possibly from a previous stroke, even though he looked to be in his early forties. He wore a tan cap and had an arm-length stick in hand.

"This is my land," the man shouted. "Nobody tells me I have to go."

"The Russians are on their way. You don't have much time to get to safety."

An artillery shell hit at the northern-most section of the area, punctuating Robert's statement and spewing a great gout of dirt and grass into the air.

"Do you think that I am afraid of them?" The man shook his stick to the north.

"It doesn't appear so." Robert had to think of a way to convince the man to leave—quickly. He didn't have time for that, though. They had to place as many mines as they could before the shelling reached their position.

"What about your family?" Robert asked.

"I sent them off to stay with my sister and her husband. But I won't be run off by a bunch of communist hoodlums. Or by you Americans either."

"No," said Robert, "I can see that you wouldn't, but what about the obligation you have to support and protect your family?"

"This land has been in my family since my great-grandfather's day. It is the heritage of my family. I have an obligation to protect it."

Robert cast a glance over at Shaw, who had his arms crossed, staring at him. He needed another mine. "The land is safe. The land will still be here when the war is over. And if you are alive, then you can help your family to return the land to what it was when your ancestors farmed it. I think you owe it to your great-grandfather to find a place to stay safe so you can rebuild the heritage of your family here."

The man harrumphed. "I suppose I could hide out in the wine cellar until after the fighting is over."

Robert placed his hand on the man's shoulder. "Please, do that. I'll pray that all of your ancestors will look over you."

Another shell exploded. This one landed less than a mile away.

The man cast a scowl in the direction of the explosion and returned the way he had come. His steps were slow and defiant, with his head held high and the stick still clutched in his fist.

Before the dust of the latest explosion had settled, a large contingent of armored vehicles appeared on the road. Dozens of Austrian armored fighting-vehicles rushed down the A22 in full retreat, weapon turrets facing toward the rear. Men stood in the turrets, ready-to-fire. Scattered within the column were a handful of SK-105 Kurassier tanks and M-109 howitzers.

Robert looked to Shaw, expecting him to signal their withdraw from the field. Instead, he impatiently motioned for another mine.

Was the man deaf and blind?

They had ten to fifteen minutes, at most. Then the entire Russian Army would be boiling into the valley, right into the fields of fire of the US and Italian troops that had set up behind him. This was not the place to be once the shooting started.

Robert grabbed a mine and ran toward Shaw. He looked for the farmer to see how far the man had gone. Not far at all. Robert mentally urged him to pick up the pace.

As soon as the mine was in Shaw's hand, Robert dashed back to the ordnance vehicle and pulled out another one for Cohen.

More shells fell in the valley, following the column of retreating Austrians. The shells fell more frequently now, getting closer to where the engineers were working.

The traffic from the north slowed to a trickle. Three Leopard tanks were the last of the vehicles to appear at the far end of the valley. Not only were their turrets reversed, but they were also firing.

Robert had just handed Shaw another mine when a shell hit about two hundred meters from them. The blast thundered in Robert's ears and he dived for the ground. He could feel a second explosion through the earth beneath him.

"Time to go," said Shaw.

Shaw continued to work, digging a hole for the last mine and placing it inside. By the time he finished, Cohen had joined them, grinning. "I wish we could stick around and find out how the Russians like our little surprise."

"I bet you would," said Shaw. "Take Williams and secure the rest of the mines for travel. We'll have a chance to use them at Trento."

The Leopard tanks had almost reached them when Robert, Cohen, and Shaw readied the last of the mines for travel and then piled into the ordnance vehicle. Artillery rounds fell all around them, showering them with geysers of brown dirt and green bits of the grapevines that were being uprooted in the explosion. Some of the blasts were close enough to rattle Robert's bones. His ability to hear anything besides the booming of near misses had long since failed.

Shaw turned onto the A22 and sped away, passing the slower armored vehicles of the defeated Austrian Army. The soldiers in the turrets wore expressions of such abject misery that Robert hoped never to see the like of it again.

I wish I were home.

"You should try to catch some sleep," said Shaw. He glanced back at Robert. "It won't be much more than a nap, but it'll help because we're going to be busy when we reach Trento."

It didn't sound like a joke. Nothing Shaw said ever did. But how could he seriously think that a person in their current situation could fall asleep? Robert's ears still rang from the artillery bombardment they just exited, and the Russian army was not far behind.

═══════

Robert's body rocked back and forth.

"Williams." A familiar voice sounded nearby.

Again Robert's body shook, this time it continued until he opened his eyes. Shaw stood outside the ordnance vehicle, his arm on Robert's shoulder. "Wake up, Williams."

It took a moment for Robert to realize where he was—and what was going on. He wiped cooling drool off his face. A great fog filled his head, making each of his movements seem sluggish.

"Move it," Shaw ordered.

Robert's muscles responded to the command even though his mind still groped for an anchor point in the real world. The last thing he remembered was Shaw telling him to catch some sleep. And apparently that's what had happened.

"You have about ten minutes to get something to eat," said Shaw. "Make sure you do. We may not get another chance to eat for a long time, and you'll need your strength."

That meant more work. Robert wasn't sure he could go on. He wondered if they would shoot him for disobeying a direct order if he couldn't move. If they did, then at least he could sleep.

"Oh yeah," Shaw continued, "I have this for you."

Robert tried to focus his eyes on the object Shaw held in his hand. It looked like a letter. A subtle hint of perfume tingled in his nose. His mind cleared a little.

"A batch of supplies arrived while we were in the field," said Shaw. "We may not be getting any more for a while. Anyway, it included mail. This one's addressed to you."

Robert snatched the letter away from Shaw.

21

Sarah checked her watch for the umpteenth time. Logan had scheduled a 10:00 a.m. meeting with a comedian they had hired. At a quarter till, the comedian had arrived, but there was no sign of Logan.

That struck Sarah as extremely odd. Logan arrived at work early every day. He normally waltzed into the office, whistling, smiling, and generally acting more good-humored than anyone had a right to act that early.

A quick scan through her emails failed to produce any messages to explain his absence. Ditto for any voice mail left on her phone. She still had fifteen minutes before it turned into a real problem. Walking the comedian back to the conference room, getting him coffee, and talking up his talent might buy another twenty if she took it slow and easy.

In the meantime, Sarah planned to track down her missing coworker. No sooner had she punched his number into the phone than Logan stumbled into view. He wore the same set of clothes that he had worn yesterday, except they were wrinkled. Red, bleary eyes and a day's worth of scruff on his face added to the whole image of a man with a serious problem.

"Logan?" Sarah hurried to intercept him. "Are you okay?"

"Do I look okay to you?"

Sarah hesitated. Her first instinct was to lash back at him. Instead, she took a deep breath and then spoke. "No, you don't. You look horrible, and I asked because I'm worried about you."

Logan rubbed his eyes and sighed. Then he motioned Sarah into his office. "The IRS is auditing me. They've frozen my bank account and blocked my credit cards."

"Can they do that?"

"Of course they can. They are the stinking I-R-S. They can do whatever they want because they are a government agency and they control the money. I'm screwed."

"Why would they do all of that to you? It's not like you're a terrorist or a drug dealer. That seems pretty extreme."

"I don't know." Logan closed his eyes and leaned his head back. "My best guess is that someone in the office reported me because of the argument we had last month. That's all it would take since under the current administration the IRS is treating Christians like criminals."

"You think this is part of some conspiracy?"

Logan lowered his voice and leaned in closer to Sarah. "The government has done it before—used the IRS to target their political rivals. What would stop them from going after anyone who thought differently than they do?"

Memories of her father talking about just such a scandal silenced any further argument. The idea that either of the parties had the ability to use the IRS as a political tool chilled her. She wrapped her arms in front of her, hoping that would be enough to combat the goose bumps that had formed there.

If what Logan said was true . . . everyone should be scared. It meant that each American citizen ran the risk of being targeted by the government whenever the other side of the political divide was in power. The fact that the President heartily approved of the action made it even more frightening.

The possibility that the audit may have been triggered over a petty argument with a coworker bothered Sarah. Working at Media Slick had made it harder and harder to retain the values she had always followed. Not that she was ready to find her parents and live in a tent, but this development made her really consider looking for a new job. The glamour of the industry had definitely faded in light of the way personal advancement was placed over the needs of others.

Sarah laid a hand on Logan's shoulder. "Maybe it's a mistake. Things tend to look worse than they really are when we first run into them. How about we focus on work right now and worry about the audit later?"

That sounded lame.

Logan gave her a look that said he didn't believe it either, but he nodded his head and then combed his fingers through his hair. "Can you keep Pokey busy while I hit the bathroom and clean myself up a bit?"

"Absolutely." Sarah spun around and speed-walked toward the lobby, happy to have some time to think about how she could assist Logan. The two of them had become good friends during the few months she had worked at Media Slick.

She didn't know much about how the IRS operated. Until this year, she hadn't even paid any taxes. Most likely, she would be a great big zero when it came to helping Logan with this problem. If only her dad were around; he'd have some ideas.

Pokey looked up from an old copy of *People* magazine when Sarah walked into the room. He had droopy eyes and a face that seemed to sag around the mouth. His clothes made a different statement altogether. A designer suit and a red power tie boldly announced that this man had something to say and demanded your attention. The odd combination of laid-back looks and serious fashion defined Pokey to the core.

"The conference room is ready." Sarah smiled at Pokey as she resisted the urge to adjust her clothes to fit perfectly on her body, an achievement that seemed natural for the comedian. "Logan is gathering up the materials he's going to need and will meet us there."

"Revolution." Pokey stood up and followed Sarah. He sounded a lot like Eeyore from *Winnie the Pooh*.

"I'm sorry, what was that?" Sarah asked.

"Revolution is the solution." The words came out long and slow.

The solution for what? For Logan's problem? No, of course not. Pokey didn't know anything about the tax audit. Did he?

"All right, you have me hooked," said Sarah. "If that's the solution, then what is the problem?"

"The only problem that matters." Pokey stopped in the middle of the hall, gave her the droopiest look she had ever seen, and then hit the next line with exact comedic timing. "My imminent domination of the world."

Sarah snickered. If Pokey was this funny all the time, today's meeting should prove rather interesting—if not productive. She opened the conference room door and motioned him inside. "Can I get you anything? Coffee? Water?"

"Is it the Water of Victory?" A tone of normalcy entered his voice.

Sarah imagined that this might be how Eeyore sounded if he ever had an occasion to get excited. "Sorry, we're fresh out of that. We only have bottled water."

"Bottled water will be fine." The sound of doom had returned.

Sarah turned, took a step, and nearly ran into Logan. He looked marginally better with his shirt tucked in and hair combed. Nothing in his demeanor indicated he was ready for the meeting with Pokey, though.

She motioned Logan down the hall where they could speak without anyone overhearing their conversation.

"If you want . . ." The words flowed out of her mouth on their own. A part of her whispered that she should mind her own business, but it didn't feel right leaving a friend to face a problem alone. ". . . I can meet with Pokey. We went over the specifics of the assignment together so I feel pretty confident that I could handle this on my own."

Logan's mouth tightened, his eyes narrowed, and his face turned a bright red.

That was not the reaction Sarah expected.

"I didn't expect you to be in on this too; we're both believers. Are you trying to replace me?" Logan raised his voice. "Is that the plan? Work with me long enough to understand what I'm doing and then slide right in and take over. That way Joel can get rid of me without any downside to the deal."

How could he think that?

"That's not it at all," Sarah said, not sure how to defend against his misguided claim. "I just want to help."

"I'll bet. You want to help me right out the door. Is that it? Except it's not going to work. You can go right back to whoever put you up to this and tell them that I'm not leaving without a fight."

Logan pushed her aside, stopping at the door to adjust his tie. He glanced over at Sarah and said, "I don't want you in this room with me. I don't want you to talk to my people from now on. In fact, I don't want you to talk to me either. So take a hike."

Openedmouth and stunned, Sarah stood alone in the hallway, staring at the closed conference room door, wondering how the situation had gotten so terribly out of hand.

She shuffled toward Brooke's office. Besides getting a fresh set of assignments for the rest of the day, Sarah hoped that her friend could make sense of what was going on with Logan. She plopped down on the chair in the office and waited for Brooke to get off the phone.

"Is there a problem?" Brooke asked when she terminated the call.

"Logan."

"I thought I heard him shouting. Do I need to call the police?"

"No!" But was that really true? "He's just upset because he found out that the IRS is auditing him."

"Oh, that," said Brooke.

"Did you already know about the audit?"

"Of course. I'm the one who reported him."

None of this seemed right. It felt like an episode of the *Twilight Zone* where her friends had been secretly replaced overnight by evil aliens. Why would a person set out to ruin a coworker's life because they disagreed with their political view? You didn't even do that to your enemies.

"That seems pretty drastic. It isn't as if he threatened anyone. He just had a little more to drink than he should have and offered his opinion on the subject. The only thing he's guilty of is making his point in a loud manner."

When Brooke swiveled her chair so it faced right at Sarah, a dangerous glint filled her eyes. "People with mind-sets like his are dangerous. We have to do what we can to make sure small-minded bigots aren't in a position to force their way of life on the rest of us. Besides, if he hasn't done anything wrong, there's nothing for him to worry about; the audit will only be a minor inconvenience."

Minor problem. Major problem. It didn't make a difference. Brooke shouldn't throw another person to the wolves over a heated argument or a difference of opinion on how the government should operate.

Based on the reaction Brooke had whenever the Mormons were mentioned in the news, Sarah had to wonder if she might end up in the same situation as Logan. How long would it be before Brooke targeted Sarah for her religious beliefs?

22

"This isn't exactly what I had in mind when I prayed for help," John told Becky. The two of them stood at the entrance to the mine, looking out at a snow-covered Camp Valiant. Snow falling in early October was odd enough, but the region never received three feet of snow all at once, even in winter.

"I don't know," said Becky. "It isn't too cold inside the mine. Besides, the bad weather might just get rid of the Dorganites."

John put his arm around his wife. The fact that she continued to see the positive in any situation continued to inspire and amaze him. He didn't have that kind of optimism, but at least he had her. "You're right. I'm just worried about how this will impact our work. We need to have those buildings done before winter sets in and the snow is slowing us down. Speaking of which, I better take a look around and see how close the work crews are to finishing what needs to be done inside the buildings."

"I have faith that you'll find a way to get everything done. You always do." Becky patted John on the chest and then rose on her toes to give him a kiss.

John followed the fence line toward the gate, watching for Dorganites. The group had breached the fence on a couple of occasions, but John suspected that his posting guards next to all the important supplies in camp had discouraged them from any real mischief. He wasn't sure how long that would last, though.

When John was about halfway to the gate, the snow stopped falling. Although the sky was still cloudy, John could see all the way across camp and hear the pounding of hammers and the buzz of power tools. He spotted Cody playing in the snow with other children his age.

When he reached the trailer, John found Paul Young standing on the steps, scanning the area outside the camp with a pair of binoculars.

"See anything?" John asked.

"Apparently the Dorganites aren't hardy cold-faring folk," said Paul. "Not that I blame them. I wouldn't want to be camping in this weather either."

"Guess that snow turned out to be a blessing after all. What about the National Guard troops?" Even as he asked, John could see a squad of the soldiers huddled together just past the gate.

"Still at the same spot. They look miserable. I almost feel sorry for them."

"It's not their fault that someone in Washington sent them out here," said John. A brief pang of pity for the soldiers hit him. Two days ago these same men pointed guns at the members of the camp. Had anything gone wrong, John's family could have been killed. And yet, he felt a strange compassion for them. "Maybe we should make a gallon of hot chocolate and take it over to them."

"Sort of a welcome to the neighborhood gift," said Paul. His expression made it obvious that he didn't approve.

"Not everyone on the other side of that fence is our enemy. In the days to come, Camp Valiant is going to need allies. Who knows what some hot chocolate or a warm meal might mean to these soldiers. When everything falls apart and people are rioting in the street, a kind word might be all it takes to persuade them to join us—perhaps even to accept the gospel."

"You make a pretty decent point." Paul scuffed a trailer step with the tip of his shoe. "I'll go make some chocolate."

Fifteen minutes later, the two of them walked out the gate and approached the soldiers in a slow, nonthreatening manner. John held the container of chocolate out in front of him, hoping the guardsmen didn't mistake it for a homemade bomb.

"It's pretty chilly out," John called out to the soldiers. "We thought a couple of cups of something hot in your belly would help you warm up a bit."

"You got any coffee?" one of the soldiers asked.

"No." John laughed. "Just cocoa."

"I guess that'll do." The soldier waved for them to approach, eyes wary.

Each of the soldiers downed a cup of steaming cocoa and then held their cups out for more. The one who had first spoken to John waited for his refill and then asked, "You guys really think the world is going to end?"

"That isn't exactly—"

"Post One, we have company," squawked a radio on the soldier's hip.

A soft thwump-thwump-thwump of a helicopter sounded, still hidden by the clouds, but getting closer.

"Excuse me, sir?" The soldier seemed perplexed at the announcement.

"I have been notified that an inbound helicopter contains a VIP," said Lieutenant Martin. "They will be landing close to your position. When they arrive, you'll be at attention and that post better look orderly. I am on my way now."

The soldier placed the radio back on his hip and said to his companions. "You heard the man! We have a VIP due for imminent arrival. Get this post in shape."

All eight men scrambled to secure the area, cramming empty MRE packages into their backpacks, stowing personal electronic devices into their pockets, and adjusting their uniforms. When Martin arrived three minutes later, the guards were standing at attention, stealing quick glances in the direction of the incoming helicopter.

The lieutenant climbed out of the truck and thoroughly inspected the post before walking over to the gate where John and Paul stood watching the flurry of activity. Martin did a double take, looking at Camp Valiant, scanning the area outside the fence, and then once again studying the camp.

"It there something wrong?" John asked.

"The snow." Martin pointed to the ground inside Camp Valiant.

"Yeah, I know," said Paul. "Weird isn't it? This area never gets snow this time of the year. So much for global warming."

"No," said Martin, "that's not what I meant. I have men posted in key points all around your perimeter and there is three times as much snow everywhere else as there is inside your camp. It's like you're sitting in the eye of the storm."

"That is something," John agreed.

Thoughts of snow vanished with the arrival of the helicopter. It pivoted as it approached, showing the presidential seal embossed on the side. It occurred to John that calling their guest a VIP may have been an understatement.

Why would someone that important be here?

The helicopter settled on the ground, and the door slid open. Four Marines jumped out and scanned the area as if they had dropped into a combat zone. Only when each of them had given a thumbs-up did stairs unfold and Calvin McCord step down. The Vice President had a rugged face, a Kirk Douglas dimple, and steely-blue eyes that took in the scene before him with a quick glance. But the thing about him that stood out the most was the pistol strapped to his hip.

"Lieutenant," said McCord, "I assume you know who I am?"

"Yes, sir." Martin snapped a crisp salute.

"Then we can skip the formalities and get right to business. The President has asked me to come out here and find out exactly what's going on. Based on what little I know of the Mormons, I find it difficult to believe that these people are in open rebellion. What's your assessment of the situation?"

"I received instructions to locate to this position and guard against any hostile activity perpetrated by the residents of Camp

Valiant. On our arrival we searched the premises for weapons and then seized them. The Mormons—" Martin glanced over at John, his expression betraying an inner turmoil. "They have cooperated with us all during the operation. I have no reason to believe that they pose a threat to the nation's security."

"What about the weapons you confiscated?" asked McCord.

Martin signaled one of his men and the soldier picked up a duffle bag, brought it over to where McCord stood, and set it on the ground. The Lieutenant opened the bag and displayed the weapons. "Three shotguns, a hunting rifle, two pistols, and a bow."

"That's it?"

"Yes, sir. To the best of my knowledge this is it."

"Not really the kind of arsenal you'd expect from a subversive group." McCord ran a hand over one of the shotguns. "More like what a bunch of campers might pack to defend themselves against coyotes or snakes."

Martin sighed. "That's along the lines of what they told us as well."

McCord rested a hand on the grip of his pistol. "These are dangerous times, Lieutenant. If anything, I'm surprised that a group this size didn't have more weapons."

"Yes, sir. The war in Europe is enough to make anyone consider carrying a little extra protection with them."

"Have you noticed them acting strangely?" McCord asked.

"They sing a lot," said Martin.

"Sing?"

"I mean, *a lot.*"

"Who is the person in charge of Camp Valiant?" asked McCord.

"John Williams," said Lieutenant Martin, pointing at John.

John handed the empty cocoa cups over to Paul, dropping a couple in his haste to ready himself to meet the Vice President of the United States.

Bracketed by the Marines, McCord trudged through the snow toward the gate. When he got within twenty feet he called out, "Mr. Williams, would you please join us out here. The President has sent me to find out what's going on."

John unlatched the gate and strode to meet the Vice President. Probably about the last thing he expected to happen during the day, or any day, was a visit from the VP, Calvin McCord. His mind raced to remember any tips on protocol for meeting one of the country's leaders.

Do I call him Mr. Vice President or Mr. McCord?

If John tried to shake hands, would those Marines tackle him to the ground?

"Mr. Williams," said McCord, "I have been told that you and your people pose a threat to the American way of life. Is that true?"

"With all due respect," said John, "whoever gave you that idea didn't know what they were talking about."

McCord chuckled. "I've thought that myself from time to time. Well then, if this isn't a rebel base or a terrorist training camp, what exactly are you doing out here?"

John could already imagine the kind of reaction he'd get from telling the Vice President that they were out here in preparation for the end of the world. Sometimes it even sounded odd to John, but for someone who didn't believe the Church was true, it must border on the truly insane and bizarre.

"We believe that the situation around the world is going to get worse and may include another civil war here in the United States. In preparation for that event, we have built this farm and others like it. That way, when things fall apart we can feed everyone."

McCord stiffened at the mention of civil war. "What makes you think that?"

"My talking about all of that must make us sound like a bunch of conspiracy nuts," said John. "We're not; it just doesn't take a genius to figure out the direction everything is headed. We just want to protect our families."

"Good tactical move," said McCord. "Gather your forces for mutual defense, keep your people fed, and then wait for the shooting to stop. When it's all over, the Mormons are in a position of power. If it plays out like you think it will, you could have excess food to barter."

"That isn't what we plan to do. The food we grow will be for anyone who needs it—provided they are willing to live with us in peace. We're doing this to help people, not force our way of life on them."

"You plan to feed everyone?" McCord looked skeptical.

"I don't know about everyone," said John, "but as many people as we can."

"Is that so?"

"Sounds crazy, doesn't it?"

"A little bit," said Mr. McCord as he looked past John to the camp. "Before I make up my mind about what to do with you, I'd like a tour of your camp. I want to see for myself what you people are really like."

"In that case," said John, sweeping his arm to indicate the area behind him, "welcome to Camp Valiant, Mr. Vice President. Allow me to show you around."

John led Mr. McCord, accompanied by four Marines and Lieutenant Martin, through the gate. They started with the construction trailer, which now served as command post, visitor center, and secondary camp kitchen. The interior was cluttered with equipment they had brought in from the snow as well as the food supplies they used for meals during the week.

McCord looked the trailer's interior over, his gaze lingering on the picture of Jesus hanging on the wall. He stopped in front of each of the inspirational posters, which Becky had insisted adorn the wall. The "Family Photo" poster depicting people of all races, and the "When You Fall, Fall on Your Knees" poster, depicting George Washington kneeling in prayer, seemed to especially capture his attention. The VP gave an almost imperceptible nod.

They went to the warehouse next. At Mr. McCord's request, John gave a detailed listing of the equipment they stored in the building and the long-term plans for it. McCord stayed alert throughout the process, occasionally checking a box or crate when John listed the contents. When they finished, Mr. McCord nodded. "I see that there are still several more buildings to visit."

"Yes," said John. "The workshop and the dorm are finished. Two more of the buildings are just about ready to use. I guess it doesn't matter which one we see first."

As the group left the warehouse, John felt a prompting to introduce the Vice President to the people in camp. Bill Summers, Wayne Crawford, and Shane Dawson were inside the workshop. John made sure to offer some background information on each of the men and describe the project they were working on. This added a considerable amount of time to the tour, but McCord didn't object.

Becky, Helena Reidhead, and the work crew wives were in the dorm. Again John introduced whoever was in the building to the Vice President. McCord stopped in front of an inspirational poster that stated, "Who is your hero?" and depicted a man with a bow in one hand, and carrying a deer over his shoulder. McCord looked at Becky and asked, "Does this represent someone important in your religion?"

"That is Nephi," said Becky. "He hunted for food while his family traveled through the wilderness. His success was tied to his faith in God. When I look at this poster, it reminds me that Heavenly Father provides the way for His children to survive and even prosper."

"Sounds like my kind of hero," said the Vice President.

The group visited each of the unfinished buildings and then moved on to the tents. Mr. McCord took much less time inspecting them. During the walk to the mine, John pointed out the fields they would be farming the following spring.

"That is a pretty good-sized chunk of land," said McCord. "How many people do you expect to feed from what is grown here?"

"Possibly 125,000 people," said John. "Of course, there are other camps being set up all over the country. Maybe even all over the world."

As they entered the mine, John spotted his children. It wasn't every day that you had the opportunity to show off your kids to the Vice President. "These bright, outstanding individuals belong to me. This is Lucas. These are the twins, Jesse and Elizabeth. And here is my youngest, Cody."

Mr. McCord bent over and asked Cody, "What do you think of all this? Do you like living here?"

"It's all right." Cody shrugged. "I wish we had a television and some video games to play, but we get to play outside a lot and I made a bunch of new friends."

The Vice President shook hands with the rest of the Williams family and then motioned for John to continue the tour.

John opened a few boxes that held packages of food, but Mr. McCord gave them only the briefest examination. When they reached the end of the mine John said, "That's it, Mr. Vice President. You have seen our entire operation. I hope that it answered any questions about us that you might have had."

"It did." McCord spun around and led the march back to the gate. "I don't see how you people are any threat to the country. In fact, you might even be an unexpected asset in the months ahead.

"Lieutenant Martin, you will give the Mormons their weapons back. As soon as I get back to Washington, I will make sure your unit is reassigned to some place where they are needed. In the meantime, I expect you to stand down and await those orders."

"Yes, sir." Martin threw McCord a quick salute.

Mr. McCord glanced over at the lieutenant. "And thank you for having the sense to request clarification of your assignment when you noticed that these people were not dangerous. We need more officers like you."

"Thank you, sir." Martin let a smile slip but quickly recovered.

"Mr. Williams . . ." McCord stopped at the gate and faced John. "Good luck to you and the rest of your people, and I'm sorry for all the trouble."

Out of habit John extended his hand to the Vice President. "Thank you for taking the time to visit us. I certainly didn't expect that."

McCord took the offered hand and shook it. He boarded the helicopter, the Marines boarding immediately after him. Then the door shut and the helicopter lifted into the air, disappearing within minutes into the clouds above.

As soon as the whumping of the rotor blades faded in the distance, a heavy snow started to fall, pushed along by a freezing wind. John said good-bye to the lieutenant and then sprinted to the trailer to get out of the weather, his mind still replaying the events of the day.

The Vice President himself had visited Camp Valiant. That had to be important. Dare John hope that the visit marked an end of the government's opposition to the Saints gathering? And if that were the case, what obstacle would be thrown at them next? What could be worse than close government scrutiny?

Those were thoughts for another day. John made a cup of hot chocolate and then settled down at the kitchen table in the trailer, looking over the progress reports from the construction crew.

The wind howled outside.

Worried about the safety of his people, John walked out into the storm. He organized everyone in the workshop into teams and sent them out to pass the word to take shelter until the storm was over.

Paul Young ran into the workshop. "Lieutenant Martin is at the gate and wants to talk with you."

What now?

Pulling his jacket tightly around him, John trudged through the blowing snow. When he spotted the lieutenant, he wondered about Martin's early comment about Camp Valiant sitting in the eye of the storm. Ice crusted on Martin's uniform.

"If you're bringing our weapons back," said John, "that could have waited until after the storm. In fact, I'm having a hard time thinking of any business that couldn't have waited until the weather cleared."

"I-I-I," Martin stammered from the cold, "need your help."

23

*R*obert,

How do you do it?

How do you stay so calm while the whole world is falling apart? It's not as if I'm a ditzy airhead that panics whenever anything goes wrong. I like to consider myself a strong and capable woman. But we're in the middle of a man-made apocalypse. No one is safe—anywhere.

What amazes me is how comfortable I feel with you. Even though you are thousands of miles away, you can write a few lines in a letter to me and I feel safe. That's never happened to me before. I mean, I felt safe with my father when I was a child and still do to a lesser extent, but this is different.

Thanks for those scriptures you had me look up. It must be a Mormon thing to hand out verses in response to questions people have about life. If I was having problems cooking a roast, I half expect that you'd find a line out of the book of Gastronomical on how to do that. Well, with everything that is happening right now, that Mormon thing doesn't seem so bad—or even weird.

What verses do you have that deal with being underpaid,
underappreciated, and overworked?
Love,
Sierra

Robert's smile, as large and as wide as he'd ever had, persisted through a second reading of the letter. He felt as if Sierra was sitting right next to him. It made him comfortable and warm inside. He could sit all day with her.

It was really he who needed to thank her. As much as he enjoyed the letters from his family, they just didn't compare with the ones from Sierra. She was the one who kept him going when he felt like hiding in a deep dark hole until the war was over. He loved her dry wit and how she did her own original thinking. When she made a choice, she did it only after carefully examining all the options.

He *needed* to marry that girl.

He hoped she wanted to marry him.

"Williams!" Shaw called out as he and Cohen approached. "You'd better join the rest of the unit. They decided not to allow us to blow up select sections of the town as part of the defenses."

Cohen gave his little cartoon-weasel chuckle. "We even guaranteed that when the Russians hit town, the town would hit them back—like a ton of bricks."

"Yeah," said Robert. "It's hard to believe they said no to that."

Cohen shook his head and smirked.

"Anyway," said Shaw, "from the radio chatter I heard over the NATO channels, the Italians have been doing a pretty good job up north. From their location on the mountain looking down on the A22, they have knocked out dozens of main battle tanks and a ton of armored troop carriers, but it doesn't look like they're going to hold out much longer. Mayo has everyone working on defensive positions. Find out from Sergeant Wojcik what they need you to do. Cohen and I are going to see if anyone has some spare explosives they would be willing to part with."

"Maybe even voluntarily," said Cohen.

"I suggest you keep your rifle with you from now on," Shaw told Robert. "You're going to need it."

The two NCOs headed toward where the remnants of the Austrian army had reportedly set up. Robert folded the letter and tucked it away. He found Wojcik directing work teams as they established defensive positions.

The defensive positions amounted to piles of rubble that had been moved from the ruined buildings in Trento to the streets at the edge of town. Stacked as high as a man's chest, they would allow the soldiers to fire at the enemy with some measure of protection and would inhibit the passage of enemy vehicles. About two hundred meters out, regular infantry were digging foxholes in the soft dirt of the fields just north of the SS12.

Wojcik spared a glance toward Robert and said, "Team up with Gutierrez." Then he marched off, shouting orders to each of the soldiers he passed, telling them how to improve the defensive position they were working on.

Robert's eyes burned from lack of sleep; they felt as if someone had scoured them with sandpaper. He could barely keep them open. His movements were sluggish and his limbs dragged at him, their weight pulling him toward the ground. He trudged over to where Gutierrez was operating a bulldozer.

"Hurry it up, rookie." Gutierrez had dark rings around his eyes but looked a lot fresher than Robert felt. "Do you know how to drive any heavy machinery?"

"Yeah," said Robert. The fuzzy state of his head made it hard for him to remember what it was called. "One of those things that are like this except smaller."

"You mean a Bobcat?"

"That's it," said Robert, feeling stupid. "When I worked construction, I ran one of those all the time. But . . . I don't have an operator license."

"You've got to be kidding me!" Gutierrez laughed. "The whole stinking Russkie Army will be coming down that road pretty soon, and you're worried about operating a Bobcat without a license."

"What if Captain Mayo finds out?"

"If you manage to live through this, who cares what the captain has to say about it? He'll probably pin a medal on your chest. Now get busy. Take Feldstein with you. He knows which streets the captain ordered blocked."

Robert followed Gil to where a pair of Bobcats and a mini-excavator sat. His mind fumbled through memories of the construction work he had done a few summers back. He wasn't exactly sure if he knew how to operate the machine anymore.

"How'd the field trip go with the Boom Brothers?" asked Gil.

"Good. I mean, I don't know . . . maybe just okay. We still had a lot of mines left when we took off out of there. The Austrians came screaming out of the north and then artillery started falling on our position. I'm surprised we didn't get hit."

"Any fight that you can walk away from is a good one. Just think about moving this rubble where it needs to go, and you should forget all about nearly getting blown up."

"Gee, thanks."

Gil slapped Robert on the back. "No problem. That's what buddies are for."

Trento had plenty of rubble from the quake. An hour passed and Robert moved enough bricks and stone to make it difficult for Russian vehicles to pass this way. Gil was right. Keeping busy did prevent Robert from reflecting on the shelling or about how tired he was.

The fatigue couldn't be ignored entirely. He made mistakes. Once, he dumped a load of bricks on top of a foxhole dug out earlier in the day. Thankfully, no one was inside when he did. It was only when the Bobcat clipped an already damaged building and caved in a wall that Wojcik came over.

"You're done, Williams."

"I'm sorry, Sergeant," Robert sputtered through lips that felt thick and numb from his lack of sleep. "I'm doing my best."

"I know," said Wojcik. "All of us have our limits. Grab your rifle. I'm going to take you to your combat post. You can sleep there until the Russians arrive."

Robert muttered something that almost resembled words. He picked up his rifle in one hand and followed Wojcik through the streets, barely keeping his weapon from dragging along the ground.

He didn't notice the screaming fury of American F-16s overhead.

He didn't notice the appearance of the retreating Italian Army on the roads north.

He didn't even notice the artillery bombardment creeping ever closer to town.

24

The trip to Camp Valiant still hovered in Calvin's mind. Boggs may have intended it to be a wild-goose chase with a group the President considered religious fanatics, but it had rejuvenated Calvin instead. It had showed him that the country still held good people with just and admirable intentions.

Although it seemed unlikely, Calvin had a feeling that he and John Williams might cross paths again. But he couldn't imagine what series of events might lead to another meeting with the Mormons. As far as he was concerned, the matter was duly investigated and no further monitoring of them needed to be done.

A knock sounded on the door and Kyle Dalton entered without waiting for an invitation from Calvin. "I think you'll want to see this."

"Intel on the war in Europe?" Calvin asked.

"That situation isn't looking so good right now. This"—Kyle held up a CIA folder—"is scarier if you ask me."

The warm feelings of a moment ago fled, chased by the icy hounds of fear. What could possibly be scarier than another world war? Calvin snapped up the folder and looked through it.

A picture of Mr. Acero stared right back at Calvin. Most of the folder held the dossier of a Russian spy named Vasily Akhromeyev.

"You must have rattled him that morning you intercepted him on the lower level," said Kyle. "He left the building in a hurry and didn't bother to hide his face from the cameras. We got a good image of his face, and I was able to search our database and come up with a match."

"Any idea who he was meeting with?" asked Calvin.

"Yep. At least, I have a pretty good idea." Kyle leaned over and flipped through the documents in the folder until he uncovered a list of visits by the Russian agent. "As you know, President Boggs is not much for early morning visits, but he happened to be here for several of them on the days that Mr. Acero was on the guest list. The President's calendar was rearranged every time the Russian agent visited the White House."

"Are you telling me that the President of the United States is meeting with a Russian spy?" asked Calvin. Boggs and he had been bitter political rivals over the years, but Calvin had hoped that his suspicions about the President being a traitor would prove wrong. The idea that the leader of the country might betray all of them left Calvin more than a bit shocked.

"That's what it looks like. What do you want me to do about it?"

Calvin pulled his fingers through his hair. Kyle had been right; this information complicated the entire situation for the United States, at home and abroad. It was one thing to have foreign agents operating within Washington, but it was another for them to be working with the President. And on a personal level it was an absolute nightmare.

A scandal of this nature could very well throw the United States into utter chaos, pitting both political factions against one another during an already volatile time. If Calvin went public with the information, America would suffer. The best hope for a reasonable resolution of this scenario was to confront Boggs with it and hope the President wasn't the kind of politician who would order Calvin killed to keep his secrets safe.

"Do you have another copy of all this?" Calvin asked.

"Are you kidding?" asked Kyle. "This is the biggest dustup since

Watergate and you're wondering if I made copies to ensure I don't disappear in the middle of the night?"

"All right, it was a stupid question." Calvin gathered up the papers and put them back in the folder. "If something happens to me—you get to call the shots on all this."

"If that was meant to be a joke, it's not funny."

"None of this is."

Calvin gave Kyle a ten-minute head start and then headed for the Oval Office. As soon as he stepped out of his office, Agents Bowers and Hancock joined him. Their presence had annoyed him most days, but today it slid icy knives down his back. Calvin wondered if they might be ordered to take care of Boggs's little political problem for him.

"It looks like you're headed to see the President," said Bowers.

"Are you planning on stopping me?" Calvin asked.

Neither agent answered.

"Since he sent me all the way out west to see the Mormons"— Calvin held up the folder as if it contained a report on Camp Valiant—"I suspect he might want to hear what I found out—don't you think?"

Agent Bowers dropped back and used his cuff mic to announce the Vice President's intended visit with Boggs. Hancock gave a noncommittal grunt and continued marching just behind Calvin.

"The President is busy at the moment," said Ms. Wilks when Calvin arrived at Boggs's office. "However, if you would like to wait, I believe he will see you when he finishes his current business."

Coming from Ms. Wilks, that was a giddy exchange.

Calvin sat . . . and wondered. Had Boggs found out the real reason Calvin had come to speak with him? Did the President know that his secret meetings with a Russian spy had been discovered? Was the unusual level of cooperation from Ms. Wilks and the VP's own security detail merely a holding action until Boggs could make arrangements for a more permanent solution to his problems?

Plenty of ideas flowed through Calvin's mind as to what Boggs and the spy could be doing together. None of them good. Most of thcm outright scary, like the possibility that Boggs was working with the Russians on a scheme to legitimize their invasion of Europe.

An hour passed. Then two. Interns and aides arrived with packages and messages and promptly left. None of the people in the room spoke to Calvin. At last, the door opened and Boggs motioned Calvin inside.

"What did you find out about the Mormons?" Boggs asked, although he didn't seem interested in the response. He leafed through a stack of papers on his desk.

"Whoever told you they were a threat has some sort of agenda against them."

"Can you be sure of that from such a short visit?"

"I spoke to their leader, and he has a son serving in the military in Italy. The sheriff in the nearest town vouches for them being the best kind of neighbors. Other than a few guns they use for hunting, they are unarmed. Their purpose for being out there is to grow food—for everyone—in case the country falls apart. I wish we had more people like them."

"Very well," said Boggs as he signed a document in front of him. "I will take your suggestions under advisement. Unless you have anything else of importance that you need to speak to me about, I really need to get back to work."

Calvin paused, tapping the folder in his hand against the desktop.

Boggs stopped his signing and looked up.

"I know about Mr. Acero."

Calvin carefully watched Boggs's reaction. The President's hand twitched, causing an uncharacteristic blemish in his signature. His eyes flicked from the Secret Service agents in the room to Calvin and back. He chewed on his lower lip for just a second and then straightened up.

"Alvarez, Simpson," Boggs addressed his security detail, "I would like to talk to the Vice President alone, please. That goes for Bowers and Hancock as well."

All four of the Secret Service agents looked at one of another with quizzical expressions and then filed out of the office. Boggs waited until they had left and shut the door behind them before looking straight at Calvin.

"Does anyone else know about this?" Boggs asked.

"If you mean, can you get rid of me and sweep the whole thing under the table—no. I've made arrangements for the information to go public if an unfortunate accident happens to me."

Boggs closed his eyes and slumped back in his overstuffed chair. "Do you think so little of me, Calvin, to even consider that as a possibility? Obviously, you do."

That was not the reaction Calvin had expected. Something about the situation didn't match up with what Calvin thought was going on. Sensing that there was more to come, he waited for Boggs to continue.

"The United States is balancing on the edge of a precipice," said Boggs at last. "I have had to make some hard decisions in the interest of saving this country from the forces that threaten to rip it apart, both internally and externally. If only you understood the tremendous stress I have endured as part of my effort to lead America back to the forefront of great nations."

"Tell me about Acero, or can we do away with that and just call him by his real name—Vasily Akhromeyev?"

"You have to understand how close we are to having riots in every major city across the country. As it is now, not a single day goes by without a gun-toting citizen opening fire in an office or on the street or rampaging through a school. Or a mob descending on a grocery store. Or an attempted bombing at an airport. Local law enforcement is undermanned and overworked. How long can this go on before they decide they have had enough and walk off the job?"

"The Russians are part of the problem," said Calvin. "The latest evidence shows that they were behind the Texas bombing in an effort to throw the country into another civil war. With them stomping through Europe, it's become obvious why they wanted us at each other's throats. Keeping that in mind, why are you meeting with the enemy?"

Boggs opened his desk drawer and pulled out a pack of cigarettes.

He put one in his mouth and attempted to light it, his hands trembling so bad that he couldn't operate the lighter. After three flicks of his thumb, he tossed the lighter back in the drawer but left the cigarette in his mouth. "Smoking is prohibited in the building anyway."

"Akhromeyev?" Calvin steered the conversation back to the Russian agent.

"The Russians have threatened to attack the oil fields in the Middle East if we get involved with the war in Europe. As long as we stay out of the conflict, our supply of oil will continue to flow uninterrupted. They even convinced Iraq to lower the price of oil we get from them. We cannot afford to have our oil supply reduced at this time."

"So you let those troops in Germany die, without support, all for cheaper oil."

"No!" Boggs buried his face in his hands and shook his head. "That's not what was supposed to happen. They promised it would only be a small border skirmish, just enough to convince the European Union that the Russians were serious about keeping control of Ukraine and the pipeline. It was just supposed to be a show of power." Boggs's voice came through his hands, muffled and weak. He looked up at Calvin. "I only wanted what you wanted—to keep America safe."

The man had made a major mistake. He had turned a blind eye to the needs of the country's NATO allies and the problems of Europe in general. Tens of thousands of people had died, partly due to his decision to accept the terms that the Russians had dictated to him. Boggs had made a hard decision, and it went wrong.

Calvin had just as hard a decision ahead of him. By all rights, Boggs deserved to have the whole world know about what he'd done and let him face the consequences for his actions, but that was just as likely to throw the entire country into an emotional frenzy and trigger widespread violence. More American lives would be lost due to his incompetence.

Or Calvin could keep his mouth shut about the secret deal with the Russians and work with Boggs on fixing the problem.

"You made a deal with the devil, all right," Calvin announced, "but this is where you tell him the party is over."

"The Russians are not going to be happy about that," said Boggs.

"They might as well start getting used to it; there's going to be a lot of things that we do that they're bound to not like."

"We?" asked Boggs. "Not you? All it would take is for you to hold a press conference and tell everyone what I have done and that would be the end of my presidency. As Vice President you would take over and have free reign to run the country as you see fit."

"What good would come out of turning you in? The way I look at it," said Calvin, "all of us have hit bottom; you, me, the country. The healing and the rebuilding have to start somewhere. It might as well start with us."

"You and I working together?"

"That's the idea. You whip your party into line, and I'll do the same with mine."

"Do you really think this will work?" asked Boggs.

"I guess we'll have to wait and see."

25

Angels blasted trumpets of war from the heavens, demons pounded drums of destruction on the ground, and the earth *shook*.

Robert woke up and opened his eyes.

Early morning sunshine lit cobbled streets littered with bits of brick, stone, and even broken furniture. Looking about, he could see that someone had propped him against a two-story gray brick building. Ahead of him a soldier crouched behind a pile of rubble.

No. Not just a soldier. Gil.

Pops and bangs from all around him suddenly transformed into the sounds of small-arms fire; the staccato of assault rifles and the triple spats of M-16 bursts.

Boom!

A building to the left of his position exploded. Chunks of stone and mortar cascaded onto the street, followed by the collapse of one wall.

"Snap out of it, Williams!" Gutierrez shouted from the other side of the road. "The Russians are about to knock on our front door, and I don't plan to let them in. Pick up your rifle, and get ready to fight."

Robert fumbled for his M4 carbine. Then he launched himself

forward, but his legs weren't quite ready to move, and he ended up plunging into the pile of rubble where Gil had taken cover.

"You okay?" Gil asked.

Robert nodded, ignoring the pain in his knee where it had rammed into a brick. The rest of him managed to hit the bricks with greater resiliency.

"We let you sleep for as long as we could," said Gil. "The Russians started shelling us about thirty minutes ago. I'm surprised you didn't wake up then."

Pain from the throbbing knee actually helped clear Robert's head. He and Gil were positioned on the right side of the street, facing north, while Gutierrez and Johnson had the left. The four of them formed one of twenty-four fire teams in the unit. Robert worked with Gil, who sported an M16 with a M203 grenade-launcher attached. Gutierrez served as team leader. He and Johnson had the M249 machine gun in place and were getting ready to fire.

Robert scanned the area in front of them. The SS12 highway stood about 500 meters out from their position. Beyond that, the mostly open fields between Trento and Gardolo could be seen under the raised expressway, composed of rows and rows of green vines hemmed in by thriving oak and beechnut trees. Farther to the right, the space between the two towns narrowed to only a few hundred meters. Russian troops approaching from that direction would have cover until they were well within the range of NATO weapons.

A pebble hopped along the ground, accompanied by the clatter of metal tank treads on the streets in front of them. Dust vibrated on the cobbled stones. Even the brown brick fragments that littered the street bounced. Vibrations rose through the soles of Robert's boots to his jaws, which already chattered with fear and adrenaline. Trails of dust drifted down from the ledges of the upper stories of nearby buildings.

An explosion and a cloud of smoke from its turret cannon announced the arrival of the first Russian T-90 tank. It pulverized a fence and a couple of small trees into splinters as it rolled into sight.

A wave of Russian BMP armored personnel-carriers followed in its wake.

Robert fought the urge to run. His heart was pounding heavily in his chest.

One of the BMPs had barely broken into the open when it erupted into a fireball that rose like a flaming mushroom into the sky. Somewhere further down the line, a second armored vehicle exploded, spewing yellow fire and black smoke.

More Russian vehicles raced across the open fields, losing a few more of their number along the way. When they reached the SS12 overpass, the BMPs stopped and disgorged the troops inside.

Johnson opened up with the M249 machine gun. Russian soldiers from the nearest armored personnel-carrier fell under the withering onslaught before they found cover and returned fire.

No sooner had the enemy troops gone to ground than Gil pumped a grenade into the middle of them. The blast tossed two of the Russians completely out of their protective spot and incapacitated a couple more. In a matter of seconds, the enemy squad had been all but destroyed.

Untouched, the Russian BMP armored personnel-carrier bored down on Robert's position. A turret-mounted 30mm cannon fired on them, shattering bricks and tearing away at the mound of rubble that protected Robert and Gil.

It would be only a few moments before the cannon chewed through the debris.

Gutierrez popped up and fired an AT4 anti-tank rocket. Leaving a trail of smoke, it streaked toward the BMP and smashed into the front of the vehicle, turning it into a smoking wreck.

A hail of bullets stitched a line across Gutierrez's chest, slamming him against the wall of the nearest building. He grunted once and then slid to the ground, motionless.

This wasn't the movies. Someone Robert knew had just been killed in front of him. Rage toward the Russians for murdering a member of his team battled against a sense of nausea at witnessing his first murder. The rage won out. Without thinking, Robert stood up and fired at the remaining members of the squad who had killed Gutierrez. A lucky shot took out one of the Russians and a burst from Johnson's M249 machine gun silenced the rest.

Somewhere in the back of Robert's mind, he realized that he had just killed a person. Part of him wanted to throw down his gun and shout for forgiveness. A nagging sensation told him that in the years to come this would be a moment that would haunt him, but right now, he didn't have time to think about it. Three more BMPs moved toward him.

They were down a man and had used their only weapon that would affect the incoming armored vehicles. It was time to get out of there.

"Fall back!" Robert called out.

Cannon rounds tore chunks out of the building wall behind Robert, showering him with stone splinters and forcing him to dive for cover. All three of the remaining fireteam members were pinned down.

A thunderous boom of a tank cannon sounded from their right, shaking the ground and scoring a direct hit on the lead BMP that shredded the enemy vehicle into scraps of metal and body parts.

As the flaming remains of the armored vehicle fell to the ground, Robert, Gil, and Johnson grabbed their gear and sprinted down the street. They ducked into a building through a large gaping hole that hadn't been there before the battle started.

"I can't believe they still have this much armor left after the beating they took up north," said Gilbert as he threw himself behind the tattered remains of a dark wood dining table inside the building. "Sooner or later, they have got to run out of tanks."

"Hopefully, before we do," said Johnson. "I think you forget the NATO forces got beat just as bad. The 31st Air Wing lost half their planes covering the retreat. We sure could use them now."

The Russians had smashed through every army they faced. Robert wondered if they could be stopped. From what he'd seen so far, it didn't look like it.

"I think this is their last push," said Gilbert. "They've faced heavy resistance all the way here. If we can stop them today, I doubt they have anything left to reinforce the line."

Bursts from a 30mm cannon sounded outside.

Robert peeked from a spot inside the shadows of the building. One of the BMPs crawled over the pile of debris they had just vacated, crunching bricks under its thick tires, and then slowly moved along the street.

Johnson set up the M249 inside the blasted remains of a kitchen and pointed it toward the hole in the wall. Both Robert and Gil pressed themselves against the inside of the wall, positioning themselves where they could see what was going on outside without being seen.

The BMP rolled past them and stopped. A soldier in the turret rotated 360 degrees, slowing to peer for several long seconds through the hole in the wall. When he completed the scan, he pounded on the roof of the vehicle with his fist and the back doors opened.

Gil stepped forward.

Something inside Robert told him to move up and support Gil. He did.

Before the first of the Russian soldiers could jump out of the BMP, Gilbert pumped a grenade through the open doors and then dropped to the floor. As the grenade sailed through the air, Robert pulled the trigger on his carbine twice and put two bullets into the chest of the turret gunner.

A hand grabbed Robert from behind and pulled him down.

The grenade exploded inside the armored vehicle, killing all of the soldiers.

Robert coughed as he sucked in a lungful of smoke that smelled of burning diesel.

"We've got to move," said Gil. "I'm pretty sure there was a third BMP with these guys. They'll be looking for whoever did this to their buddies."

Robert poked his head out a window on the far side of the building. It didn't look as if the Russians had advanced to this point yet. He handed Gil his rifle and climbed through. A quick scan to his left and right confirmed that the way was clear—for now.

In quick succession Gil and Johnson handed their weapons and extra ammo outside to Robert, who set them on the ground and readied himself to help his teammates out of the building.

Gil scrambled through the window like a monkey escaping a cage.

Just as Johnson placed his hands on the windowsill, an explosion rocked the building, billowing dust and hurling lethal fragments of stone and wood. Johnson stiffened for a moment and then went limp.

Robert and Gil each grabbed an arm and pulled Johnson out of the ruined home. A large piece of wood stuck out from Johnson's back. He didn't grunt, groan, or move when they laid him on his side. Robert grabbed Johnson's wrist and checked for a pulse. There was none.

That was it. Johnson had been alive one moment and was dead the next.

People died all the time. It had never occurred to Robert how suddenly the spark of life could be snuffed out. In the time that it took a person to snap his fingers, he could find himself experiencing the afterlife firsthand.

Gil grabbed his M16 and spare ammo from the pile of equipment at their feet, jarring Robert out of his thoughts.

Robert slung his M4 carbine over his shoulder and then picked up the M249. As he bent over, he spotted the glint of metal around Johnson's neck. Soldiers were only supposed to remove dog tags if their unit was leaving the body behind. At this point that seemed like a very real possibility.

"We don't have time for this." Gil nudged Robert with his elbow. "You can pray for him later. Right now, we have to worry about staying alive."

Robert snagged Johnson's dog tags, wondering if he shouldn't have done the same for Gutierrez, but a stream of 30mm cannon rounds tore up the cobblestones only a few feet away. Stony bits of the street stung their faces like a swarm of angry bees.

The two of them bolted in the opposite direction of the enemy fire. They rounded a corner without bothering to look if the northern end of it was filled with Russians. A zig and a zag sent them down yet another street that was offset from the others, placing a row of buildings between Robert and Gil and any enemy soldiers to the north. At least, until the Russians advanced this far.

Behind them, Robert heard the roar of a BMP engine getting closer. Tires crunched on the debris-filled streets as the vehicle rounded a corner and gained on them.

Another barricade had been erected at the far end of the street. A unit of Austrian troops manned the position. As the BMP turned the final corner, one of the Austrians stood up and pointed a rocket at the Russian vehicle.

Robert flopped on his butt like a baseball player sliding into base. Gil just dove headlong along the cobblestone street.

The rocket whooshed over their heads, waves of heat licking them as it passed. It streaked down the street and struck the side of the BMP before the vehicle could complete its turn. A pair of explosions rocked the armored troop carrier as first the rocket detonated and then again as the fuel tank ignited.

Gil spat blood on the ground. His face-first slide had resulted in a busted lip and nose. These minor injuries didn't slow him down in the least, for as soon as the rocket passed overhead, he popped up and sprinted for the barricade, yelling for Robert to follow.

The two of them vaulted over the barrier just as a wave of Russian soldiers poured into the opposite end of the lane. AK-74s popped and a line of bullets pinged off the debris next to Robert's right hand. He dropped on the other side of the brick mound and readied the M249.

"*Willkommen*," said one of the Austrians as he fired on the invaders.

A combination of the M249 and the Austrian MG3 machine gun blunted the Russian advance. Without armor to lead the way, the enemy troops were cut down as soon as they moved. Even when they managed to find cover, the heavy weapons dug them out. At least a platoon of Russian troops risked their lives to advance along this street.

The firepower that the M249 spit out simultaneously amazed and sickened Robert. For the moment, he was glad to be on this end of the deadly device, but he knew that the images being etched in his mind would not fade with time. The smells of smoke and gunpowder, the rattling booms of gunfire, and the visions of bloodied men tossed aside like broken dolls would likely haunt his dreams for the rest of his life.

It looked as if they might hold this position.

Then Robert ran out of ammunition for the M249.

As he crouched behind the barrier and switched back to his M4 carbine, the Austrian to his left toppled over, a bullet hole square in the middle of his forehead. And then the soldier to his right fell backward.

"Sniper," Robert yelled. He turned and scanned the area in front of the barricade, looking for where the shooter was firing from. Seconds later he spotted the sniper and snapped off a series of shots in that direction. He failed to hit his target, but the near misses caused the Russian to back away from the window.

When he changed magazines in the M4, Gil lobbed a perfectly aimed grenade into the building, blowing the sniper and portions of the wall into the street below.

"*Zuruckgreifen*," hollered an Austrian NCO. Then he turned to Robert and said, "Fall back. We can't maintain this position any longer."

Gil sent a couple more grenades down the street, hunkering behind cover until two rattling *whumps* sounded. What was left of the ragtag allied unit retreated. A pair of soldiers laid down suppressive fire to cover the withdrawal and then, in turn, another group of soldiers did the same for them.

That set the pattern for the rest of the day. Fight and retreat. Troops reformed with the remains of other units that had survived. By the end of the day, the conglomeration of American, Italian, Austrian, and even a few British soldiers had been pushed back to the center of town. Only one of the Austrian soldiers they originally joined up with had survived. Gil had long since exhausted his supply of grenades.

A large number of soldiers, covered in grime and dust, set up in and around the plaza where the Americans had first arrived. It seemed appropriate for Robert to return to this spot. The beauty of the Fountain of Neptune, the bell tower Torre Civica, and the Piazza Duomo all reminded him of the love he had for this country and the Italian people. If he was meant to die, then it felt right that he do so within sight of where he had helped Enzo, Lucy, and little Gianna to retrieve their parents' bodies.

"Williams. Feldstein." Sergeant Shaw approached them. "Come with me."

Robert gave a nod to the collection of soldiers he had been fighting with for the last couple of hours. He didn't even know their names, but he felt a kinship with them. They had survived when so many others had died. So many.

"You can resupply out of our ordnance vehicle," Shaw continued. "Then you can get something to eat and catch some sleep. It doesn't look like the Russians are going to push any farther today. As far as tomorrow goes . . ."

Shaw didn't finish the sentence. He didn't need to.

They walked to the far side of the plaza, feet dragging. Four Humvees were parked along the street and with them were American soldiers. Robert estimated their numbers at about a platoon's worth of men. That wasn't many when compared to the amount of men they had started the day with. Still, the Americans had fared better than their NATO allies.

Robert grabbed a large metal box of ammo and found a spot to sit and reload the magazines for his M4. Then, not expecting to see the ordnance vehicle again, he dumped the rest of the loose shells into his pack. Gil loaded up on grenades. He even handed Robert a few.

"I got to say this for the army," said Gil. "They sure know how to show us soldiers a good time. I can't remember when I had this much fun."

"What I can't figure out," said Robert, "is after all we've gone through today, how you have enough energy to make sarcastic remarks like that. I'm so tired that I don't think I even care if I eat or not. In fact, I can't even remember when we last ate."

"Yesterday. At least I did. You were busy reading love letters."

Robert looked through his pack and found a mangled Snickers candy bar. He figured he could manage to stay awake long enough to eat that. Anything else would require too much effort to open and possibly heat.

A movement from across the street caught his attention. It didn't move like one of the soldiers who surrounded him. He snapped up his carbine and leveled it at the figure moving toward him.

Robert watched as the person walked closer. Finally, he recognized Cora.

"If I'd known that you would react that way to bread and cheese," said Cora, in Italian, "then I wouldn't have brought any for you and your friend."

Cora hobbled over to Robert with a wicker picnic basket in hand and a sweet smile on her face. Gianna accompanied her, holding the hem of Cora's dress as if she were afraid of being swept away should she let go.

"You shouldn't be here." Robert blinked his eyes, wondering if he were seeing things or perhaps had fallen asleep and this was nothing but a dream. He looked over to Gil and found him watching the exchange. If Robert was dreaming, then it appeared that he wasn't the only one experiencing this vision.

"This is my home," said Cora. "Where else should I be?"

"I just meant that it isn't safe. The Russians are here, shooting at people. If you have friends in another town, you should go there while you can. And if you're not worried for your own safety, then do it for the children."

"The Russians have no interest in killing us. What good is this town to them without people to raise crops, make wine, and ship it to their leaders in the north? Besides, the Spirit tells me that this is where I need to be."

After a long day of fighting with the Russians, Robert just didn't have the strength or the desire to argue with this woman about where she belonged. "You brought us food?"

"Not much," said Cora. "Just some bread and cheese. Even that has to taste better than those horrible rations they give you soldiers. That isn't real food."

Bread and cheese sounded good. Robert's mouth already watered. He took the offered basket and split the fresh food inside with Gil. Robert bit down on a crust of bread and closed his eyes as the flavor took him back to happier days when he ate food like this on his mission and shared a message of love with the strangers he met.

"Will you be able to stop the bad people?" asked Gianna.

Robert wondered that himself. They had spent half the day fighting and the other half running away from the Russian assault. An eternity had passed since this morning, and yet the events of the day felt as if they had taken only few minutes. Trento was the last best place to stop the Russians, and it didn't look as if the NATO forces could hold out through another day of fighting.

"I don't know," said Robert. "My friend, Gil, mentioned that the Russians took heavy casualties. Their advance might be on the verge of stalling, but unless we think of something tricky—it doesn't look good for us."

"What kind of a trick?" asked Gianna.

"Maybe if we attacked their fuel and ammo supplies, we could slow them down until more help arrived. But in order to do that, we would have to drive right through the middle of the enemy lines."

"Not if you took one of the mountain roads," said Cora.

"I thought the only way north was through the Adige Valley." Robert straightened up, the food in his hand momentarily forgotten.

"No," said Cora. "That is just the easiest. There are dirt paths that are inaccessible most of the year and too rugged for the average car even when the snow has melted away. You can take them all the way to San Michele if you know the route."

"Do you know the way?" Robert asked.

"I have never had the need to take the mountain roads," said Cora, "but I have a friend who knows them quite well."

A thought bloomed in Robert's mind. Small. Powerful. It refused to give way to reason, growing instead into a full-blown plan. An awful but beautiful plan.

26

An eerie quiet hung over the offices of Media Slick. With Joel and Brooke both out of town for a commercial shoot and Logan on "special" administrative leave, there was a hollowness to the building. But at least Sarah had plenty of time to catch up on the mundane paperwork and follow-up tasks for the exciting stuff the company was doing.

The problem with filing was that while it kept your hands busy, it left your mind free to focus on other things—like the war in Europe and whether Robert was still alive. All this time Sarah had thought her brother was safe, away from combat, digging ditches or building shelters for orphans in Turkey. Why would they put a construction worker with a gun in a real war?

If she hadn't gotten a letter from him, she wouldn't even have known he was close to the front where all of the real fighting was going on and from where bodies were starting to be sent home. Of all of her family, Sarah felt closest to Robert. He didn't judge her and didn't try to tell her how to live her life.

She worried about the rest of her family too. Living in tents during an intense snowstorm reminded her of the stories about the pioneers she heard as a child. For a lot of those rugged trailblazers, the story ended in tragedy. Is that what was in store for her parents and siblings?

I have to do something to bring them back here where it's safe.

Chloe screamed from the front reception area, shattering the silence.

A gunshot rang out.

Sarah froze.

Two more shots followed.

Gangbangers. An angry client. A random shooter.

Thoughts sped through her mind, none of them sticking. Just a rattled reaction to the sound of gunfire.

Run. Hide. Call the police.

That was it. Call the police.

She ran over to Joel's desk and picked up the phone. Her hands shook like a branch during a storm. They shook so much that she dropped the receiver when she punched a button for an outside line.

Sarah left the receiver dangling from the desk and tapped 9-1-1 on the keypad.

Another scream pierced through the wall of the adjoining office. It sounded like Olivia. *Bam. Bam.*

Shut the door and lock it. Then hide.

Sarah's legs felt rubbery and nearly buckled when she took the first step toward the door. What if the shooter came through as she tried to lock it?

As she reached for the handle, a figure rushed through the opening and collided with her. Sarah screamed as she flew backward and landed on the floor.

Ethan reached down and attempted to help her back up as Ashley bounded into the room and slammed the door shut. Then just as she reached for the lock, Logan came crashing through.

"You destroyed my life!" Logan shouted. His words slurred. His eyes were wide and bloodshot. He smelled unwashed and reeked of alcohol. He held a pistol in his hand and waved it about wildly as he spoke. "Why?" he asked as he stepped up to Ashley. "Why did all of you do it?"

Ashley stood her ground. She licked her lips. "Think about this for a minute. We didn't all report you to the IRS. Just Brooke. You want her—not us."

"It doesn't matter." Logan pointed the gun at Ashley. "All of you knew about it. You sicced your government dogs on me because all of you wanted to see me humbled. I lost my house. I lost my money. I lost my wife. I have nothing else to lose. But you do."

"Stop, Logan." Ashley raised her hands in front of her as if she were halting traffic. She stood straight and looked him in the eyes. "Brooke was wrong. Totally wrong. Don't make the situation worse. You still have a chance to do the right thing."

"No!" Logan shouted. "Don't blame this situation on me. It's not my fault. I'm the victim here."

Then he pointed the gun right in Ashley's face and pulled the trigger.

Bam.

A scream tore itself from Sarah's throat. She turned her head so wouldn't be able to see Ashley's body. Sobs worked their way up from her chest, but she fought against letting them out. It seemed important that she not cry.

Logan stepped over to Ethan and pressed the barrel of the gun against his forehead. "What about you?"

Ethan blubbered.

Horrified, Sarah watched the two men, unable to turn away or close her eyes. Ethan kept working his mouth to speak, but all that came out was "P-p-p-p."

"No pithy remarks about my social flaws?" Logan's face had turned a purplish-red and his eyes burned with a fierce anger. "Go ahead. Tell me how I deserve to have the government rip my life apart. Tell me how all of this is my fault."

Ethan closed his eyes and sank to the ground. "P-p-p-please."

"It's not my fault!" Logan screamed. "All of you have forced me to do this."

Bam. Bam, bam. One, two, three times Sarah watched Logan pull the trigger and then stood there as the body toppled over.

The smell of burnt gunpowder filled the room.

Then Logan turned and faced Sarah.

Fear paralyzed Sarah. Her eyes remained fixed on the smoking gun.

I don't want to die. Please, Lord, help me.

Logan raised the pistol.

"Heavenly Father loves you," said Sarah. The words flowed out of her mouth without any conscious thought. She knew they weren't hers. She prayed they were being given to her by the Holy Spirit.

Logan hesitated. His hand shook.

"I love you," said Sarah.

His face twitched. Tremors rippled along Logan's bottom lip. He shook his head and lowered the gun. "It's not my fault."

The same prompting that had provided words for Sarah now hushed her. She stood there and lifted her gaze to Logan's face. Silent. Fearful.

"It's not my fault," said Logan, his words almost whispered, his head bowed.

In the distance a siren sounded.

Logan jerked his head up and screamed, "It's not my fault!"

Then he put the gun to his own head and pulled the trigger.

27

As hard as the wind blew inside the camp, John could hear it howling like a banshee in the area beyond the fence. He doubted that the guardsmen out in that storm had prepared for a blizzard this time of year.

"When the storm hit," said Lieutenant Martin, "I called all of the squads in from their posts. Two of them have not returned. We have radio communication with them, but they can't find their way to us in all of this wind and snow, and we, of course, can't find them. I've told them to stay wherever they are rather than risk them wandering even farther from our position."

"Someone needs to find them and quick," said John. "They won't last long in this weather. How can we help you?"

If Lieutenant Martin was embarrassed to ask civilians for help, his personal struggle with the cold masked any signs of it. His arms were tucked in close to his body, and he was hunched over. Rather than turn his back to the gale, Martin faced John and the fury of the wind. The man had to be desperate for help.

"You know this area better than we do," said Martin. "I have no right to ask you, but will you help rescue my men?"

"I know the area pretty well," said Paul. "Back when we had

shotguns, some of the work crew hunted rabbits on our off time. Curtis knows the area better than I do, but I'm willing to go out and look for them."

"Wait a minute," said John. "That's no spring shower out there. I want you to understand that you're risking your life if you go."

"Are you going?" asked Paul.

"Yes," said John. "I'm in charge of the camp and it's my responsibility to look after the welfare of anyone here and that includes visitors."

"As the assistant to the Director of Defense it's my responsibility to make sure you don't get yourself killed," said Paul. "You wait here and I'll go get Curtis. It may take a couple of minutes for me to talk him into helping the soldiers."

"I suggest you mention to him how awkward my troops will feel when he rescues them," said Lieutenant Martin. "That should provide a little payback for our confiscating his shotgun. He can even walk beside me during the rescue and rub it in."

John quickly interjected, "That won't be necessary, Paul. Just ask him to turn the other cheek and help us save the lives of several men."

Paul dashed off toward the dorm.

"What about the rest of your men?" asked John. "I can't imagine that any of you prepared for a blizzard. It may be a bit crowded, but I think I could fit all of you in the warehouse. You'll be out of the wind and snow, and we can bring in a couple of heaters."

Martin stared at John for a long moment. "Why are you helping us?"

"Because that is the kind of people we have been taught to be."

"Thank you for being that kind of people," said Martin. The lieutenant hesitated again. "We don't have to sing—do we?"

"Let's just find your men and then we can discuss the matter." John grinned.

Paul returned with Curtis.

"So the soldier boys got themselves lost." Curtis wore the first smile that John had seen on him since the guard arrived.

"This is serious business," said John.

"You bet it is," said Curtis. "If we don't get them out of this weather soon, the lieutenant will be writing next-of-kin letters for his lost troops. Where are they?"

"Post Three started back to our main camp but decided they had no chance of finding it in the storm. They returned to their post, which was approximately fifty meters away from the northeast corner of your property. "

"It should be easy enough to find them," said Paul. "What about the other group? Do you have any idea where they are?"

"They were posted on the far side of the camp, opposite the front gate. I don't know where they are now, though. During my last radio contact with them, they stated that they had found a tree in a gully and were using it for cover from the storm."

"Anything unusual about the tree?" asked Curtis.

"Private Pugh said something about the limbs of the tree were missing on one side. Possibly from a lighting strike."

"I know the place," said Curtis. "That's pretty close to the spot we selected for the agriculture shed."

John worked on a plan in his head and finally said, "Let's split into two teams. Paul, Lieutenant Martin, and a couple of the National Guard troopers will go after the men in the northeast corner. Curtis and I will take a couple of the soldiers with us and attempt a rescue of the other group."

"I'll go get my men and bring them into camp," said Lieutenant Martin.

"Good," said John. "That will give us time to bundle up and get whatever equipment we need for a rescue mission in the snow."

───────────────

Freezing wind sliced through the protective layers of John's clothing, even though Becky had insisted he don enough shirts that he could barely move his arms. His face numbed within seconds of climbing over the fence where Curtis felt they were most likely to find the lost guardsmen.

meters. If that isn't enough we can come back and get some more posts."

"Hope it works," said Curtis. He looked skeptical.

John set out in the direction of the tree. Or at least the direction Curtis thought the tree was located. He played out the rope as he walked, often stumbling on the rough terrain. When he reached the end of the rope, he took a hammer out of his pack, grabbed a fence post from Private Backus, and then pounded the post into the ground. A red ribbon attached to the top of the post flapped excitedly in the wind.

Private Backus signaled the second half of the rescue team to join them.

Several minutes later, Curtis arrived, pulling himself along the rope, hand over hand. The soldier accompanying him coiled the rope up as they walked.

Though he was only thirty yards away from Camp Valiant, John could no longer see the fence, or any part of the camp for that matter. Wind-driven snow prevented them from seeing any farther than a few feet in any direction. Doubts about the plan nagged at John.

The team repeated the process. Once. Twice. Three times. Neither John nor Curtis were sure they still headed in the right direction. The best they could do at this point was to keep going until they ran out of fence posts and then range as far as they could with the rope, hoping to run across the missing soldiers.

John had just finished securing the sixth post when Lieutenant Martin announced, over the radio, that they had successfully recovered the other group and were headed toward the warehouse.

When they reached the end of the rope for the seventh post, John fumbled the hammer and dropped it in the snow. He spent valuable time tucking his hands into his jacket pockets to warm them up enough to keep a grip on the hammer.

The ground turned out to be too rocky to sink the post. John moved several feet to his left and tried again with the same result. Moving to the right proved marginally better, but it still took nearly five minutes to secure it.

"If you want," said Private Backus, "I can hammer the next post."

"You do that."

As soon as they reached the end of the rope the eighth time, Private Backus pulled out the last post and slammed it into the ground, sinking through the snow and several inches into the dirt below.

That figures.

"I guess I should have had you doing it all along," said John.

"Nah, I think I just got lucky and struck a sandy spot."

Once Curtis and the other guardsman arrived, all four men trudged through the snow, looking for the tree. With about half the rope played out, they came across a snow-filled gully.

"This is it," said Curtis.

"Are you sure?" asked John.

"We're north of the tree. I hope we have enough rope to reach them."

John trudged forward another couple of yards until the vague silhouette of a tree loomed over them. The lost guards lay huddled together, mostly snow-covered, at its base.

All four of the rescue party plowed through the snow.

Private Backus and his companion pulled the lost soldiers to their feet and ordered them to walk in place, flap their arms, anything to get the blood pumping through their bodies. Then they wrapped them with extra blankets.

All but one of the lost guards responded to the field treatment for hyperthermia. Private Backus and his companion volunteered to carry the unresponsive soldier back to camp. That left John and Curtis to wrangle the rope by themselves on the return trip, John at the front again and Curtis bringing up the rear.

John forged through the storm alone, his mind drifting to stories about the pioneers as they crossed the plains late in the fall and the tragedy that befell them. They, too, walked on legs stiff from the cold, fingers and toes tingling. How did they manage? John had a round-trip of a little more than six hundred feet and he didn't know if he was going to make it. How did they travel like this for miles?

Without realizing it, John reached the end of the rope. He spent a moment looking for the post and then, keeping the line as taut as possible, he marched to his left. Going much farther than he expected to go in order to find the post, he reversed direction.

Too bad he hadn't kept track of the number of steps he took or the amount of time he spent traveling the one direction. Then he could be sure when he reached the spot where he had started. John trudged through the snow until he was certain he had passed his starting spot and gone far enough to have found the post.

Nothing.

Curtis and the soldiers must think him lost. And he was. The guardsmen were in bad shape and needed shelter. John's stumbling about in the snow without a clue as to where to find the next post put all of their lives in danger. The plan had seemed so reasonable when he came up with it. Besides, who would've thought that anyone could have this much trouble finding a flagged fence post only thirty yards away?

John switched directions again, planning to intensify his search for the post. He took about a dozen steps and tripped, falling on a snowy mound that turned out to be a watermelon-sized stone. A sharp pain shot through his shoulder from where it struck the rock.

Panic welled up inside him. Something had gone wrong with his rescue plan, and he didn't know how to fix it. He started to rise and then decided against it. Since he was already on his knees he might as well say a quick prayer to keep his knees from freezing.

Calm settled over John as he finished the prayers. He placed his hands on the ground to aid his attempt at standing and spotted a strand of red in the snow. John grabbed the ribbon and pulled on it. The missing fence post broke free of the snow.

John closed his eyes and thanked God.

Instead of attempting to hammer the post into the ground, John grabbed a few large rocks and piled them on top. Worried that the post might wiggle free when the others followed the rope, John piled on a couple more big stones.

Then all he had to do was notify the others.

Except that Private Backus and the radio he carried had stayed behind in order to help his weakened companion. The next time he planned a rescue mission, he really needed to think things out better.

John staggered through the snow, following the rope back to the others.

"We thought you got lost," said Curtis.

"Maybe we can talk about it back at camp," said John.

The extended wait had reduced everyone's ability to traverse the snowy terrain. They stopped twice on the way to post number seven. John and Curtis each wrapped an arm around the waist of one of the lost guardsmen who couldn't walk and helped support his weight. He didn't know about Curtis, but John barely managed to propel himself forward. In his head, he kept reminding himself that they only had to travel another hundred yards.

They made it to post six without any problems, finding it almost immediately. John left the guardsman at the spot where the rope played out and searched for post five. It took only a couple of minutes to locate the fence post with a red ribbon snapping in the fierce wind. He retrieved the guardsman, attached the rope to the post, and signaled the rest of the group to join them.

Post four. Post three. Post two. The slicing wind continued to buffet the men, making it harder and harder to take another step. Only when John tied his end of the rope to the first post did he sigh in relief. They were almost home. Another fifteen minutes and all of them could relax inside one of the heated buildings of Camp Valiant.

John uncoiled about half the length of rope when the fury of the wind abated. It was as if he had stepped through an invisible barrier that blocked the worst of the storm. Having witnessed the "eye of the storm" himself, John had no doubt that this was the hand of God protecting His chosen people, just as He had when Moses led the Israelites out of Egypt. Did this mark the beginning of a new age of miracles?

Ahead of him lay the dim outline of the fence and group of people gathered there.

"John?" Becky called out from the middle of the group. "Is that you?"

Hearing the voice of his sweet wife gave strength to John's legs. He sprinted across the remaining terrain and wrapped his arms around her.

"What about the rest of them?" asked Bill Summers.

Only then did John look back to see what had happened to the guardsman he had helped along. The guardsman limped along, slowly, but under his own power.

The rest of the group shuffled into sight a few minutes later. Lieutenant Martin checked each of the soldiers as they arrived and then made arrangements for them to be carried to the warehouse.

John took Becky's hand and headed for camp.

"I was starting to get worried you weren't going to make it," said Becky.

"Me too," said John.

28

"You must have suffered serious head trauma during the battle," Mayo bellowed.

Robert had to admit that the man made a good point.

"There must be well over twenty thousand viable troops still functioning in the Russian 20th Guard and you want me to send a handful of men with explosives, behind enemy lines, on a suicide mission to blow up their fuel and ammo supplies. Is that correct?"

"Yes, sir." Robert struggled to restrain his tongue. After all that had already happened today, he didn't need a dressing-down from his commanding officer for offering advice, but the words came out anyway. "The thing is, Captain Mayo, we have to try because our forces can't hold out for another day."

"What makes you think you're in any position to judge that?" asked Mayo.

"I think seeing the events of the day firsthand has given me a pretty good idea of what's going to happen tomorrow—sir." Speaking up like that to Mayo surprised Robert. It wasn't like him to stand boldly before authority figures and resist their challenges. He guessed that dodging bullets all day might have something to do with his newfound confidence. Or had the constant encounters with death brought on an emotional numbness?

"I like the plan," said Cohen with a crazed smile.

"So do I," said Shaw.

Mayo looked the two NCOs over as if searching for serious head wounds, his head shaking the entire time. Then his gaze drifted over to where the wounded Americans were being tended, next to a line of tarp-covered dead. A frown replaced the headshaking.

"The three of you lunatics may think this is a good idea, but I don't like it one little bit." Mayo glared at each of the three in turn. "That doesn't mean you aren't right. I don't see that we have any other choice. Do we have enough explosives to seriously disrupt their supply line?"

Shaw nodded toward Cohen. "The corporal appropriated ordnance from the Italian engineers before they were moved well back of the front line. We have enough to hurt the Russians—for a while. They can always bring up more, but I think this mission, if we succeed, will buy us a couple of days."

"Very well. You will operate as two independent teams," ordered Mayo. "That means you'll need to find a fourth man to assist you with the actual explosives work as well as taking a pair of drivers for the two Humvees you'll be using on the mission. What about a guide?"

"One of the locals has volunteered to show us the path through the mountains," said Robert. "As soon as we reach the A22, on the far side of the mountain, we can split up and search for supply targets. Our guide can remain behind on the mountain paths until we return—if we return."

Mayo motioned them over to his command vehicle, pulled out a map, and laid it flat on the hood. "We don't have any satellite surveillance of the area, so I can't tell you where the Russians have positioned their supply depots. Luckily, the Russkie Army is nothing if not predictable. Based on their standard logistical procedures, I can give you a pretty good idea of where to look."

The captain spent nearly a half hour going over possible locations for the fuel and munitions depots and finding the best ways to approach them. When he finished, he folded up the map and handed it to Shaw. "I guess I won't need this tomorrow. If we get pushed out of Trento, we're done. You can leave as soon as it's dark. Good luck."

"Thank you, sir." Robert saluted Mayo, but the captain had already done an about-face and was marching toward a group of officers from the combined forces. For the first time, Robert noticed that Mayo walked as if he carried a heavy weight on his shoulders, taking slow, almost ponderous steps. He stopped once and rotated his shoulders as if adjusting the load.

Which was worse: facing death on the front line or witnessing the deaths of dozens of men under your command? Ultimately, each of those deaths must add pounds to the burden he carried as the ranking military leader in this area.

"Snap out of it, kid," said Shaw. "I asked you if you had any suggestions for the last member of our foursome?"

"Yeah," said Cohen. "Maybe someone you don't like so much."

Just like Cohen said, it made more sense to bring someone along that he didn't care about. Then if the team died during the mission, the responsibility for suggesting that anyone come along would be less traumatic.

How had he come to a point where his head was filled with thoughts like this?

"Give me a second," said Robert and then he turned and walked over to where Gil was sitting. Cohen's comment rattled around in his head, but he couldn't shake the feeling that Gil was the right person to go along.

Gil looked up. "I'm not sure I like that look on your face. Please don't tell me you've done something crazy like volunteer for some stupid suicide mission."

Robert chuckled. "It's worse than that. I'm going to ask if you want to go along."

The smirk Gil usually wore faded. He looked down at his hands as he tossed a small rock back and forth. "If there's one thing you learn in the army, it's not to volunteer."

"I guess I don't blame you," said Robert. In a way he felt relieved.

Gil's head tilted up again, the smirk was back. "Lucky for you, I'm a slow learner. Not only that, but sticking it to the Russians sounds a lot better than just sitting here waiting to be killed."

"Who's the crazy one now?" Robert turned to the engineers and called out. "Gil's going with us."

"That works," said Shaw. "Grab your buddy and get ready while Cohen and I round up a pair of drivers. And see if you can't track down our mountain guide. We need to be rolling in less than fifteen minutes."

Robert sat in the back of the lead Humvee along with Antonio. The elderly Italian claimed to have used these very same roads to elude Italian law enforcement as he carried contraband into the country. That had been long before he joined the LDS Church.

The Humvees crept along the mountain pathways in the dark. Both of the drivers wore night-vision goggles to help them navigate the treacherous dirt roads—if you could call them roads at all. Because the Humvees were wider than the vehicles Antonio normally used in his clandestine travels, the right wheels rode dangerously close to the edge of the path and the steep drop-offs beyond. Twice the vehicle had shifted weight suddenly, putting Robert's heart in his throat and sending rocks tumbling down the cliff.

"What do you think of your plan now?" Cohen asked.

As crazy as it seemed, Robert was convinced that this is what he needed to do. He looked Cohen straight in the eyes and said, "I'm pretty sure this will work."

At least, I hope it will work.

"With that kind of enthusiasm," said Cohen, "I'm glad you're working with me rather than Shaw. We might make it out of this alive. And won't my mama be happy about that."

Robert thought about his own parents. How would it affect them if he died?

"This is it," Antonio announced in Italian. "The A22 is straight ahead. If you want to find the spots you showed me on your map, one vehicle will have to turn left here and the other will need to turn right."

Both vehicles stopped and the men climbed out. Shaw unfolded the map and compared it with the instructions Antonio gave him. They were close to one of the locations Captain Mayo had pointed out to them. The second was farther away. Shaw decided that since the second location was farther behind enemy lines, Cohen and Williams would search for targets in that direction. In the meantime, Shaw and Gil would hold for twenty minutes before heading out on their own. If the captain was right, then both teams would reach their targets about the same time.

"One last thing," Gil said as Robert turned to climb into his own Humvee. "Thanks a bunch for suggesting me for this suicide mission."

"Don't mention it," said Robert. "I'm sure you would've done the same for me." He closed the door on the vehicle and hoped that he hadn't just closed the door on their friendship.

———————

Progress had been slow, much slower than Robert expected. The trip through the mountains had taken most of the night, leaving Robert plenty of time to stare into the dark and worry about the thousands of ways the mission could fail. Now, they traveled on a dirt road that paralleled the A22, stopping all too frequently so Cohen could exit the vehicle and scan the immediate area for signs of a supply depot.

Dry-mouthed, Robert sat and waited for Cohen each time. His ears, hypersensitive in the dark, found only the sounds of insects buzzing and chirping in the night.

An hour before dawn, they found a fuel supply stashed away from the main road, but relatively close to the dirt path they followed. Cohen decided not to risk detection by moving the Humvee any closer. Instead, he loaded Robert down with most of the explosives and detonators and the two of them set off on foot.

Cohen held up a hand.

Robert halted.

"Do you remember how to set these explosives?" asked Cohen.

"Yeah." Robert nodded. "I think so. But I won't have to because you're going to do it—right? I mean, I'm just here to carry all of this equipment for you."

"That's the plan." Cohen's voice lacked its usual laid-back tone. He handed a couple more packs to Robert and pulled out a KA-BAR fighting knife. "If I'm not back in ten minutes, you're on your own. Try circling around to the far side of the fuel convoy and set the charges like I showed you. Spread them out so they're hard to find; then get out of there."

"I will," Robert said, nodding again, "but you're coming back—right?"

"Yep, that's the plan." With that said, Cohen slipped into the night, leaving Robert behind to wonder if he really did remember how to set the charges.

Someone coughed in the distance. Elsewhere, the faint sounds of conversation gave proof of the Russian presence. Each disturbance in the still night reminded Robert he was behind enemy lines and surrounded by hostiles.

And right now, he was alone.

No. It just seemed that way sometimes. The thought that no one was ever really alone calmed him. Wherever he went and whatever he did, God accompanied him.

Robert settled down and focused on scanning the immediate area for enemy soldiers. A soft crunch of gravel alerted him that someone approached. He raised his pistol, unsure if he should defend himself with it, knowing the sound of gunfire would alert all of the Russians in the area to his presence.

"Holster that pistol," Cohen ordered in a low voice, "and follow me."

Crouched low, Cohen slunk through the darkness like a panther on the prowl.

Robert copied the NCO's movements as best he could, but he ended up making as much noise as if he had walked normally. They stopped next to a fuel tanker with a big red star on the side. A pair of bodies lay on the ground, tucked underneath the tanker.

"Hand me the first package," whispered Cohen.

The order snapped Robert's attention back to the task at hand. It wasn't as if he hadn't seen plenty of dead bodies over the last few days, but realizing that Cohen had knifed two men stunned him. Robert slipped off his pack and handed him the first explosive.

Cohen crawled under the nearest tanker and went to work, unhindered by the darkness. In a few seconds, he finished and stood back up. Robert barely had a chance to watch for any approaching guards.

"Got it," Cohen whispered. "On to the next one."

They repeated the process four more times in the following ten minutes. Robert handed over the explosives and almost before he could shoulder the backpack into place, Cohen finished setting and arming the bomb.

Robert turned to leave and heard footsteps.

Cohen laid a hand on Robert's shoulder and pulled him back into the shadows. A pair of soldiers walked casually past their hiding spot. Robert listened as the sound of the footsteps continued past the truck. He and Cohen waited a few moments more before they moved on stealthy feet toward the next target.

The two of them hardly made a sound as they crept through the gap between two of the tankers. Robert thought he had finally caught on to the whole stealth thing. Then, as they rounded the front of the target vehicle, they came face-to-face with the guards that had just walked past them.

Cohen's hands shot forward, grabbing one of the guards, spinning him around, and clamping a hand over his mouth before the

Russian had a chance to react. Then he struck with his combat knife. Once. Twice. Three times.

Robert and the second guard reacted simultaneously. The Russian pawed at the strap on his rifle, fumbling to bring his weapon to the ready.

Backpack still in hand, Robert swung it by one of the straps and slammed it into the soldier's head. The soldier flew backward while his rifle tumbled to the ground.

Robert dove for the rifle.

Letting the body of the first soldier drop to the ground, Cohen rushed the second guard. He dropped on top of the Russian and shoved his hand over the guard's mouth. As the wily NCO raised his KA-BAR to attack, the guard pulled his own knife. Both men sunk blades into one another simultaneously.

Cohen pierced the Russian's chest. The guard stiffened and then stopped moving.

By the time Robert retrieved the rifle and returned to Cohen, the fight was over. The NCO rolled off the dead Russian but didn't get up.

"You said you remembered how to set the explosives," Cohen wheezed.

"Yeah, but that's your job." As soon as he said it, Robert regretted the words. They sounded selfish, when really he just wanted Cohen to be all right.

"Not anymore." Cohen struggled to speak. "This is it for me."

"No. I can't leave you here. I'll carry you back to the vehicle."

Cohen raised a hand. "Give me the rifle. I think I can hold on long enough to cover you. As soon as you hear any shooting, plant the last of the explosives and get out of here."

"But you'll die . . ." Robert didn't know how to finish what he wanted to tell him.

"Then you better take these." Cohen fished his dog tags out from under his uniform and handed them to Robert. "Get moving. If you don't get the rest of these explosives planted, the Russians are going to keep rolling over the top of us."

Robert took the tags, noting how they glistened red in the moonlight. He stuffed them into his trouser pocket and then got up. His heart screamed at him to stay, but he knew that he had to do whatever he could to stop the Russian advance. Afraid to look back at Cohen, he picked up the pack containing the remaining explosives and snuck along the line of fuel tankers.

Unlike the demolitions he had first encountered in Ankara, these explosives had been rigged beforehand. All Robert had to do was plant one in the undercarriage of the tanker and arm the detonator.

Simple, right?

What had taken Cohen seconds to do took Robert almost two hand-trembling minutes to accomplish. A sense of relief washed over him as soon as he armed the first package. He scanned the area for guards patrolling along the line of tankers and then crept toward the next target.

He placed five explosive packages before shots rang out in the night. Robert's instincts told him to drop the pack and run as fast as he could away from the Russian camp and into the dark. Instead, he crouched and hurried along the line of trucks until he reached the last tanker, skipping all of the other intended targets. He rolled underneath the truck and hooked the backpack to a protruding part on the engine.

The sounds of gunfire stopped. That had to mean Cohen was dead.

Voices shouted in Russian. Lights popped on and raked the area around the camp, looking for intruders. Neither the voices nor the lights had reached Robert's position—yet.

Robert sprinted away from the trucks. He hoped that the lack of shouting in his immediate area meant that no one was close enough to hear him running. Out of the corner of his eyes, he watched for spotlights moving in his direction.

In his haste to get away, he tripped over rocks, bushes, and who knew what else, until his foot failed to find any ground at all, and he tumbled down the side of a steep gully. The collision with the ground at the bottom knocked the wind out of him.

He opened his mouth and tried to force himself to breathe, but he couldn't. A spotlight passed over his location as he rocked back and forth in the safety of the shadows below. After what seemed like hours, he pulled in a long, deep breath.

The sounds of engines starting added to the angry chorus of shouts back at the enemy camp. Robert might be safe from the roving spotlights for the moment, but eventually the Russians would send out patrols. If only he could see in the dark, he could follow the gully away from camp and then worry about working his way back to the Humvee.

Night-vision goggles.

How could he have forgotten about those? Robert strapped them on and activated the goggles. The world sprang into green brightness. He stayed crouched and ran along the gully until it started to rise with the mountain.

Risking a peek over the top, he gathered his bearings and then scrambled out of the gully in what he hoped was the direction of the Humvee. He placed whatever rocky mounds he could find between himself and the enemy camp. After a few hundred meters he gave up stealth and ran as fast as he could, leaving the lights and sounds of pursuit behind.

"Where you going?"

Robert's heart leaped into his throat. The unexpected voice had surprised him. It came from about thirty meters to his left and a bit behind him.

"Are you planning to run all the way back to base?" Robert recognized the voice of his driver.

When Robert turned in that direction, he spotted the Humvee. He dashed toward the vehicle. "We need to go. Now."

"What about the corporal?"

"He didn't make it. And neither will we if we don't get going."

Robert opened the Humvee door and dove inside just as the driver gunned it to life. The driver had had the presence of mind to turn the vehicle around while they were gone and all they had to do was drive forward—quickly.

A mighty rumble sounded from behind them. Robert turned to see huge orange blossoms lighting the night. They were both beautiful and horrific. Even as far away as the Humvee was from the explosions, the ground shook from the destructive power that Robert had released from the enemy fuel reserves.

In the shadows of the flames, Robert could see the silhouettes of Russian vehicles headed their way.

29

Calvin McCord and Nelson Boggs pulled up to the United Nations building in the Presidential limo. The Secret Service team that protected both of them formed a small army, like bees swarming the queen.

As Calvin climbed out of the vehicle, his suit jacket pulled away, revealing his nickel-plated M1911 pistol strapped to his hip.

"We agreed that you would remain unarmed in Washington," said Boggs.

"You suggested it," said Calvin. "I didn't agree."

"Please, Calvin, we have come so far in such a short time. The NATO alliance is falling apart and the image we project at this summit is vitally important. Having the Vice President show up armed for war gives all the wrong messages."

Calvin thought differently. Packing heat might show the rest of the world how serious the United States was in their new resolution to support their allies in Europe. An image of strength could even deter Russia from following through with their threat to attack the oil fields in the Middle East.

Then again, Boggs made a good point. There was such a thing as looking too eager for war. Unwilling to damage the newly forged bond of cooperation between the President and himself, Calvin unstrapped his holster and placed the weapon back in the limo. He adjusted his jacket and walked beside the President, smiling and doing his best to look statesmanlike.

To give Boggs his due, this is where the politician really shined. He had a knack for connecting emotionally with his audiences, making them feel the passion that he felt. All Calvin had to do this time around was nod his head with all the talking points. He hoped this event marked the reversal of fortunes that would lead to prosperity and peace once again.

They approached the entrance of the UN building. Part of the security detail moved ahead to take control of the doorway. A couple of officers spread out to urge the press to back away, giving the agents room to properly assess any threat.

A man stepped out from the sea of reporters, wearing a long coat and sunglasses. He pulled a gun out of his coat pocket and in one quick motion fired at the wall of human flesh that protected the President.

In quick succession, three Secret Service agents dropped to the ground.

Agents Bowers and Hancock grabbed Boggs by the arms and pulled him away from the crowd, away from the gunman. The rest of the security detail stepped between the Presidency and the assassin, pulling pistols as they moved.

The assassin wrapped an arm around the neck of a reporter who had been standing next to him, pulled her close to his body, and used her as a living shield. He continued to fire, wounding two more agents.

People screamed. Some ran. A few flopped onto the sidewalk. One man stood just a few feet away, frozen to the spot, his mouth gaping.

Calvin turned to follow Boggs inside the building and spotted Vasily Akhromeyev working his way out of the crowd. The Russian hesitated for a fraction of a second as he locked gazes with the Vice President.

The man shooting it out with the Secret Service was only a distraction.

Akhromeyev grabbed a man fleeing the rampaging gunman and forced him toward the President, shoving him at the last second.

Agent Bowers braced for the impact and then pushed the bystander aside. Before the agent could turn again to face the real threat to Boggs, the Russian shot Bowers twice in the face.

Calvin reached for his M1911, slapping his side before he remembered that he had disarmed at the President's request.

True to Secret Service training, Agent Hancock threw himself in front of the President rather than exchanging gunfire with the assassin.

Akhromeyev put a trio of shots into the agent's chest and then another in his forehead as Hancock pitched backward.

Calvin dove for the weapon Agent Bowers had dropped.

Bam! Bam!

Pistol in hand, Calvin rolled into a kneeling position to fire. Focused only on taking out the Russian agent, Calvin pulled the trigger and shot Akhromeyev at point-blank range. The power of the bullet caused the Russian's body to jerk to one side.

It took four more shots to put Akhromeyev down. Calvin continued to pull the trigger until the pistol dry-fired. A quick glance showed that the Secret Service had killed the first shooter and were checking the crowd for further threats.

Only then did Calvin look to check on Nelson Boggs. The President lay on the ground, blood pooling around him. Akhromeyev had shot Nelson Boggs twice in the head.

The people in the crowd continued to shout the same message. "The President is dead! The President is dead!"

30

Soft light filtered through half-drawn shades in the office of Jean Hampshire. The effect was supposed to soothe emotionally distraught patients during their visits, but it made Sarah sleepy more than anything else.

"This is the last of our scheduled counseling sessions," said Jean. "If you feel that you need more time with me, I can arrange for that to happen."

Even though Sarah still had nightmares about the shooting, she didn't think more visits with Jean would help. She doubted that any mortal had the power to ease her suffering. Only time would dull her pain. "I can manage from here."

"Then let's make the most of our session today," said Jean. The middle-aged woman smiled at Sarah. A practiced smile.

A patronizing smile, thought Sarah. The homey office, the casual clothes Jean wore—they all were imitations of friendship and love. Every word Jean uttered was measured to convey a sense of warmth and caring to her patients. And the worst part was that with Sarah's parents gone, Jean represented the best available option for advice.

"What are you feeling today?" Jean asked.

Sarah fidgeted with the bottom button on her sweater. A whole emotional storm rattled around inside her. Guilt tormented her for surviving the ordeal while those with her had not. She alternated between an overwhelming relief because she lived and crushing guilt for feeling that way. None of which she felt like sharing with a stranger. Knowing that Jean would persist with her gentle rubber-hammer of persuasion until Sarah offered a problem they could discuss, she grabbed one and tossed it out for examination. "I was wrong."

"About what?" Jean leaned forward in her chair, her hand reaching out as if it might magically extend across the table sitting between them and console Sarah with a concerned pat on the shoulder.

"When my parents left the city for the great Mormon gathering, I thought I would be safe here. I thought they were the ones in danger. Now I realize that no place is safe anymore. For the first time in my life, I understand what it meant when my Church leaders talked about the hearts of men growing cold."

"You have experienced a horribly traumatic event," said Jean. "It's natural for victims to have a strong reaction to a fight-or-flight situation and perceive more threats in the world around them. Take a moment to ask yourself if it is realistic to believe things are actually any more dangerous than they were a few weeks ago. If you can admit that you have only become more sensitive to the possibility of danger, then it will be easier for you to overcome your fears."

And there it was: the reason why further therapy sessions would be a waste of time. No matter what Jean said, the world had become a more dangerous place. War. Crime. Natural disasters. A rich person might stick her head in the sand and ignore their presence, but no one could completely escape the effect of those plagues.

Sarah's family had always shared hand-me-down clothes, but this year they couldn't even afford to replace the shoes that her brothers had outgrown. The arguments among the Media Slick workers had grown more intense over whose turn it was to pay the bar tab, but Ethan was driving a brand new BMW X1 the last time he came to the office. It seemed that the greater the wealth, the easier it was for the privileged to convince themselves that nothing at all was wrong with the world.

Maybe Mom, Dad, and the other LDS aren't as crazy as I thought.

"Sarah."

Jean's voice brought her back to the here and now.

"I understand what you're saying," said Sarah. "Thank you."

"From what I've heard," said Jean, "you still have a job at Media Slick. They have agreed to let you take as much time as you need to recover and then return to work."

Of course they would. How would it look to the public if the company fired the lone survivor of a workplace shooting spree? They really had no choice except to support Sarah and hope she didn't go to the media with any juicy, behind-the-scenes gossip about the company.

The media. A shudder ran down her back. Newspapers, magazines, television stations, and bloggers from all over the country wanted an exclusive story about the rampage and especially how Sarah had survived the face-to-face encounter with the killer. They hovered like vultures looking for a bit of death to report. All it took was another multiple-homicide to pull their attention away and leave her alone.

"I won't be going back to work there," said Sarah.

"Well then, will you be moving back home with your parents?"

Sarah tapped her fingers on the arm of the stuffed chair. Several versions of how that discussion with her father might unfold went through Sarah's head. All of them ended in a manner that left both her and her family in a worse situation than what they currently faced. Sarah wanted to rush into her father's open arms and have him tell her that everything was going to be all right, but she had to be realistic. If her parents found out what had happened, they would insist that she stay with them where it was safe, but Sarah did not want to live in a primitive camp, hiding from the world.

"My parents and I don't see the world in the same way. They have gone to where they believe they are safe, and I have stayed here in the place where I grew up, a place that feels safe to me."

"I'm glad you see things that way," said Jean. "One last item before you go. As horrible as all of this is, I think it's important that we don't judge Logan. We can agree that what he did was wrong, but in the end all of us are victims. All of us have reasons for doing what we do, and I think it will help you to let go of the hurt if you can understand that."

Anger flared within Sarah. Right was right. Wrong was wrong. It seemed that society was growing all the more willing to confuse the two. She fought back the urge to lash out at Jean and tell the therapist she was full of baloney—she did not want to have her sessions extended because of an outburst. Tears formed in her eyes, irritation with Jean and the world at large having blazed a trail for the rest of her pent-up emotions to follow. If Sarah was going to get out of here while still reasonably composed, she had to go now.

"I'll keep that in mind," she said as she stood up. The woman had no idea what it felt like to be in her situation. It hurt. Hardly a moment went by when Sarah didn't think about that day, watching her coworkers die. She needed to get out of there before Jean had the chance to offer any more of her learned advice.

———————————

Sarah decided what she loved about moving into a new apartment was that it represented a chance to leave the unwanted past behind and look ahead to the future. However, it still meant unpacking all her stuff and finding a place to put it.

The studio was slightly bigger than the bedroom she used to share with her sister but quite a bit smaller than Brooke's apartment. Sarah now owned a hide-a-bed couch, an overstuffed chair, a clothes dresser that served as a television stand, a small coffee table that doubled as the dining furniture, and a bookcase. Some of it was used. All of it was cheap. At least it matched—more or less.

Brooke had voiced a minimal protest over Sarah moving out, but the words had no sincerity in them. The truth was that Brooke was just as happy to have Sarah out of the apartment as Sarah was to leave. Looking back, Brooke had never been a real friend. At best, she had needed a person to help defray her expensive lifestyle and walk in her shadow. It was only a matter of time before the disgust Brooke had felt for Logan and his Christian beliefs was turned onto Sarah.

Sarah's father had always said to learn from your mistakes and move on. That was exactly what she planned to do.

She opened a box and pulled out a handful of books. Her favorite collection of pioneer stories came out on top, the cover reminding her of how she admired the brave men and women who risked so much to travel west. They faced storms, starvation, disease, and angry mobs for the opportunity to live and worship the way they wanted.

In a way, that description fit Sarah too. She had experienced something every bit as challenging and dangerous as what the pioneers had encountered in pursuit of a life of her own making. And like them, she needed to suck it up and forge ahead.

I am a modern-day pioneer.

Sarah placed the book of pioneer stories on top of the bookcase, with the cover facing out where she could see them from anywhere in the apartment. The image strengthened her, driving the fear she had felt since the attack to the deep shadows of her heart where it lurked unfelt, but still present. One day, she hoped, the horror would leave her completely.

She identified the next book as soon as her fingers touched the fake leather cover—the four-in-one scriptures her parents bought for her sixteenth birthday. A sense of comfort settled over her as she opened the book. Her lips mouthed the first line of chapter one without even needing to read it.

"I, Nephi, having been born of goodly parents . . ."

Nephi certainly knew all about trouble. Although he was many centuries dead, Sarah had an idea that he could offer much better counsel on how to face the challenges that lay ahead than Jean or Brooke or the talking heads on television. Reading how he dealt with the problems in his life would almost be like having a discussion with him. Maybe it was time for the two of them to get properly introduced.

"Hey Nephi, I'm Sarah."

A heavy chunk of darkness lifted from Sarah's heart as she began to read.

31

Robert looked back down the mountain trail at the raging fires that were all that remained of the enemy fuel depot. The flames illuminated a few BMPs close to the inferno, but prevented him from spotting any Russian vehicles that might be in pursuit of the saboteurs. Because of the heat from the fires, night-vision goggles would be just as useless in determining how closely behind the enemy units followed.

In the distance, a second fire burned. He hoped that meant Shaw and Gil had succeeded in their mission as well. Against outrageous odds, both teams had struck blows against the mighty Russian juggernaut. Robert hoped it was enough to slow down the Russians, but the other fire could just as easily be a secondary target with his two friends lying dead on the ground— just like Cohen. He shuddered.

"Any sign of our guide?" Robert asked the driver.

"No sign of anyone."

The local who had shown them the back way through the mountains hadn't been at the spot where they left him. Robert hoped Shaw had picked him up already. That would mean that at least part of the other strike team had survived the mission and were on their way to Trento.

If that were the case, then Robert's vehicle was the caboose, so to speak. And since the driver was busy driving, that left Robert with the full responsibility of fending off any enemy attacks. Without a weapon turret on the Humvee, the best he could manage was an M16. He turned around in the passenger seat, grabbed a rifle and extra magazines from the back of the vehicle, and then sat back down.

Even though the weapon would be useless against an armored vehicle, Robert felt better holding it in his hands. Sort of like a metal security blanket—that shot bullets.

They bumped along the mountain path as the sky lightened with the approaching dawn. By the time the sun poked its first rosy fingers above the horizon, they had almost reached the halfway point back to Trento.

On the plus side, having more light made it easier for the driver to navigate the path. But it also made it easier for the Russians to spot them. The lighter it got, the more time Robert spent facing backward, watching for the first signs of enemy pursuit.

Almost twenty minutes passed. Sweat trickled down Robert's face and neck even though it wasn't particularly warm. At any moment he expected to see a BMP crest the pinnacle of the mountain behind them. Instead, a MiG-29 jet fighter soared into view.

The MiG made a course correction and dived toward them.

"Take evasive action," Robert shouted, "we have a MiG after us."

"The only place to go is off the side of this mountain!" the driver yelled.

A flash and then a trail of smoke marked the launch of a rocket. It streaked toward them, leaving Robert only seconds to react.

He reached over and yanked the steering wheel hard to the right. The Humvee plowed into the mountainside, tilting the vehicle as the wheels attempted to ride up the rocky wall.

Then the whole world shook violently and fell. A near miss of the rocket flipped the Humvee over and slammed it into the mountain. The vehicle slid down the slope to finally rest on the trail, settling on its roof.

Robert's head buzzed. Smoke and flames filled the vehicle, although he had a difficult time making either of them out through the blurred eyes. He wasn't sure which way was up, or down, or even where he was.

But a nagging voice in his head told him to move.

When he tried to adjust his position, a searing pain shot through his leg. He stopped squirming and focused on getting his bearings. The haze in his head started to clear.

Move!

Robert wiped at his face. His hand came away bloody. Through the red blur that was his vision, he noticed a window. Grabbing the frame with both hands, he hauled himself through it.

Move! Faster!

He scrambled as best he could, squeezing along the narrow space between the Humvee and the mountain. Using his hands, he pulled and dragged himself over the rocks and bushes on the mountainside until he slipped and fell sideways into a rocky crack.

The shallow cleft in the rock was just large enough to conceal Robert.

Autocannon shells tore into the Humvee, rattling it with their massive concussive energy. The vehicle exploded, sending gouts of fire washing over the entrance of the crevasse where Robert lay hidden.

Robert reached out in an effort to rescue the driver from the burning heap, but the vehicle tumbled down the mountain. If only he'd reacted a little quicker, he might have saved the man whose name he didn't even know.

The air reeked of singed hair, burnt rubber, and dust. Robert licked his lips and tasted blood. He heard the howling jets of the MiG as it made another pass overhead. And then nothing.

He stayed in the cleft and checked his injuries. Something had passed through the calf of his right leg, he had a gash on his forehead, and the exposed portion of his left arm had minor burns. All of it hurt, but he was alive.

The MiG didn't return.

Tearing strips from his shirt, Robert bandaged his leg and head as best he could. The leg wound still seeped blood but not too badly. He was more worried about whether it would support his weight. Wounded or not, he had to get out of there.

Placing his hands against the crevasse walls and using his arms to support part of his weight, Robert stood, wincing at the pain in his leg. A wave of nausea washed over him as he stood fully upright, and a woozy sensation in his head caused him to wobble.

He leaned against the rock and steadied himself. He didn't have time to wait until he felt better before pushing on. If he wanted to evade any Russian troops that might be pursuing him, he had to deal with the pain, the nausea, and the dizziness and just keep moving.

There was no sign of the driver on the path, or anywhere else. Just bits of torn and burnt parts from the Humvee before it went over the ledge. Maybe the others hadn't made it either. For all Robert knew, he could be the only one who survived the mission.

If he survived.

Strange. He faced the very real prospect of death and it didn't match his expectations. Not that he had dwelt on the subject. Why focus on the bleak and unexpected when there existed so much good in the world? He felt tired. The fears that had been his stealthy companions since he arrived in Italy had vanished during the MiG attack and had not returned.

Robert had been so sure about joining the army. A steady paycheck, assistance with his education, and even some engineering work. The idea had seemed crazy to him at first, but each time he prayed about it he received an answer that this is what God wanted him to do. Then the war started.

Horrible, horrible war.

War would deprive his parents of a child. Just like it had for the thousands of parents who had children die on both sides of the conflict.

War had ravaged the land and people of Italy—as well as others. Already he wondered which images would be the ones that stayed in his mind: those happy days of service from his mission, or the tragedy-filled scenes of the war?

How he hated war.

Robert limped along the mountain path, progressing slowly, but refusing to take any breaks. The Russians BMPs might still be on their way.

Sure enough. Robert had only made it about halfway down the mountain when he spotted the first of the Russian troop carriers at the top. If anything, it surprised him that it had taken them this long to arrive. All he could do was quicken his pace and hope to reach the bottom before they did. At least there he might be able to hide among the vinemeters and carefully work his way back to his unit.

He tried running. That placed too much stress on his wounded leg and worsened the bleeding. Instead, he settled for a limping fast-walk. Every few steps he looked over his shoulder to check the progress of the Russians.

A half hour passed, and the enemy had closed to within a few hundred meters. Robert wasn't going to make it. The only thing that had kept him alive this long was the rugged terrain. It made it difficult to spot a slow-moving target like him. Now he was nearly out of intervening obstacles to cover his retreat.

He didn't want to die. If he died, he couldn't marry Sierra. A scene of the two of them holding hands, looking into each other's eyes, and committing to become one unfolded in Robert's mind.

A hail of bullets spattered against the rocks to Robert's right, shattering stone in a storm of gray and brown fragments.

Robert dropped to the ground and scrabbled forward on all fours.

Ahead, the mountain curved away from him. If he could make it to that ridge he would be safe for a little while longer, perhaps giving himself enough time to find a hiding spot. What he really needed was a miracle.

He offered a prayer as he scuttled along.

Another burst of automatic fire splintered stone just above his head.

Steeling himself for the pain, Robert launched from his crouch like a runner out of the starting blocks. He sprinted for the ridge, his wounded leg screaming in protest at the misuse. At the last moment, he dove over a boulder and slid headfirst along the dirt path.

On the other side, less than fifty meters ahead, sat a Humvee. A camouflage net had been thrown on top of it. Shaw and Gilbert stood next to it, weapons aimed in his direction.

"I told you!" Gil belted out the words loud enough for Robert to hear them even from that distance. "That boy has God on his side."

"Move it, Williams!" Shaw shouted and then pounded on the roof of the Humvee with his palm. He grabbed the netting and pulled it off the vehicle, while Gil raced toward Robert.

How was it even possible that they were here?

Robert forced himself upright and limped toward Gil as quickly as he could. The run had worsened the wound, his leg barely supported his weight. He hobbled a few meters and then tripped and fell.

Gilbert helped him up and draped one of Robert's arms over his shoulders. The two of them ran an odd three-legged race toward the Humvee. They needed to get inside the vehicle before the Russians came around the mountain bend.

One of the Humvee doors stood open while the engine idled. Shaw grabbed a shoulder pack and dashed to the side of the mountain. He placed something behind a medium-sized boulder and then uprooted a mountain shrub and covered the pack.

Gil nearly threw Robert inside the vehicle and then jumped in after him. The driver didn't wait for Shaw, he engaged the engine and started forward. Shaw took a few steps, grabbed the sill of the door, and swung his feet inside. Gil had already moved to the other side of the Humvee and was leaning out the window, covering their withdraw with his M-16.

When the BMP finally appeared, Shaw lifted a remote detonator and aimed it at the enemy armored vehicle. He waited until it pulled alongside the boulder with the pack before pressing the detonation switch.

An explosion rocked the BMP, lifting it on one side. It teetered for a moment.

Robert held his breath as he watched. They only had one shot at this. He knew the blast wasn't powerful enough to destroy the BMP. If it came back down on all wheels then the Russians would be able to shoot them.

Tip. Tip. Fall over, Robert chanted in his mind.

Slowly, the BMP continued to roll, right off the path and down the mountain.

Robert exhaled the breath he'd been holding.

Shaw lowered himself into a seat and glanced over at Robert. "That's cutting it close. Two more minutes and we wouldn't have been here."

"You mean we still had two more minutes?" asked Gil. "If I'd known that we would've taken our time."

"Thanks for waiting," said Robert.

"No problem," said Shaw. "I would've been willing to wait longer except that Captain Mayo just gave us the order to return to base. Command has decided to withdraw all American troops from Italy."

32

M r. President."
    Calvin continued to look through reports on the civil unrest that had paralyzed the country since oil shipments from the Middle East virtually stopped. The deal Boggs had with the Russians died with their assassin. Now, Calvin was hip-deep in a nation-wide panic that had resulted in daily riots. The civil war he had worked so hard to prevent was almost upon them. This time it would not be fought over slavery or the North controlling the South. The impending war in America would be fought over resources. State against state. City against city. One residential block against another.

"Mr. President." This time the press secretary tapped Calvin on the shoulder.

"Were you talking to me?" asked Calvin. At times it still hadn't sunk in. Nelson Boggs was dead and that made Calvin the President of the United States. A position he never wanted. Possibly a position he had no business taking over.

"Yes, sir," said Jacqui Isaacson. "Everything is ready for you to go on the air. We will go live in five minutes."

"Thank you." Calvin dismissed Jacqui and picked up the speech she had prepared for him. A fine speech, full of flattering words and impressive ideas. But not the one he intended to deliver. He pulled out a folded and crumpled page of notes and looked them over one last time before his public debut as the President.

The entire nation waited in desperate anticipation to find out what their new President intended to do to solve the many problems. None more so than his fellow politicians in Washington. They felt the wind of change in the air—and feared it.

If one man could alter the political landscape, Calvin intended to be that man. Left. Right. Conservative. Liberal. He didn't care. All of those were unnecessary labels. What America needed right now was patriots. Men and women willing to do what was right and let the consequences follow. As far as he was concerned, right now there were no political parties. The men and women in Washington needed to set aside their differences and help him save the country. He could not allow partisanship to pose a threat to the country and his plans for its recovery.

Jacqui leaned into Calvin's office and raised a hand with two fingers lifted.

Calvin stood up and removed his suit jacket. Strapping his M1911 pistol on his hip, he made sure to position the weapon so that it stood out and then walked out of the office he had been using.

As expected, the White House staff gasped as they spotted a gun-toting President headed for the pressroom. The Secret Service agents he had personally selected to form his security detail gave each other a quick look and then shrugged before falling in behind the new President.

Jacqui rushed toward Calvin. "What are you doing? You can't wear a gun for the State of the Union address."

"Sure I can," said Calvin without breaking his stride. "As the commander in chief, I am authorized to carry a weapon if I see the need to do so. After watching Nelson die in front of me, I see that need."

"That's not what I meant," stammered Jacqui. "It doesn't look right. What are people going to think when they see the President of the United States wearing a gun?"

"I'm betting on them thinking the situation we face is serious." Calvin rolled his sleeves up to the middle of his forearms and walked out to the podium. He waited for the cue to speak, thinking how it should be Nelson standing in front of the country giving this message.

Jacqui held up one hand and silently counted down . . . Four . . . Three . . . Two . . . One. A red light on the camera announced that Calvin was live in front of hundreds of millions of people.

"The squabbling stops here."

Calvin unclipped the mike from the podium and walked around to where the cameras could see a full view of him and the pistol on his hip. He wanted the nation to know that this wasn't politics as usual. He needed them to understand that the country faced a difficult and uncertain road ahead of them.

"As of this moment, I renounce my political affiliation. I am not a Republican. I am not a Democrat. I am the leader of a country that is on the verge of absolute collapse because we cannot get past all the labels we hang on one another. There is only one classification that should concern any of us at this point: we are Americans."

The audience in the room applauded.

Calvin cut them off with a wave of his hand. "All the slogans, mottoes, and feel-good speeches are not going to help us out of this situation. We have to stop this senseless bickering and work together to solve the serious issues facing the country right now. I intend to use my considerable resources as the President of the United States to bridge the divide that has separated us for so long."

Some of the crowd even stood when they applauded this time.

Calvin had wanted to avoid the usual hollow politics that had become the norm in the White House, and here he was sounding every bit like the men he swore to oppose. That had to stop.

"I think, maybe, that you misunderstood me," said Calvin and waited for the applause to die down. "This will not be an easy process. The country has sunk too far into a sticky quagmire for our problems to be solved with pretty speeches. I guarantee that in six months I won't be popular, but I will make the hard choices. I will make the decisions necessary to take back control of our destiny as a great nation.

"President Nelson Boggs and I had more than our fair share of disagreements during the time we worked together. His loss could not have come at a worst time. All of us will sorely miss his diplomatic skills in the trials ahead. The mantle of leadership has fallen on me, and I am here to announce my first official act as President.

"Because of the high levels of civil unrest, the local police forces and National Guard units have been stretched to their limits. If the winter is as unnaturally harsh as meteorologists have predicted, the government will not have the manpower to deal with the situation. I have made the decision to recall our armed forces. The brave men and women of the military will be coming home. Europe will have to band together in order to solve the problems created by war with Russia."

A roar of questions burst from the crowd. Cameras flashed. Hands raised.

Past presidents may have handled the situation differently, but Calvin decided that the rest of the speech could wait. He pointed to a woman eagerly waving her hand back and forth.

"In the days to come, a lot will be said about the way you dressed for your first appearance as President. Does the wearing of a gun have some special significance that you'd like the public to know?"

Calvin rested his hand on the grip of the pistol. "I intend it to serve as a symbol to powers both foreign and domestic that Lady Liberty, and I as her champion, will not submit quietly to tyranny. Anyone wanting to destroy the Constitution will have to go through me first."

33

John finished his normal morning patrol of Camp Valiant, ending where he began, at the front gate. No holes in the fence. No missing crates of supplies. No members of the camp missing. And no hordes of unbelievers lined up along the fences.

He stepped inside the trailer and turned on the radio to the local news station. In the last few months he had relied on it more and more for information about what was happening around the world and specifically about the war in Europe. Robert hadn't written them in over a month and that worried John.

". . . Russian troops continue to push into Northern Italy. NATO forces have so far been unable to stop the 'Red Juggernaut,' as the Russian President has taken to calling their military. Inside sources indicate that the alliance of nations is starting to fracture.

"Meanwhile, on the home front an early and severe winter has critically affected the fall harvest. Stores expect shortages in the months ahead. Public response to the news has been—"

Bill Summers entered the trailer, walked over to the kitchen, and grabbed a glass of orange juice. "You know the news isn't going to get any better."

"It doesn't hurt to hope." John turned the radio off. "If the work crews can do such a great job finishing those buildings in all the snow we've had, anything's possible."

"I suppose," said Summers. "They're motivated. The longer it takes to get these buildings constructed, the longer it will be before they can benefit from them. I'm surprised they're already halfway done with the chapel. I didn't think we'd even get started on that until spring."

"Besides," said John, only half listening to Bill, "I'm worried about my son Robert. I haven't received a letter from him for several weeks now. As far as I know, he could be right on the front line. It sure would be nice to get a letter from him telling me he's okay. A message from my oldest daughter would be great too."

A double honk of a car horn sounded outside. John looked out the window and spotted Sheriff McKinney's cruiser. The sheriff climbed out of the vehicle and walked around to the trunk.

"Wonder what kind of trouble is brewing now?" asked Bill.

"Only one way to find out," said John as he set down his glass of juice and walked outside. "Good morning. At least, I hope it's a good morning."

"Don't know about that," said McKinney, "but it should be an interesting one."

John opened the gate and joined the sheriff at the back of his cruiser. Four long wooden crates sat in the trunk. "What are those?"

"That's the interesting part. These boxes are addressed to you, and they have the President's name on them. They must be important so I decided to deliver them myself. But that's not the only reason I drove out here. If you've been listening to the news lately, you know that the country is on the verge of declaring martial law. When they do, I'm hoping that the town of Greenville can work together with you folks, sort of a mutual protection pact. If that's all right with you."

"Thanks, Sheriff," said John, taken aback by the town's willingness to cooperate with the Saints. He expected a begrudging acceptance of the Mormons, but never an alliance or a friendship. It certainly was what both communities needed.

"I think that is going to be the key to surviving," said John. "Count us in."

"Good," said McKinney. "Now one of you want to give me a hand unloading these crates? They're heavy."

John grabbed a wooden cross section on the lid and lifted. The sheriff hadn't been exaggerating; the box weighed at least two hundred pounds. They moved all four of the crates out of the back of the cruiser and onto the ground. Bill ran to the workshop and returned with a pry bar. Wood creaked as Bill pried the top of the box off, revealing several M14 rifles in packing material.

"There are two cases sitting in the front seat. My guess is that'd be ammo to go along with the rifles," said McKinney.

"Is the President allowed to send us weapons?" asked John.

"Don't know," said McKinney, "but he did."

John pulled a letter from one of the crates and unfolded it.

> *Mr. Williams,*
>
> *My mind continually drifts back to the visit at Camp Valiant. While I don't have any interest in your religion, I was impressed by the caliber of your people. The United States of America was founded by hard-working families who came here to forge lives where they could worship in peace and in doing so established the values which have guided us for more than two hundred years. I see that within your community. I see good people willing to help their neighbors. I see parents who love their children and children who love their parents.*
>
> *A cancer has infected our great country. Every day I see the evidence of it all around me. I reached a point where I wondered why I bothered to fight the system and the encroaching evil that threatens the American way of life. But when I visited Camp Valiant my reasons for becoming a public servant all flooded back to me. I serve to protect people like you.*
>
> *A storm of civil chaos is brewing, and we have no*

*guarantee that the war in Europe will not become a war
in the Americas. The days ahead promise to be quite horrible. I hope these guns will help you retain control of the
food you will be growing and distributing to your neighbors. They should come in handy for keeping your people
safe. When this is all over, perhaps you will permit me
to visit once again and sit with your families and enjoy
the warmth that you share with one another. Until then,
pray for us all.*

—Calvin

*P.S. I took the liberty of checking on your son Robert.
He is alive and well in Italy, but he will be returning home
soon. His commanding officer has recommended him for the
Distinguished Service Cross. I have it on good authority that
the request will be granted.*

Tears formed in John's eyes. He couldn't wait to tell Becky and
the rest of the family the good news about Robert. John folded up
the letter and placed it in his shirt pocket. The worst of the troubles still lay ahead for members of Camp Valiant, but at least they
wouldn't face them alone.

34

A pair of soldiers loaded Robert into a stripped-out Humvee. The vehicle had been field-modified to function as medical transport for the wounded on the trip to Vicenza. He barely felt the jostling. The painkillers, he realized, had kicked in. As his suffering faded, a powerful urge to sleep tugged at him.

Captain Mayo poked his head in through one of the doors. "Before we take off, I wanted to congratulate you on a job well-done. Frankly, I didn't think you boys had a ghost of a chance to succeed."

"Did we stop the Russians from advancing?" Robert asked.

"Don't go taking all the credit," said Mayo. "Destroying those fuel and ammo depots wouldn't have been anything more than a bump in the road if our troops hadn't fought as bravely as they did. You just happened to be the last straw. At least for the moment, the Russians are not showing any interest in pushing farther into Italy. Who knows what they might decide to do tomorrow."

"Then we should stay and help," said Robert.

"Listen, Williams," said Mayo. "We've been chewed up and spit out. We're done here. Besides, we don't have enough troops to make a difference. So, sit back and enjoy the ride. And that's an order."

Captain Mayo saluted him and then withdrew from the vehicle.

Gil climbed in next to Robert, shutting the door behind him. The Humvee rumbled to life.

"Are you injured?" Robert asked.

"Nah." Gilbert stowed his M-16. "The medic said you were going to be okay and that it was all right if I rode with you. Nobody else from my original unit made it."

As bad as Trento had looked when they arrived, it looked much worse now. The remaining American military vehicles formed a column and wended through the streets, headed for the air base in Vicenza.

"Are we really going home?" Robert asked.

"That's the word command passed down. From what I've been able to gather, things are a real mess back there. They need us to help keep the peace. It looks like we will be leaving the war in Europe just so they can drop us in the middle of the hostilities in the good old U. S. of A."

"But . . . we will be going home." Robert said it more to himself than Gilbert. The painkillers made it hard to focus on the discussion, his thoughts kept drifting to the realization that he had survived the war in Europe. He was going to live. He had a future ahead of him.

With hands that felt as if they were made of lead, he reached into his shirt pocket and pulled out the pictures he kept there. Enzo, Lucy, and Gianna looked up at him from the top photo.

He had felt all along that he needed to return to Italy. Once upon a time, he thought it was for the purpose of finishing his mission here, but now he knew better. Guided by the hand of God, Robert had helped save Italy from falling to the Russians. His actions had given these children a future.

A warmth spread through his chest that had nothing to do with the pain meds.

Then he swapped pictures and gazed at Sierra.

I have a future.

DISCUSSION QUESTIONS

1. What responsibility do true believers have to help those who do not gather?

2. If asked to give up your right to bear arms, would you surrender them or fight?

3. Would it be better for the Saints to gather in the cities or to establish separate communities like Camp Valiant?

4. What is going to happen to those Saints who refuse the call to gather and are left behind?

5. What do you think about the President of the United States carrying a gun?

6. Under which conditions would it be all right to refuse a call to help our NATO allies?

7. At what point do our domestic problems justify turning our backs on the events happening around the world?

8. Will all of Christianity be targets of persecution in the last days or only select denominations?

9. What would it take to humble you to the point where you would listen to the difficult messages God has for us?

10. What item or activity could you not leave behind or give up?

ABOUT THE AUTHOR

RANDY LINDSAY is a native of Arizona. He lives in Mesa with his wife, five of his nine children, and a hyperactive imagination. His wife calls him the "Storyman" because he sees everything as material for a good story. Randy's first novel, *The Gathering: End's Beginning*, was published in 2014. He has also been published in several anthologies during 2013–14. If you want to find out more, you can check him out at RandyLindsay.net.